PRAISE FOR

The Perfect Son

"[A] perfect summer thriller. . . . The author's ability to create a sense of escalating unease is one of her most notable achievements. . . . The twist in *The Perfect Son* is a big one."   —*The Columbus Dispatch*

"A powerful, unpredictable debut thriller about a mother's attempt to re-assemble her life from the shards of tragedy. Lauren North's skillful narrative casts everyone as a suspect and keeps the reader guessing until the final, emotion-packed pages."   —David Bell, *USA Today* bestselling author of *The Request*

"The thriller is told in two alternating time periods that come together at the very end, with a very big twist."   —Betches.com

"A fast-paced psychological thriller."   —Book Riot

"[An] emotionally harrowing debut. . . . An intimate, unbalancing mix of grief, paranoia, gaslighting, maternal protectiveness, and profound compassion."   —*Publishers Weekly* (starred review)

"A heartrending evocation of grief that packs a devious punch. It left me reeling."   —Lesley Kara, author of international bestseller *The Rumor*

"As satisfyingly intriguing and page-turning as you could possibly want. An emotional read—the end is a shocker!"   —Emma Curtis, author of *When I Find You*

"Beautifully written psychological suspense about the power of love after a life-changing loss. A sense of impending doom and foreboding gripped me from the first page. . . . The ending is stunning and powerful."
—Mary Torjussen, author of *The Closer You Get*

"A captivating, suspenseful thriller that draws you in—with a twist that will take your breath away." —T. M. Logan, author of *Lies*

"Taking a page from *The Woman in the Window* by A. J. Finn, *The Perfect Son* by Lauren North is a perfect psychological thriller. . . . This tour de force novel is shocking, grief stricken, and a little too realistic."
—Fresh Fiction

Lauren North

ONE
STEP
BEHIND

BERKLEY

New York

BERKLEY
An imprint of Penguin Random House LLC
penguinrandomhouse.com

Copyright © 2020 by North Writing Services Ltd.
Readers Guide copyright © 2020 by North Writing Services Ltd.

BERKLEY and the BERKLEY & B colophon
are registered trademarks of Penguin Random House LLC.

Library of Congress Cataloging-in-Publication Data

Names: North, Lauren, author.
Title: One step behind / Lauren North.
Description: First edition. | New York: Berkley, 2020.
Identifiers: LCCN 2020007107 (print) | LCCN 2020007108 (ebook) |
ISBN 9781984803863 (trade paperback) | ISBN 9781984803870 (ebook)
Subjects: LCSH: Psychological fiction. | GSAFD: Suspense fiction.
Classification: LCC PR6114.O7784 O54 2020 (print) |
LCC PR6114.O7784 (ebook) | DDC 823/.92—dc23
LC record available at https://lccn.loc.gov/2020007107
LC ebook record available at https://lccn.loc.gov/2020007108

First Edition: September 2020

Printed in the United States of America
1   3   5   7   9   10   8   6   4   2

Cover art by Hanna Valui/Alamy Stock Photo
Cover design by Faceout Studio/Amanda Hudson
Book design by Katy Riegel

For Laura, Nikki, and Zoe

ONE
STEP
BEHIND

CHAPTER 1

Wednesday, June 12

Jenna

My heart is beating machine-gun-fire fast as I reach out to undo the new dead bolt at the top of the front door. I move to the chain next with the fluid movement of doctor's hands—calm and steady—masking the truth, keeping the shaking fear deep inside. I used to think I was invincible. I used to think nothing could rattle me, but that was before.

Where will you be today? Leaning against a tree in the park opposite our house, standing in broad daylight? Or will you be a shadow watching out of sight? A feeling I can sense but not see? How many e-mails will you send? How many ways will you find to torment me today? The questions are like caffeine hits to my exhaustion. I can't have slept for more than three hours last night. My eyes itch, my muscles ache with heaviness, but at least the fog is clearing over my thoughts. Three hours. It feels like less.

"Are we walking or driving, Mummy?" Beth asks from behind me.

I turn around and feel the love well up inside—a visceral heat. I wish I could shield them from you. Nine-year-old Beth, and Archie, six almost seven, are standing ready at the bottom of the stairs, school shoes on, dark green book bags looped around one shoulder. Archie is a miniature version of Stuart with shaggy brown hair and a wide toothy grin. He's wearing gray shorts and a white polo shirt with a grass stain on the collar that hasn't washed out. His arms and legs have tanned a golden brown in the weeks of endless sun.

Beth is more like me with her fair skin and the red freckles that sprinkle the bridge of her nose. Her green gingham summer dress is the new jumpsuit style, so she can do cartwheels and handstands without the boys seeing her knickers. Strands of dark orange hair are falling out of her ponytail and over her face, but I've given up trying to neaten it. She gets her independent streak from me too.

There is no last-minute scramble for reading books, no final cramming of spellings for the test, no lost items to hunt for in our house. They've been conditioned from the get-go in efficiency and routines. I'd love to take the credit but it's Christie, our child-minder, who's done it.

"It's really hot. Can we drive?" Archie asks, dragging out the final word in the whiny voice we dislike so much, but can't seem to get him to stop.

"Good idea, let's drive," I say, as though walking was ever an option.

There's an instant sigh of relief around us, as though the hallway itself has been holding its breath. It's your fault of course that my son is so scared. I've done all I can over the last year to hide my fear from them. But then you disappeared for a week in May. Seven whole days of not seeing you. No e-mails, and none of your sick gifts left on my doorstep either. I was a spring uncoiling—slowly, slowly—hoping beyond hope, day by day, that you'd given up. Day seven fell on a Monday, one of the first warm days of the year and my first school run in ages, and Stuart wanted to take my car in for a service, so we walked the half a mile to Greenstead Primary School. But then you know that, don't you? You were waiting in the doorway of the corner shop, two roads away from the school gates.

We turned onto the road and there you were, just meters away from us. Watching. I tensed up so tight that the world spun and I grabbed Archie's hand and then Beth's and we ran flat out, running for our lives, it felt. I stopped only when I realized I'd dragged Archie to the pavement and he'd grazed one of his knees.

We skipped the playground lines and went straight to the office, a mess of tears and blood and fear. Mr. Bell, the head teacher, was a wave of calm and kindness over our panic. He sent Beth to class and Archie to the first aid room for a Band-Aid before sitting me in the staff room with a strong cup of tea that I slopped all over the new carpet because my hands were shaking so badly.

It was only later, when I grabbed a spare minute during the night shift to phone Stuart, that I learned about the book bag. "Archie thinks he dropped it when you were running. I'm sure someone will hand it in." They didn't though. You took it. Another piece of us, of me, that's yours now.

I lie awake at night thinking of Archie's reading diary and the comments back and forth between Miss Bagri, Archie's teacher, and me or Stuart. The little notes that are meaningless really but somehow feel so personal, so telling in your hands.

A final big deep breath in before I down the last dregs of tepid coffee from my mug, grab the car keys, and ready myself to open the front door.

"Wait here," I say, throwing a glance back to Beth and Archie, who know without me telling them that they're not to move until I've checked the doorstep.

I yank open the heavy wood door a few inches, just enough to peek out without the kids seeing the tiled doorstep.

It's a doll's head today. One eye is open and staring up at me. The other has been burned into a melted hole.

I bite the side of my mouth, keeping my scream inside, and slam the door shut.

"What is it, Mummy?" Beth asks.

"It's nothing." Of course she knows it's not nothing. It's always something, but how can I tell my children what's out there, what you're doing to me? I run through the house and grab one of Detective Sergeant Church's clear plastic evidence bags.

"Go wait in the living room," I say, shooing Beth and Archie away.

They move without complaint and when I'm sure they're gone, I open up the front door and scoop the doll's head into the bag, careful not to touch it. I can taste the coffee rising at the back of my throat, but I work quickly, desperate to get back to the kids and make things normal for them. At least there's not a glass this time, smashed into a thousand shards for me to sweep up.

When the bag is sealed I shove it into my purse to drop at the police station on my way past. Then I wash my hands three times and, pulling myself together, I step into the living room, forcing a bright smile. "OK. We can go."

I open the front door again, wide this time, and the heat hits us. Like the residue of candy floss on fingers, it coats our skin in a sticky film. No sea breeze today, nothing to take the edge off the heat wave. Both kids leap over the step and land on the path as though an invisible evil lurks on it. It's an effort not to do the same.

We hustle to the car, parked further down the road than I'd have liked, but with no driveways, the cars on the road are packed tight on both sides, like Starbursts in a tube, and we can't always find a space right outside our house.

The street is a row of fifty semidetached houses the same as ours, built a hundred and something years ago in dark red brick, all facing out to the park with its boating lake, playground, and many, many places for you to hide. We're three roads back from the seafront where the property prices quadruple.

Our estate agent, Wayne, has boasted sea views from our house which is laughable really. If I stand on a chair at Archie's window and crane my neck then maybe I can catch a glimmer of the green estuary and the slow cargo ships making their way toward London, but I've not corrected him. The sooner we move, the sooner we'll be far away from you.

The moment we're in the car I lock the doors, allowing myself a quick inhale of breath before it starts again. Road, mirrors, windows, road. My gaze flicks between them, staring at every parked car, every tree, every doorway we pass searching for the outline of your figure, a glimpse of broad shoulders and dark hair.

We stop at a traffic light, the green man beeping in time with my indicator as the children and parents flock toward the school. There is laughter and shouts of "Hello." They look so happy, so oblivious. They have no idea how fragile their lives are, how quickly everything can be stripped away.

The green man disappears. The last stragglers dart in front of our car. My hand reaches for the gear stick, my left leg already easing off the clutch, and that's when it happens. I feel you before I see you. That strange sense of being watched that is now sickeningly familiar.

Not now, I plead to you in my head. *Not with Beth and Archie in the car. Please no.*

Then I spot you. You're standing on the pavement, tucked a little way behind a tree on the other side of the road. Your phone is in your hand, and it's the screen you're staring at, not me. But then you look up and our eyes meet. *I'm watching you, Jenna,* that look is saying.

I freeze. Inside I'm screaming at myself to reach for my phone and take a photo of you, something the police can use to figure out who you are, but my muscles won't react. All I can think about is keeping Beth and Archie safe.

For the longest second the only noise is the tick, tick, tick of the indicator. It sounds so slow compared to the beating of my heart. A horn blasts from behind me. I jump at the noise, a yelp escaping my throat. The traffic light has turned green.

"What's wrong, Mummy?" Archie whispers from the backseat. I've scared him.

"Nothing, darling," I reply, my voice too high. I spur into action, pulling the car over to the side of road and parking askew on the curb. I have to get a photo this time. My hands are slippery with sweat but I cut the engine, dig my phone out of my bag, and open the camera.

"Where is he?" Beth asks, her voice sounding so young now, so full of the same fear surging through me, and I feel myself tearing in two, longing to be the mother she needs, the one who will always protect her, and knowing I can't. How can I keep her safe when I don't know who you are? Or what you want from me?

"Get back," I whisper. *He's there. He's right there.* The car behind me honks again—a final beep of *What the hell are you doing, lady?*— before driving around me, blocking you from view for a moment. When the car is gone, so are you. Only the fear remains.

CHAPTER 2

JENNA

Every muscle, every joint, every single cell in my body vibrates with the urge to run. I can taste it in my mouth—a stale bitterness, like unbrushed teeth. We may be a more advanced species than most animals but our basic instincts are still the same—the surge of adrenaline, the fight-or-flight response.

All I want to do is take Archie and Beth and run away and never come back. And we are running. Stuart keeps sending me links to houses in a village ten miles away. But he doesn't get it. Ten miles isn't enough to get away from you. We need ten thousand miles and an ocean between us. I could get a work permit for almost anywhere in the world. It wouldn't just be a new house, it would be a different way of living. I haven't told Stuart how I feel yet. He's been right by my side through all the horrors you've thrown at me and I don't know how to burden him with this new request. Once we've found a buyer for the house, then I'll say something.

There are two viewings scheduled today. Stuart is taking a long lunch to show the buyers around the rooms that have been our home for the last decade. No FOR SALE sign, of course. I can't have you finding out our plan.

Another car passes us. I drop my phone and glance across the road. The street is still empty and so I do the only thing I can do—I drive away, I carry on.

The moment we're parked outside the school I tell Beth and Archie to sit tight and play on their tablets, then I step out of the car and call the police. I don't want the kids to hear this. They are already so aware of you and what's happening. Flashes of Archie's tearstained face and pleas for just one more bedtime story flood my thoughts. He never used to be scared of the dark. Beth will never admit to being scared too, but her sudden mood swings—angry one moment, desperate for cuddles the next—tell their own story.

The call is the usual back-and-forth. When, where, what, followed by a "We'll send a patrol car." I'll get a call tomorrow or the day after from DS Church—the nasally voiced detective who's managing my case. She'll tell me they've struck out again.

"Ready to go, kids?" I ask, finishing the call and opening Archie's passenger door.

As they grab their bags and clamber out I feel my skin itch again with the heat and the feeling of being watched that will follow me now for the rest of the day, the rest of my life I think sometimes.

We're swept toward the school by the tide of parents and children. I spot Christie walking just ahead of us with the train of children she's had over for breakfast this morning, along with her own daughter, Niamh. Beth and Archie skip ahead to join her and their friends and I hurry to catch up and try not to feel ditched.

When I think about leaving Westbury, Christie is always my first thought. She has taken care of Beth and Archie in her home since Beth started school five years ago, wiping their noses, their bottoms, and their tears with a motherly love I'll never find in childcare again. Plus, they adore her and she says yes every time we need her to.

"Hey, sweetheart," Christie says to Beth as she reaches her side.

Christie is in her midthirties with long brown hair she wears in a messy bun. She's always smiling and always wears baggy jeans and a loose T-shirt.

"Christie, I got ten out of ten on my spelling test yesterday." Beth's voice is bouncing with a joy I rarely hear.

"That's wonderful." Christie holds out her arm and Beth moves closer, the pair hugging as they walk. I feel a strange mix of happiness and jealousy seeing them together like this. I'm glad Beth loves Christie. It makes our childcare situation so much easier, and yet I can't help wishing it was me Beth was hugging right now.

The bell rings as we step through the gates and into the playground and four hundred children sprint to their class lines. I kiss Archie first and hold him close. "Have a good day, Archie. I'll see you . . ." I jump forward in my head, wading through the sludge of tiredness to remember my shift pattern this week. I finish at nine thirty tonight, then another twelve-hour shift tomorrow—seven till seven. "Tomorrow night, hopefully." I emphasize the final word and squeeze Archie a little tighter. He might be only six but Archie knows as well as anyone that I can't simply walk away at the end of the day like Stuart can on his building site. A&E doesn't work like that. "Or Friday, OK?"

"Bye, Mummy," Archie says, pushing me away a little.

I bend down and lean close so his classmates don't hear. "Remember not to hold it, baby. If you need to go to the bathroom, just ask. Mrs. Smith or Miss Bagri will take you."

He nods distractedly, his mind already in the classroom.

Archie's class starts to move and I step over to Beth and the year four line. She sees me coming and gives a small shake of her head. No hug today then. The realization stings for a moment but I push it away. Beth is growing up and I have to respect that, regardless of how much I want to hold her right now. "You didn't tell me about your spelling test. That's really great, well done," I say, shoving my hands in the pockets of my trousers.

"I forgot," she says with a shrug.

"Well, I'm proud of you." I smile as brightly as I can. "Have a good day."

"Don't forget the ribbon, Mum," Beth says, eyebrows rising up and head tilting forward in a way that makes her seem older than nine.

"Ribbon? What ribbon?"

She gives me her trademark sigh and eye roll. "I need an egg box, an empty cereal box, and some red ribbon for a Father's Day gift we're making. I told you about it at the weekend. We need it on Friday."

I nod. "Right. Yes, of course." There's a vague memory of a conversation about ribbon. Beth caught me as I was collecting a letter from the doormat, pulse racing, vision blurring, wondering if it was from the postman or you.

"You will get it, won't you?" Her face changes and she's suddenly so small, so nine again.

"Yes, yes. I haven't forgotten," I lie. "Your class is moving. You need to go."

"And it's non-uniform day on Friday," she says, ignoring me.

"I know. You've told me ten times this week. You saw me write it on the calendar. Your dad's taking you to school on Friday and he knows too. Plus, Beth, you're old enough now to remember yourself, aren't you?" I know she's thinking of the time when Archie was in reception and she was in year two. One of my rare drop-off days long before you, when my only excuse was juggling family and work. I'd missed the letter in the book bags about a non-uniform day, raising money for the hospital, of all things. Beth and Archie had been the only kids in a dark green and white uniform next to a parade of purples, pinks, and blues. They'd both cried as they'd gone into school.

Beth flashes me a quick smile before racing off and joining the end of her class. I wait until she's disappeared around the corner and allow the relief to sweep through me. Beth and Archie are safe. You can't get to them in school. It's only me now.

I turn away and join the bottleneck of parents trying to get through the gate and look around for Christie or a familiar face to join in the polite "how's things?" parent chat, but I don't recognize a single mum.

"Hi, it's Jenna, right?" a voice says from beside me.

I'm already nodding as I turn to face the woman. She's slim in skinny cutoff jeans and a black vest top. Her shoulder-length blond hair is deadly straight and shining with health. She's early forties like me but looks more youthful somehow. I peer at her forehead, searching for the lines, but her skin is smooth and taut.

"Yes."

"Hi, I'm Rachel Finley, Lacey and Freddie's mum." She must register my blank expression because then she adds, "Lacey and Beth are best friends, and Freddie and Archie seem to be heading the same way. I was hoping we might bump into each other."

"Oh right, yes, of course. It's nice to meet you at last," I reply as though I know what she's talking about.

"Look, no pressure, but I'm chair of the PTA and we're absolutely desperate for new members. I wondered how you felt about joining? You don't have to decide straightaway. There's a mums' night out coming up. You can come along if you want and just have a good time. Here." She pulls out some folded pieces of paper from her bag and hands them to me. "It's just some more information and our contact details, in case you want to think about it."

I can feel myself staring openmouthed at Rachel, trying to find the nicest way I can to say no, because it is a no. There is no way I have time to bake cakes or raffle prizes. "Er . . . it's just I work a lot so I'm really not sure I have time."

"No worries. Just think about it. I'd better run. See you at the party on Saturday?"

"Wouldn't miss it." I stretch my lips into a smile and watch her stride away, wondering who this woman is. Has Beth mentioned a Lacey recently? There was a girl she kept talking about a few months ago, but I'm sure her name began with a *T*. Am I that out of touch with my own children?

Too many drop-and-runs at Christie's house. Too many assemblies, sports days, parents' evenings that have clashed with a shift I couldn't swap, leaving Stuart to do the brunt of it. But school is the tip of the iceberg when it comes to my absence as a mother.

I missed Archie's fifth birthday party at the aquarium. I missed Beth's gymnastics competition and the third-place trophy she received. Twice I've worked on Christmas Day and missed seeing their faces as they rushed downstairs to find their presents under the tree. But it's the little stuff that eats at me the most—the family dinners, the laughter at bath time, the learning to tie shoelaces, games of Go Fish.

Sometimes I kid myself that it won't always be this way, but it will. It's one of many sacrifices I've made for the job I live and breathe. Stuart and I went into starting a family with our eyes wide open to the juggling act ahead of both of us, but unlike Stuart, it's me who carries the burden.

The guilt has grown year after year, from the first settling-in session at nursery when I left a screaming, red-faced, four-month-old Beth. It's grotesque and spiky, this guilt I feel inside; a mound like the outer shell of a horse chestnut—hard and sharp—jammed in my stomach.

And all of that is before I consider what you've done to me, what you've stolen from my life.

As I slide back into my car, I feel my phone vibrate in my bag. A wave of nausea crashes over me but I dig my phone out anyway. An e-mail alert appears on the screen, then another and another. Five in total. All from different e-mail addresses. All from you.

My eyes dart around the road, looking beyond the parents and the school traffic, searching for you. The fear is as real as if you're reaching into my car and wrapping your hands around my neck, squeezing tighter and tighter until I can't breathe.

CHAPTER 3

Sophie

I'm walking fast, trainers bouncing on the pavement with every stride. My eyes are down, fixed on my phone. The screen is tilted away from the bright glare of the sun and I'm scrolling through Instagram, looking at photo after filtered photo of celebrities and people I barely know. I've no idea why I bother, and yet I never stop.

My head is full of the clients I have booked for the rest of the week. I make a mental note to remember a roller for the IT band strengthening one of my clients needs tomorrow. And there are two new mums who've booked a block of six sessions together which start this week. They want to burn off the extra pregnancy weight while their babies sleep. I'll have to get to Fairview Park early tomorrow to grab a shady spot for them.

Today I'm on my way to Manor Road and a forty-six-year-old woman who talks nonstop for the entire session, no matter how many lunges and squats I make her do. She doesn't need me to tell her how to exercise or to stand over her barking orders. She spends hours in the gym each week. But I guess she's lonely and likes the company.

I wonder if I should ask how her affair is going. She talks about it often enough, but it doesn't feel quite the same as the "How are the kids?" and "What plans have you got for the weekend?" questions I usually ask.

I'm always surprised how much my clients tell me about their lives. Personal trainers are like hairdressers, I think. There's a false intimacy, as though we're friends when we're not. How can we be friends when they pay me to spend that hour each week with them?

The tops of my shoulders start to tingle. I forgot to put sun cream on in my hurry to leave the flat. Nick was looking at his watch and tutting about being late. I'll have red raw burns tomorrow. *Good one, Soph!*

I look up, and that's when I spot Matthew up ahead, ambling toward me in his usual way—like a tortoise—slow and steady, no rush, no care.

What the hell? is my first thought, which is immediately followed by a double take. Is it really him?

Yes is the answer. Who else would wear black jeans and a black T-shirt in this heat?

I flick a glance behind me at the two long rows of middle-class detached houses with their gravel driveways and redbrick garden walls. It's Westbury's residential suburbia. Giant Victorian houses worth a million at least, and miles from town and the restaurant where Matthew works, miles from his beaten-up terrace house that gives me the creeps on the rare occasions I visit.

There is no reason why Matthew should be on this road at this time in the morning, except me.

"You're a big sister now, Sophie. It's your job to look after Matthew. You have to promise you'll always be there for him." My mum's voice leaps into my head, making my insides lurch. I take a breath and

slow down, trying to get control of my thoughts before Matthew reaches me.

He lifts one hand from the pocket of his jeans in a lazy wave, and as ours eyes connect I wonder what's going through his mind. Are childhood memories of Christmases and birthdays, paddling pool days, and baking days with Nan rolling through his thoughts? Does he see the good memories first or the bad ones? Does he have times like I do, where all he can remember are the bad things that happened? Where his chest hurts so much it feels impossible to breathe? When all he feels is guilt? Sometimes I wish I had the courage to ask him. Then again, I wish I had the courage to do a lot of things.

I glance down at my phone. I don't have time to stop and talk to Matthew. If Nick finds out I was late for a client again he'll go crazy. Elite Personal Training is his business, his baby, it seems like most days. *"It doesn't pay to be late, Sophie. Ever. Do you get that? Now, I love you and I love that we're working together, but you can't be late for clients. We have to be better than that."*

I wanted to tell Nick that it was only one time and only ten minutes late, and it wouldn't have happened if I hadn't had to get across town on foot because he'd scheduled two appointments for me so close together and he'd taken the car. But my voice deserted me, so I just nodded instead.

Matthew reaches me and I slip my phone into my bag and push my cap up so I can see him better.

"Hey, little brother," I say, searching his face as I always do for the puny boy he used to be, but there's no sign of the terrified five-year-old who couldn't color inside the lines. Matthew is tall now—six foot. I'm only an inch shorter, but his shoulders are broad and

I always feel weak and tiny beside him, like I'm a rag doll he can pick up and fling into the nearest rubbish heap anytime he wants.

His hair is dark and short and not styled in any particular fashion, and the stubble on his face is almost enough to be considered a beard. Only his eyes are unchanged—two dark pools that seem to stare right into me.

Matthew smirks. "Little?" he asks, cocking an eyebrow.

I shrug. "You know what I mean. What are you doing here?"

"Just fancied a walk before work. I'm taking photos. You've changed your hair."

I touch my ponytail. The extensions, that have made my sharp bob into long hair that sits six inches past my shoulders, still feel strange and heavy on my head, but Nick likes them.

"What's there to take photos of around here?" I ask, throwing another look around. The street is empty. People are out at work or in their gardens. It's just me and Matthew. The rag doll feeling returns and I find myself shifting my weight to the back of my feet, adding the tiniest distance between us.

"Everything and nothing," he replies like I knew he would. It's the same bloody answer he gives anytime I ask that question. "What about you?"

"I've got a client who lives on the next road." I make a face. An apologetic frown. "I'm running late actually. I'd better go. You should come to the flat sometime. We've got some furniture now."

"I doubt Nick would be pleased to see me."

I ignore the comment. There really isn't time to get into it, and even if there was, what would be the point? My brother and my boyfriend don't get on and both of them seem to think that there is something I should do about it.

"I got an air bed for one of the spare rooms," Matthew says when it's clear I'm not going to reply. "If you ever want to crash at mine again, then you won't have to sleep on the sofa."

"Yeah, thanks." *I won't*, I add silently. I shouldn't have stayed over the last time. Nick went ballistic and we didn't speak for two days. "Are you still seeing someone?" I ask, thinking of the mention Matthew made about a woman he was dating a while ago.

"Sort of. It's complicated. Look, there's—"

"I really should go," I cut him off. "Sorry, but I'm running late."

Matthew moves then, one foot then another, drawing closer, positioning himself in my path. "You ignored my text the other day."

"Did I? I thought I replied." I know what text he's talking about. Four words that dropped down from the top of my phone screen when I was sitting on the sofa.

We need to talk!

Nick was beside me watching football, one arm looped around my shoulder. There was no way I could reply then.

"I'm sorry. I've been crazy busy. Everyone wants to get in shape for their summer holidays. Sorry."

Sorry, sorry, sorry. It feels like every other thing I say to Matthew is an apology. A hang-up from childhood I've never been able to shake. The tiptoeing around mood swings, placating arguments, softening words. I wish I could stop. I wish things could be different from the way they are.

"Matthew needs our help, Sophie. He needs all of our love."

"I'll text you later, OK?" I say, wanting so badly to move and yet staying anyway.

"Have you tried to see Mum lately?" Matthew asks, the change of direction throwing me for a moment.

"What's the point? She doesn't want to see us." Sadness stabs—the twist of a knife right in the space between my ribs. Twelve years on and it still feels like a gaping wound that won't heal. "Why? Have you?"

"Sort of. I walked past their house the other week. I saw Trevor and Mum out in their garden. They seem happy. She's had her hair cut short."

I close my eyes for a second, pulling my cap a little lower too. I hate hearing Trevor's name. I don't care what he says, I will always think that she chose him over us.

"But you didn't try to see her?" I ask.

He shakes his head.

A question pushes forward and I feel it in my throat and then on the tip of my tongue. It's the same question I wanted to ask twelve years ago when I was fifteen and Matthew was twelve. I didn't ask it then either. *Why did you do it?*

"There's something we need to talk about." Matthew's voice turns from casual to serious.

I'm dithering with what to say or do. I don't want to talk now, but I don't know how to walk away from him either. From across the road a front door bangs. My eyes follow the noise and I watch a man in a suit hurrying to his car. Something changes, like a spell has been broken and finally I can move again. "It'll have to wait. I've got to dash."

I run then, my legs stretching out and my lungs pulling in great big gulps of hot air. Only when my pace catches up with the rapid firing of my heart and I'm at the end of the road do I stop and look back. Matthew is still standing where I left him, staring after me; his phone is out, and I'm sure he's taking more of his stupid photos.

We'll have to talk at some point. Anxiety worms through my body as I start to run again, reaching my client's house five minutes late. Her car pulls onto the driveway just as I'm ringing the doorbell.

"Sorry," she calls out, leaping from the car. "I got stuck talking to the mums after drop-off. Have you been waiting long?"

"No, you're fine." I breathe a sigh of relief.

"Your hair looks amazing. That gray-blond is really in right now."

"Thanks." I smile and make myself focus on my day and my client, and the life I'm trying so flipping hard to live, instead of on Matthew, and the memories and hurt that are never far from my thoughts.

"You're a big sister now, Sophie. It's your job to look after Matthew. You have to promise you'll always be there for him."

"I promise. I pinky promise."

"Thank you. You're the best daughter a mummy could ask for, and I know you'll be the best sister too."

CHAPTER 4

To: Jenna.Lawson@westburydistrict.org.uk
From: Jennaonlylovesherself@mailpalz.co.uk
Subject: You

It's a great act you've got going on, Jenna. You pretend to love
your children, but I see the truth, and you know it! That's what
scares you the most, isn't it? That I see you for who you really
are—a woman who only loves herself.

   One day soon they're going to see the real you. I'm going to
make sure of it, so you can stop pretending now.

***

To: Jenna.Lawson@westburydistrict.org.uk
From: StuartBethArchie@mailpalz.co.uk
Subject: Us

Are you ready to meet me yet? Have you had enough of these
games we're playing?

* * *

To: AccidentandEmergency@westburydistrict.org.uk
From: Humanresources@mailpalz.co.uk
Subject: Gross misconduct

Dear Colleagues,

Please be advised that Dr. Jenna Lawson will no longer be
working at A&E due to gross misconduct.
   She is a disgrace to our profession. She is incompetent. She
is a dirty stain on our hospital and so we have FIRED her!!!!!

Best regards,
Human Resources

* * *

To: Jenna.Lawson@westburydistrict.org.uk
From: BethandArchielovedaddymore@mailpalz.co.uk
Subject: Time's running out

When are you going to DIE DIE DIE DIE DIE DIE DIE DIE DIE
DIE DIE DIE DIE DIE DIE DIE DIE DIE
DIE DIE DIE DIE DIE DIE DIE DIE
DIE DIE DIE DIE DIE DIE DIE
DIE DIE DIE DIE DIE DIE DIE
DIE DIE DIE DIE?????

* * *

To: Jenna.Lawson@westburydistrict.org.uk
From: JennaLouiseLawson1978@mailpalz.co.uk
Subject: My gift

Did you like my gift this morning? I called her Jenna. Jen for
short. What did Archie say? I bet he cried, didn't he? He really is
a crybaby. It's your fault!!! He can see right through all of your
pretending crap. Did you see the way they both ran to your
childminder this morning? Couldn't wait to get away from you.
Not that I blame them!! You know they'd be happier without
you, right?

CHAPTER 5

Jenna

The conviction rate for stalkers is less than 15 percent. I looked it up early on, before you peeled away all of my confidence and stole the last vestige of hope.

Even back then, even with the percentage so low, I clung to it. I reported you to the police, feeling so silly and time-wasting when I slid the cards you sent across the desk of the interview room with Stuart by my side. I was still trying to convince myself it was a silly joke, but they took it all seriously.

It was December. The same day I half saw you for the first time, when you were just a shadowy figure who threw that . . . that thing at me, and they wanted to know when it started.

"July," I said, realizing for the first time how long it had been going on. And then it didn't feel like a joke, it felt crazy that I hadn't reported it earlier. But it all happened so slowly, and I kept telling myself it was harmless, that it would go away.

How naive I was when I opened that first card with the pink carnations on it that you sent to the hospital. Just two words inside:

Thank you.

I remember thinking it was odd that no one had signed it, but it didn't toy with my mind in the middle of the night like the next one did a week later. The second card came through the letterbox. Same flowers on the front. Different words, and this one hand-delivered.

You're Perfect.

They kept coming after that, like you were writing out the messages from a pack of Sweethearts.

At first, weeks could go by without a single incident, but since you stepped out of the shadows in May and showed me your face, your cold dark eyes, barely a day passes without you messing with me. You're so good at appearing when I least expect it, staying around just long enough to wreak terror on my life and then disappearing before the police can find you.

"Keep a diary, Dr. Lawson," the police told me. "Write it all down. Every sighting or attempt at contact and how it makes you feel. Prosecuting harassment isn't easy. Often just a warning from us does the trick, but if it does go to court, then having a diary of each event can make a difference."

That was back when they were confident too. But how can they warn you when they don't know who you are? When they can't find you to talk to? All they have to go on is my description, and even that I was only able to give them last month when I saw you properly. While I'd love to say you're the very essence of evil, you're not. You're just so . . . so average. Average height, average build.

Dark hair, not short, not long. Jeans and T-shirt style of clothes, often a backpack. That's how I described you to DS Church.

One average-looking man in a seaside town of two hundred thousand. And that's not including the tourists who flood in and out like the tide any time the sun shines and most times when it doesn't. You aren't even a needle in a haystack, you're one tiny piece of hay.

"He'll slip up one day," they said. This was a while in, when they were no longer confident but apologetic. "Just keep doing what you're doing. Vary your routine as much as possible and the routes you take. Always carry your mobile with you."

What they didn't say, but what they meant, was that stalkers escalate their harassment. Their obsession grows and with it their need for more, and that is when they make a mistake. I read that little tidbit online late one night, shining the light of my phone away from Stuart's sleeping face so as not to wake him.

But even though I've stopped expecting it to lead to anything, I still log every sighting with the police.

FIVE MINUTES BEFORE my shift starts I walk through the hospital doors. I ignore the sign for A&E and head toward the back of the hospital. Stopping by the police station to drop off your latest gift has almost made me late, but I still have time to gather myself before I'm due to start work.

I turn a corner and then another, until I reach my destination— a set of three female toilets half-hidden beneath a staircase.

The walls are painted a garish yellow and the room smells of human waste and bleach, mingled together with the lavender air freshener that squirts out from a little box by the sinks every five minutes, but I like the quiet compared to the new toilets at the front of the hospital.

I choose the last cubicle in the row and lock the door. I drop the lid of the toilet seat and sit for a moment, feeling so tired. So spent. And I haven't even started my shift yet.

I reach inside my bag for my diary—a black A5 day planner I bought just for you. The first entry is the day I saw you standing in the park across the road from the house. It was early December when I was going to work and coming home in pitch-black darkness most days. It's hard to remember how I felt back then as I opened the front door. Alert, I suppose. Since July I'd been receiving cards and the occasional e-mail that made my blood run cold. There'd been hang-up calls to the house. The phone would ring endlessly in the middle of the night until we unplugged it and decided to go without a landline.

My head was full of the pre-Christmas panic of trying to fit in even one of the long list of festive events the school had invited parents to. Plus Christmas shopping and the set meal the A&E staff all begrudgingly paid for and went to each year, plus work itself which was a constant stream of homeless people with pleurisy or pneumonia, and office party mishaps. Not to mention the barrage of accidents from hanging Christmas lights.

I stepped out of the front door, pulling my scarf tighter around my neck and there you were. A shadow behind the railing in the park. I didn't see your face and probably wouldn't have noticed you at all if you hadn't moved, swinging your arm back and throwing something at me. It flew through the air, catching in the light of the streetlamps and that's when I saw what it was—a doll with dark red hair, like mine.

Terror shot through my body like a bullet firing from a gun. I raced back into the house and up the stairs to wake Stuart, but by the time he went out there, you were gone. We found the toy in the gutter and took it with us to the police station, along with the cards. It was the sort of thing Beth used to play with when she was younger, the kind of baby doll with the eyes that close by themselves whenever it's lying down, except this one had no eyes. They'd been picked out, and one of its arms was burned until the plastic had melted into a gloopy blob. But the worst thing about that doll, the thing that spreads dread through my body every time I think about it, was the clothes it was wearing—little green doctors' scrubs.

I skip through empty pages until I come to the first sick gift you left me in January—a pale pink box left on my doorstep with my name scrawled across the top. Beth scooped it up as she walked in from swim lessons and brought it to me in the kitchen.

I thought it was a gift from her and grinned as I pulled off the lid.

It was hair. Dark red hair, cut from a doll, the police told us later. No head this time, or body, just clumps of hair cushioned on a bed of pink carnations—Christ, I hate those damn flowers now—and burned bits of photographs.

The photos were black in places, bubbled and brown in others, but I still recognized the happy faces of my children, the family snapshots of us from holidays.

"What's in it, Mum?" Beth asked me, stepping closer.

I shoved the lid back on and pulled Beth into my arms so she couldn't look.

Stuart and I deleted our Facebook accounts after that, but it was too late. You violated me, and then you took your chance and slipped into my head, burrowing deeper and deeper until you're all I think about most days, most nights too.

The dolls became a regular occurrence after that, but you never bothered with a gift box again. The police sent everything to the forensics lab and for a while I held out hope that they'd be able to trace the dolls and who purchased them, but they were all a generic type. Easy to buy in any toy store or online, impossible to trace.

My hands turn to a date in April. The page is more creased than the rest where I've read it so many times.

> *An anonymous e-mail was sent to HR, to Don Russell, the head of the hospital, and to Nancy Macpherson, my boss, which claimed that I had sexually abused an eleven-year-old boy on a shift the week before. I didn't see the e-mail but I was told later that the details were graphic.*
>
> *I feel—*

I didn't finish the entry. I couldn't. Even now my chest feels like it's being pulled apart just thinking of that day and the ones that followed. I tried to explain to Nancy about the e-mails I'd been receiving and your harassment, wishing then that I'd gone to HR earlier instead of keeping it all to myself.

It took forty-eight hours to check the patient files, interview staff, and discover the claim was bogus. Forty-eight hours of the bottom falling out of my world. It hit me in waves of humiliation and horror, tears and anger. Still, I couldn't blame the hospital. They were just following protocol.

Stuart got excited about the e-mails, his well of optimism overflowing more than usual. "E-mails are better than fingerprints," he said. "Fingerprints have to be matched with ones already on their database, but with e-mails there will be an IP address which will lead the police straight to his front door." It didn't. You're too smart for that. You used a VPN—a virtual private network—and disposable e-mail addresses. It's frighteningly easy to do. I looked it up in the middle of the night once and even had a go at sending an e-mail to myself from a disposable account.

The escalation is scribbled across the pages and it makes my pulse race, my head spin, just thinking about it. What's next? Another visit to our garden in the dead of night? Archie came into our bedroom to shake us awake at four a.m. "Mummy, Daddy, why is there someone in our garden?" His voice was excited at first but he cried when he saw the horror on our faces and realized it was you. You were gone by the time Stuart called the police and went out there, but you'd left your mark—a scorched patch of lawn in the shape of a *J* where you'd poured weed killer on the grass.

It's been almost a year since it all began. It feels like a lifetime. I find today's date and log the sighting, fighting against the ever-growing feeling of pointlessness.

The door to the toilets creaks open and I close my diary and draw in a deep breath, another waft of bleach and lavender, before blowing it out with a puff like I blew out the forty-one candles on my birthday cake last month.

"Jenna?" I recognize Diya's voice and unlock the door to find my friend waiting for me with two Costa coffee cups in her hand. Diya is petite, reaching only to my shoulder. Her hair is jet-black and lies in a long plait down her back. She is beautiful, inside and out, and also has a wicked sense of humor and a dirty laugh, neither of which are apparent right now.

"Hey. Please tell me one of those is for me?" I smile and nod at the cups.

"Who else?" she replies, holding one out for me.

"Thank you. You're a lifesaver," I say, taking the cup and spotting the back of her hand, which is dotted with intricately painted mehndi artwork.

Diya and I met in A&E on my first day at Westbury and bonded over how similar our career paths had been. We'd both done our five-year medical degrees at London universities, followed by our years in the foundation program as junior doctors, working excruciatingly long hours and bouncing between different hospitals every few months.

By the time we'd landed at Westbury for our specialist training in emergency medicine, we felt like two female doctors in a male-dominated world, and enjoyed rising up the ranks side by side. But while I took maternity leave for Beth and then Archie, Diya kept working, moving from registrar to consultant ahead of me. The funny thing is, she is as jealous of me and my family, as I am of her and her role here.

Our friendship is another thing you've damaged. No more lunches together at the weekend, no drinks in our favorite bar in town while we put the world to rights. Diya understands, but still I know we're not as close as we once were. I don't have the space in my head to be the friend she deserves.

"It's only coffee." She laughs.

"There's no *only* about it. I didn't sleep much last night." My eyes flit to the mirror above the sinks. I look as terrible as I feel. My skin is pale, almost gray. My dark auburn hair is scraped back into a severe ponytail that sits at the nape of my neck. My eyes are watery green and bloodshot, surrounded by dark circles that match the navy of my blouse. I look unrecognizable to the woman I was a year ago.

Diya steps behind me and catches my eye in the mirror. Her face is etched with concern. "What happened?" she asks.

"Oh, the usual decapitated doll's head on the doorstep and then watching me when I'm taking the kids to school." I try to laugh, but no sound leaves my throat. I feel the familiar urge to cry and clench my jaw tight until it passes. I will save my tears for tonight.

"I'm so sorry this is happening to you. Did you take the doll to the police station?"

I nod. "I don't know why I bother though. He always wears gloves and they never find anything on it. It's starting to feel like a waste of my time and theirs." I take a sip of coffee, the hot liquid burning the tip of my tongue.

"Should you be here? Maybe you should go home."

"No. I need to work," I reply, my voice stronger than I feel.

Diya nods, understanding better than most. "Game face on then, is it?"

"Absolutely."

There's not a single thing I understand about this or you. I don't know why you've chosen me. But right now, I have patients who need me, and however scared I am of you and what is to come, however much you've taken from me, I won't let you take my passion for what I do. This place, this warren of corridors and wards, patients, visitors, doctors, and nurses, it's my haven.

So I follow Diya out of the toilets and squash thoughts of you, of my family, of everything, deep down and focus on the only thing that matters—doing my job, treating patients, saving lives.

CHAPTER 6

Jenna

It's nearly ten by the time I leave the hospital. The sun has dipped below the horizon, leaving only a faint smudge of orange and purple, like a melted rainbow in the distance. The rest of the sky is inky blue.

The streetlights on the path are the black ornate type that glow orange—a decorative feature rather than a functional source of light—and as I step into the gloom of the staff car park an unease begins to settle over me.

I look behind me to the pathway that leads back to the hospital and tell myself it's nothing. There's no one here. You've never ventured onto hospital grounds before. I imagine the CCTV cameras and security team put you off. As though trying to convince myself, I look up, searching for a camera. The car park is in darkness. There are no lights, let alone CCTV cameras like there are in the visitor parking. How did I not realize this before?

I quicken my pace, heading for the far corner where I parked my car.

The feeling of being watched creeps over me—a spider crawling up my back. My pulse races, my breath burns in my lungs to be set free. There's a noise, a clatter, like a pebble being kicked. I glance one way then the other. The darkness, like the panic, closes in.

I start to run, but my feet feel heavy as though my pumps have become a pair of Stuart's clomping work boots.

A loud whisper hisses through the night air. "Jennnnnaaa."

I gasp and stumble, my muscles freezing. I scan the outer edges of the car park, searching for the source of the voice, searching for you, and at the same time I'm desperate not to see anything, to just get to my damn car before you get to me.

"Jennnnaaaa." The whisper is like an echo coming from all around me.

Then there's a movement, a rustle of leaves from the bushes.

It's enough to ignite the panic, and now I'm digging into my bag for my car keys as I sprint forward.

"Jennnnaaa."

"Who's there?" I shout. "Leave me alone."

A lump forms in my throat. I can't breathe. There's someone behind me. Footsteps coming. I'm never going to make it.

My fingers wrap around my keys and I pull them from my bag, pointing my car key at my car. Nothing happens. "Come on," I hiss. The second time, it works and my headlights flick on automatically, blinding me for a moment as I rush toward the driver's door.

I yank it open, almost safe, and just as I'm about to dive inside, a hand grabs my shoulder.

The scream catches in my throat and I spin around, my arms flying up to protect myself from you.

"You all right, Jenna?" I recognize the mumbled Yorkshire accent and I look properly at the figure standing in front of me. It's not you, it's Thomas Carrick, one of the doctors I work with. He's eighteen months into his specialist training and a doctor I trust.

"Thomas." His name escapes as a gasp. "Did you just whisper my name a minute ago?"

"No." He takes a step back from me and glances around. "Are you . . . is everything . . ." He doesn't finish the questions he wants to ask. He never does. It's a habit Diya and I have teased him about more than once.

"Not really. I thought someone was in the car park. Someone was whispering my name."

"Was it him . . . your . . . ?" He looks around again. "Who's there?" he shouts.

My cheeks flame. I hate how everyone knows about you. All of the e-mails you've sent to my work colleagues have been mortifying.

"Let me have a quick look about," Thomas says.

I nod my thanks and watch him stride toward the edge of the car park. Every few paces he ducks down, checking around the sides of the cars he passes. He disappears into the dark and I realize I'm shivering all over.

"Couldn't see anyone," he calls out suddenly, and I jump.

"Where's your car?" I ask when Thomas has jogged back to me.

"Nowhere. My house is just over there." He points toward the road. "It's quicker to cut through the car park and hop over the wall than go the main way. Do you want me to . . . ? I can sit in the passenger seat if you want some reinforcements."

"Thanks, that's really kind, but I just want to go home."

"OK. Well, if it's all right with you, I'll wait here and watch you drive out, make sure no one jumps out."

"You really don't need to."

"I want to. Are you sure you're . . ."

"I'm fine. Thanks." I slide into the driver's seat. My hands are shaking as I push my key into the ignition and start the car.

I drive away, giving a quick wave to Thomas, who is standing where I left him, just as he said he would.

TRAFFIC IS LIGHT and fifteen minutes later I'm home. It feels like another lifetime that I unlocked the door and took Archie and Beth to school. I repeat the process in reverse, clipping the chain into place, before sliding the bolt across at the top. When it's done, I lean against the wall and take a breath, calm and steady as if it's anything like how I feel.

My feet, the small of my back, my whole body aches with the heavy exhaustion of a twelve-hour shift, of back-to-back patients, of the heavily pregnant woman who almost died and the eighty-year-old man with the stroke who did.

"Hey," Stuart calls from the kitchen.

"Hi," I reply, slipping out of my pumps and heading down the hall. My clothes feel sticky against my skin. I long for a cool shower and the sleep I know won't come.

Stuart is slouched on a stool at the breakfast bar reading one of his battered sci-fi books that I'm sure he's read ten times before. There are hundreds of them around the house—lining bookshelves in blacks and reds and yellows, stacked under the bed, boxed in the loft.

I bought him a Kindle for Christmas. It sat in its box untouched for a month before he gave it to Beth. "There's something about holding a physical book. I like the weight of it in my hands and the smell of it," he tells me anytime I moan about the growing piles of dog-eared paperbacks.

The first thing I see when I step into the kitchen is the stack of dirty plates beside the open dishwasher. I'd like to say I don't mind but I do. It's one of the things we used to bicker about—Stuart's messy side. That, and my long hours at the hospital. The "who does the most?" fight I'm sure all couples have.

I can't remember the last time we argued about the mundane stuff. You have been a sledgehammer to my life—you've stolen my ability to sleep, to laugh, to have fun, but with all that has come a wider perspective. And despite the destruction you've caused, my marriage is stronger than it's ever been. You saved it in fact.

Stuart was trying to call it quits on our marriage before you came along.

"I don't want to fight with you anymore," he said one night in early December.

Of course you don't, I remember thinking. *You never do. It's far easier for you to snipe your hurtful remarks, pile on the guilt, and ignore what's going on, than it is to face it.*

"But this isn't working for me. I want a trial separation and I want the kids to stay with me."

"What?" My head spun from Stuart's bombshell. He was leaving me and wanted to take my children with him. I couldn't wrap my head around it. "I know we've been arguing a lot—"

"All of the time."

"But things aren't that bad. This is Beth and Archie's home. You can't make them move."

"So you move out then. You're never here, Jenna. It's me that stays home with them when they're sick, me that takes them to playdates after school, me that knows what they like, far more than you do."

It was a comment aimed to hurt and it did. "Because you're a builder, and I'm a doctor. My job is always going to mean longer hours than yours. You knew that when we decided to have kids."

"Why don't you just say it? You think your job is more important than mine."

"What do you expect me to say to that, Stuart?"

"I want you to agree that the kids are staying in this house and they're staying with me. I'm their main caregiver."

But I couldn't agree. I couldn't leave my children. So round and round we went until I called a truce. "Let's give the kids one more happy-family Christmas and try to get on," I said. "If you still want to separate in January then I won't fight about it anymore. We'll do whatever's best for the kids."

It didn't feel like a truce. It felt like a stay of execution. But then the following week I opened my front door and there you were in the park throwing that doll at me. And somewhere amidst the terror, you allowed us to see what matters. You brought Stuart and me back together and we stopped seeing the worst in each other.

So now when Stuart leaves a job half-done because he wants to read for a while, I shrug off the annoyance and think of it as typical Stuart. Instead of the first words that leave my mouth being filled with sarcasm and annoyance, I remind myself that he collected the kids from Christie, he cooked their dinner, he bathed them, he read to them, he kissed them good-night. So if the kitchen is only half-tidy, if the water has been left in the bath to stain the rim, if the towels are laying damp on the carpets, then I try not to mind.

"How was your day?" he asks, looking up at me with a face

tanned a deep brown, apart from the lines around his eyes, which remain a stubborn white. I can picture him so clearly, standing in the dusty heat of a building site, paperwork bunched in his hand, laughing or smiling with the men who work for him.

When he looks at me and takes in the deepening pinch between my eyes, I wonder if he thinks of what my days are filled with. I doubt it. Stuart is happy and warm. He makes time to play with Beth and Archie whenever they ask. An eternal optimist is what I called him on the night we met, when we were both queuing at a bar in town, when Diya and I had been sick of dating doctors and went out one night in search of something different, and I laughed at his attempt to catch the barman's eyes.

But—and it really is a tiny, tiny but that I try very hard to ignore—he lives in a happy bubble and rarely thinks beneath the surface of anything. It's taken me a long time to accept this about Stuart and to see this trait as a quality. To understand it's why we fit. My whole life is spent looking beneath the surface. With patients I look beyond what they say to the tests needed. With Beth and Archie too, I second-guess their emotions. I read beneath the mumbled "fines," the "OKs," and search for the things they don't tell me. The bad days, the mean friends, the effects of a mother who is too often not home.

"My day was horrendous," I reply. "How are the kids?" I lean in to kiss his cheek. His skin is warm and he smells of lime shower gel.

"They're good. Archie got stung by a bee at break time today. He's fine though. Oh, and Beth wanted me to remind you about something, which I'm not supposed to know about, but she said you'd know what she meant."

"I do," I reply, thinking of the ribbon I mustn't forget to buy tomorrow.

"Good. They didn't eat much dinner. I think Christie gave them quite a snack selection after school. I keep wondering whether you should say something."

"To whom?"

"To Christie, about the snacks."

I shake my head. "I don't want to rock the boat. If the other kids she's looking after are eating, it will be hard on Beth and Archie not to have the same. Besides, they come out of school ravenous. Maybe we should try giving them dinner a bit later."

"All right. Let's do that. There's some pasta in the bowl for you." He nods to the worktop by the window.

"Thanks." I glance at the dish. The penne has bloated in the sauce and dried at the edges where it has been left uncovered. My stomach growls, a hollow empty sound, but the last thing I want to do is eat.

"Do you want me to heat it up?" he asks.

"Thanks, but I grabbed something from the cafeteria on my break." It's a lie. I've barely sat down, barely had time for a glass of water let alone food, but the chew-and-swallow effort feels too much.

"How did the viewings go?" I ask, rubbing my fingers into the muscles of my lower back.

"Really well. One was a couple looking to start a family and one was a single dad with older kids at high school. They liked the high ceilings and the work we've done."

It was Stuart's idea to knock through the kitchen, dining room, and living room to make one huge space going from the front of the house all the way to the back. The sofas and television are at the front, then there's the bookshelves and a log burner in the middle with two armchairs, and finally the kitchen, with bifold doors opening up into the garden. With a park across the road, the garden can be forgiven for being small. The rosebushes we planted a decade ago are neglected and overgrown, but beautiful with their yellow blooms.

The upstairs feels smaller, more cramped. Three bedrooms and just one bathroom. We had a buyer pull out last month because the master bedroom didn't have its own bathroom. They went for one of the new builds on the outskirts of town. Small rooms and thin walls, but triple the number of bathrooms.

I used to love our house, our home. I loved how central we were—a short walk to the beach and the seafront, fifteen minutes into town, a park right across the street. But now all I feel in this house is exposed. There are just too many shop doorways, parked cars, and trees for you to lurk by.

Stuart stands, pulling me into his arms and kissing my neck. "What happened today?" he asks, his breath warm on my skin.

Easy tears spill from my eyes as I take Stuart through everything you've done to me today, from the doll's head on the doorstep to the voice whispering my name.

"Oh, babe," he says when I'm done. "You should've phoned me this morning."

"I know, I'm sorry. I didn't want to ruin your day with worry. It's not like there's anything you could've done."

"Well, what can I do now? Hot bath? Glass of wine? Foot massage? After the bath of course. I know what your feet are like after a day at work."

I laugh and swipe his arm. "Oi."

We pull apart and I wipe the tears away, feeling better from Stuart's support.

"A herbal tea and bed is probably the answer," I say.

"Coming right up."

"Oh no you don't." I push him away from the kettle. "You never leave the tea bag in for long enough. I'll do it."

"Suit yourself." He flashes me his lopsided smile before stepping back to the dishwasher and finishing the tidying. "How was your day?" I ask. "Did the plumbers turn up on time?" I flick the switch on the kettle and open the cupboard in search of my favorite mug with the spots on it that Beth and Archie gave me for Mother's Day a few years ago.

And that's when I see the doll.

MY HAND HOVERS midair as my mind tries to catch up with what my body seems to already know. A chill brushes over my skin. You've been in my house. You've been in my kitchen; you've stood exactly where I am standing.

This isn't happening. I blink, willing my eyes to be tricking me. They're not.

My legs wobble from under me. I take an unsteady step back and lean my weight against the breakfast bar.

"Jenna, what's wrong?" Stuart is by my side in three steps.

"The cupboard," I say, my words shaky.

Stuart follows my gaze to the doll. It's the same generic red-haired doll you always use, but its clothes are what I can't tear my eyes away from.

"Christ." His voice is no longer mellow but alert. Hearing the change in his tone hammers home the panic circling my body and I gasp.

"Look." I swallow hard, gesturing at my trousers and navy blouse before staring again at the doll, who is dressed in the exact same outfit.

"Get rid of it, please. Throw it away."

"We can't, Jenna. He might have left a fingerprint or DNA this time."

I shake my head, hugging my arms to my body. "He's too smart for that. He's never left a single piece of evidence behind in all these months."

"He's never been in the house before either," Stuart says. "Maybe he's slipped up."

"How did he get in?" I spin around and look through to the front windows. The sky is black. With the kitchen lights on, we might as well be on a stage with spotlights pointed at us. I dart across the floor to the living room and check the windows. Locked.

Then I grab at the soft cream linen and yank the curtains shut. There's an inch gap where they don't close properly and I pull at the fabric and try to wrap them together. I knew they didn't fit when I bought them, but they were supposed to be decorative not useful. Once upon a time I liked the idea of people looking into our big front window and seeing our beautiful home. It never crossed my mind that someone like you would be looking in. Now it's all I think about.

By the time I'm back in the kitchen I'm stumbling on feet that don't feel like my own. Stuart is standing exactly where I left him, still staring into the cupboard.

"Did you leave the back doors open when you took the kids up for a bath?" I ask.

"No." He shakes his head. "You know I wouldn't be that careless. We didn't even open them with dinner because Archie was worried about a bee coming in."

"How did he get in then?"

"I don't know." Stuart closes the distance between us and I collapse against him.

"I love you," Stuart says.

"I love you too."

"Let's call the police," Stuart says, and I nod, shivering against the warmth of his body.

CHAPTER 7

JENNA

While we wait for the police to arrive we check the house, top to bottom. Under the beds, inside the wardrobes, anywhere you might be, just in case. We check the windows and the doors for any sign of a break-in too.

"I don't understand it. No one's been here except us," I say.

"Oh God," Stuart says, his voice suddenly quiet as he sinks onto the sofa. "The viewings—the potential buyers—it had to be then."

"But you were here, you showed them around. How could . . ." My voice trails off, the truth dawning slow in my exhausted state. "Stuart, no! You promised you'd do it."

"I was going to but the times got changed. One of the appointments got pushed back an hour and I couldn't leave the site for that long. We had a council inspector in today. Wayne swung by and got the keys and did the viewings for us. I told him to be extra careful."

I close my eyes for a moment against the tidal wave of anger pushing through me. *One job,* is what I think. All Stuart had to do was this one thing and he didn't, and now you've been in our house, our home, the place our children sleep. I bite the inside of my cheek until the feeling passes, and then I remind myself that it's not his fault, it's yours. Always yours.

I picture Wayne. He's a typical Westbury estate agent. Early twenties, tight suit, shaped eyebrows, and a spray tan. A talker, only drawing breath when I interrupt with a question or a remark, and then he nods his head, but I never get the feeling he's listening.

"Have you checked the camera?" I ask.

He shakes his head. "Not yet. I assumed the alert was from the viewings and forgot about it." Even as Stuart reaches into his pocket for his phone, a dread is sinking down inside me. We had the camera installed above the front door early on into your doorstep gifts. Christ, we were so smug about it too, convinced we would catch you and it would all be over in a matter of weeks.

Every time the camera registers a movement it starts a thirty-second recording. When it's done, an e-mail is sent to Stuart with a link to check the footage. So far, the videos we have of you are the top of a black umbrella approaching the door and then retreating out of sight. Sometimes we catch a glimpse of a white Puma logo on one side, but it's not enough for the police to work with. Every sports shop in town sells them.

"I've got them here," Stuart says, holding his phone for us both to see. "That's odd. There's only one. There should be loads more than this with me leaving first thing, then you and the kids, two viewings in and then out again, and us coming home."

We watch in silence. It's over so fast I don't know what I've seen.

"What just happened?" I stare at the gray screen. "Can you play it again?"

Stuart presses play and I lean closer, my eyes focused on the quick-fire movement this time. A hand, gloved in black, reaches out from beneath the umbrella and touches the camera with something and everything goes dark. It's over in seconds.

"This is insane," Stuart mutters.

We share a look before going together to the front door. I let Stuart open it, hating the feeling of cowering behind him like I'm one of those helpless characters in a cheesy '90s horror movie, the one who screams a lot and always gets killed first.

Stuart swears under his breath and I follow his gaze to the camera and the white sticker now covering the lens. It looks like a sticky label, the kind I use on the Tupperware boxes that go in the freezer to remind me what leftovers are in them, the kind you can buy from any supermarket or stationery shop.

"Can you call Wayne?" I ask Stuart the moment we're locked inside once more. "You said the first viewing was a couple, right? But the second was a man on his own? Find out who he let into our house."

"It's a bit late to call him now," Stuart replies.

"He said call anytime, didn't he? 'Day or night' were his exact words."

Stuart nods and fishes out his phone. I stare at the canvas of Beth and Archie on the wall and the glass bowl of shells above the fireplace that we add to each time we take a trip to the beach, and I wonder what you touched.

Stuart finishes his call to Wayne and rubs his hands across his face.

"What did he say?" I ask.

"Not much. He was careful to lock up after the viewings. He said the guy was in his midthirties. He must have lied about having kids at high school. Wayne said he was normal-looking, but maybe a bit weird."

"What if he made a key? Should we change the locks again?"

"He can't have made a key. These keys need to be ordered and you can't order them without a special code, which only I have. Wayne dropped the key back to me earlier. He can't get back in."

I let the tears fall then, sinking to the sofa and into Stuart's arms. Why are you doing this to me?

CHAPTER 8

JENNA

It's one a.m. before Stuart and I shut the door to the two PCs and climb the stairs to bed.

"Well, that was a waste of time," I say as Stuart follows me into our bedroom.

"What do you mean?"

"Come on. That whole 'it's not a burglary' thing. They thought I was making the whole thing up. DS Church practically said the same thing last time we spoke."

"Did she?"

"It was insinuated. Since they're having so much trouble finding him, am I sure of what I'm seeing."

"I'm sure she didn't mean it like that."

"Oh, are you now? Since you were there, were you?" I regret the words the moment they leave my mouth. I don't know why I'm trying to pick a fight with Stuart. I go to speak again, not sure if I'm going to apologize or carry on.

"You're upset, Jenna. I am too," Stuart says quickly before I get the chance, his voice calm next to mine. "But they are taking this seriously and sending a forensic team first thing tomorrow to dust the whole house for fingerprints. It's late now. Let's go to bed."

I brush a strand of hair away from my face and find my cheek is wet with tears I didn't know I was crying. I stare at the moisture on my fingertips and wonder if this is it—have I lost it? Has this new violation nudged me over the edge? I'm rational and thorough. This person—this frantic crying woman—she isn't me.

"I'm sorry," I whisper, dropping onto the bed. "I know this is affecting you too."

"You have nothing to apologize for. We'll move soon. We can even rent somewhere while this place sells. It'll be a stretch but we can do it. Once we're out of town it'll be harder for him to get to us."

"It won't be far enough," I whisper.

"What do you mean?" Stuart's eyes search mine and I know now is the time to tell him my plan.

"There's no point upheaving Beth and Archie's entire lives to move ten miles away, only for him to find us again. And he will find us. He only has to follow us home once to know where we live. We have to change our whole lives, move far away, and change our names."

"Our names? That's a bit much, isn't it?"

"Just our surname."

"I'm not running away."

"There's no other choice. We have to go somewhere he can't find us. This won't stop. He's not going to wake up one day and forget about me."

Stuart leans against the window ledge and sighs. "But the police will get him eventually. It's frustrating as hell but—"

"The conviction rate for stalking is tiny. And even if they find out who he is and arrest and charge him, the percentage of those convictions that actually result in a prison sentence is even less."

"We've got a strong case. You've been keeping your diary and we've logged everything with the police. They'll get him and he will go to prison."

"I'm scared all of the time." I choke back a sob. "And it's getting worse. Has it crossed your mind what he might do next? To me and the kids? Moving far away—"

"Running," Stuart cuts in.

"It's our only option."

"And then he wins."

"I don't care," I say. "Let him win. If I can get my life back, then someone can give him a gold medal for all I care."

"And what about my business? Am I supposed to just close it down? I started my construction firm from scratch twenty years ago. I quoted my first jobs so low I made a loss for a year just to get my reputation up as a reliable builder. Twenty years it's taken me to get to a point where people call me asking if I'll consider quoting them for an entire housing estate. My reputation isn't going to follow me to another country. I'll be starting from scratch. You can't seriously be considering this?"

Fight or flight—as usual, Stuart is choosing neither. "It's not you who has to deal with the fear I face every day. And don't tell me it's not affecting the kids, because it is. Archie is too scared to go into the toilets at school by himself. Now he's been in our house, Stuart. What if he breaks in next time when the kids are here? What if he hurts them?"

"I won't let that happen."

"Do you really believe that?" I cry out. "We have to get away. I can get a work visa anywhere in the world. We can move to

Canada or Australia. Anywhere. It'll be an adventure, a different way of life for us and the kids. It's not like we've got family here holding us back," I add, thinking of Stuart's parents, who moved away from Westbury before the kids were born. They bought a cottage in a village in North Yorkshire close to Stuart's elderly grandmother. We visit once a year in the summer holidays. Enduring five hours in the car each way for a three-day weekend. They're nice people, but they find the kids too much, flinching at every thud of feet or shout. We invite them for Christmas and other visits but they never come.

I can't complain. My parents live an hour and a half away in South London and we don't see them any more regularly. They're both dermatologists with their own private clinic, and when they're not seeing patients, they're traveling to medical conferences all over the world. I'm closer to my brother, Nathan, than to either of my parents. But I see Nathan even less. He's always on the other side of the world, working in places that need him the most.

"And what about the kids and what they want?" Stuart asks.

"They want a mother who isn't terrified every second of the day. I don't have all the answers, but I know I can't carry on like this. Just think about it, please," I beg.

Stuart stares at me for a long second, taking in my tear-streaked face, the tremble of my lips, eyes hollow and wide. Whatever he sees, it must be enough because his expression softens and he steps in front of me, pressing his hands into mine. "I'll think about it," he says. "It's late. We're tired. Let's go to bed."

Stuart moves closer, pushing me onto the bed and kissing my neck until my body relaxes and I crave the distraction he offers.

Afterward, I lie in Stuart's arms and listen to his slow steady breath. He's asleep in minutes. I close my eyes and try counting backward in threes from a hundred.

It doesn't work.

I try and think of other things—the ribbon for Beth's Father's Day gift, Archie's bee sting, our plans for the weekend—but my thoughts are a one-way train back to you. The exhaustion which has been a dark cloak over me all day has disappeared. I'm wide awake.

I've never been a great sleeper. All the studying and then years of night shifts have messed up my body clock. Though nothing has ever kept me awake as much as you have.

When I can't stand it anymore I slide out of Stuart's arms and move noiselessly to the landing.

I check on Beth first. Her covers are a scrunched-up ball at the bottom of her bed. She's flat on her back, arms out. I remember her as a baby so vividly. A tiny ball of warmth and red-faced anger. Even then it felt as though she was fighting for independence. When I gave her formula for the first time at three months old, Beth's chubby little hands gripped hold of the bottle, pushing my own away and chomping hungrily, happily, refusing to take my boob again.

And that magical baby smell—there really is nothing like it. By the time Beth arrived I'd handled babies in A&E plenty of times. I thought I knew everything about them but I was just as clueless as every other first-time mother. Just as besotted too.

I spent hours in the nursing chair in Beth's bedroom, rocking and cuddling, breathing her in. For the first time in my adult life, medicine wasn't the most important thing. And that scared and delighted me in equal measure.

In the semidarkness I catch the slight curve of her changing body and a sudden panic flutters in my empty stomach. What do you think when you look at Beth?

It's a down-the-rabbit-hole-never-to-return type of thought and I force it away.

Archie's bedroom is at the back of the house and cooler than the other rooms, but he's wrapped up in his duvet so tight that his hair is damp with sweat.

My memory of Archie as a baby is less defined. Life was different—hectic. Quiet cuddles were had late at night or in between entertaining Beth—snatches of time that were over as soon as they began. And yet somehow he still feels like my little baby. My funny sweet boy who lives most of his life fighting aliens on his imaginary planet of Bong.

I lean down and kiss his cheek and feel his breath brush my skin before I creep out of the room and down the stairs.

In the kitchen, I turn on the light. I long to open the back doors and let the night air sweep through the house, but it doesn't feel safe. My jaw clenches. I hate you for doing this to me.

I stare around my kitchen—the pale wood worktops, cream cupboards, and the matching island in the middle of the floor with four stools positioned around it. In between the worktop and top cupboards the walls are tiled with the terra-cotta squares Stuart chose for us because I was stuck at work the day the decision had to be made. Anytime I look at the tiles, all I see are the three children and two teachers who died when their school bus crashed off a bridge and fell to the road below. We saved so many lives that day, but it's the ones I didn't save that haunt me.

My gaze moves to the calendar, hanging on the wall between the fridge and the bifold doors. I made it for Stuart for Christmas, using different photos of Beth and Archie for each month. June is a photo of them arm in arm on a bouncy castle.

Our entire lives are scrawled across the pages. Stuart is blue ink, I'm green. Beth is orange and Archie is red. You've been in our house. You've seen this.

I rush forward, snatching the calendar from the wall and laying it across the island worktop. Orange and red—trampoline park party this weekend. Blue—away at the end of the month for a boys' weekend in Holland. Green—Diya's birthday drinks. Orange and red—dentist. And on it goes. A printout of my shift pattern is stuck down one side.

We might as well have given you a set of keys to our lives. You know exactly where I will be, for how long, with whom. You know when I'll be here alone and when I'll be traveling to and from the hospital. I can take different routes, I'll move the kids' dentist appointment, but it won't be enough. It'll never be enough.

Sometime in the early hours, when the dawn is breaking a yolky orange in the distance, I tiptoe back to bed and sleep for an hour. There is only one thought on my mind as my eyelids close and exhaustion pulls me into its depths—I can't live like this anymore.

CHAPTER 9

Sophie, *age 8*

Her nan's front room smells like the Travel Sweets in the gold tin. The slightly stale red and green squares, covered in powdery sugar, that her nan likes to suck on while watching *Countdown* in the afternoons.

The room is old-fashioned and hasn't changed a bit in the years that Sophie can remember and probably a hundred before that. Everything is dark brown. The carpet and the curtains are brown; so is the sideboard where her nan keeps the old board games and the posh glasses Sophie isn't allowed to touch. The sofa and armchair are brown with faded flowers on the fabric, and the wall with the gas fire is covered with wallpaper that's supposed to make it look like a brown brick wall. Even the lampshade is brown.

In a corner is a wooden TV cabinet with doors and two brass rings for handles. To watch TV Sophie has to open the doors and push a big button on the front. Not that she watches much TV at her nan's. The picture is a bit fuzzy, and anyway her nan is always doing fun things with Sophie like makeovers with her nan's old makeup bag or cupcake baking.

Her nan shuffles into the room in her pink slippers with the white fluffy trim, carrying a chocolate Swiss roll from the corner shop that her dad had rushed out to buy at the last minute. "This is a big day, Sophie. Are you excited?"

Sophie looks up from the coloring book and nods, not because she really is excited, but because that's all everyone has been asking her for the past month. Her teacher asked her at school last week. Charlotte's parents asked her the last time Sophie went for tea, and then of course there's her mum and dad, who ask her almost every day. The funny thing is that no one ever waits for an answer, like they're not really asking but telling.

It isn't that Sophie doesn't want a brother. She does. It's just weird. Everyone else's parents have a baby, but Matthew is already five. He already has a mum and dad, but because they don't want him anymore, they are giving him to Sophie's mum and dad.

Sophie was eating breakfast one morning when she was still really young, like five or something, and asked her mum why she didn't have a brother or sister like everyone else in her class.

Her mum stood at the sink with her back to Sophie and said nothing for ages. Sophie thought she was in trouble but didn't know why. Then her mum had turned, her face wet with tears, and pulled Sophie into a hug before she explained that she couldn't have any babies because something happened when Sophie was born, but it wasn't Sophie's fault. Although, the way her mum kept saying that last bit made Sophie feel like it was.

Sophie wanted to tell her mum that she'd only asked because Ashlee Greeves had asked her in the lunch line the day before. But her mum was really upset and Sophie wasn't sure if saying any of that would make it better or worse, so she said nothing.

It was soon after that chat that Sophie's mum and dad started trying to adopt. They wanted a baby, but no one would give them one because of their age and because they already had Sophie. So now someone was giving them Matthew, and Sophie should be excited.

Sophie tries to remember what Matthew is like. She met him once, about a month ago, but she knows her mum and dad have visited him more. He didn't speak, Sophie remembers. There were lots of other people there. It had been some kind of test. Her mum made her wear a dress and said if she was really good and smiled lots, then she'd get jelly and ice cream for dessert.

Her nan slides the cake onto the sideboard in the corner before giving a little shiver. "It's freezing in here today. So much for an Indian summer," she says with her usual tinkly laugh.

"It's always cold in here, Nan," Sophie says, without looking up.

"Well, let's put the fire on for a change. We don't want Matthew catching a chill on his first day."

Her nan stoops down to the gas fire and twists the gray knob at the end. Gas shushes out like air from a balloon and there's a clonk clonk clonk before the flames jump into life and the smell of sweets is replaced with burning dust.

"That's a lovely T-shirt, Sophie," her nan says, giving Sophie's shoulder a squeeze. "Matthew is going to really like it."

"How do you know?" she asks. "What if he doesn't like pink?" *I don't even like pink that much.*

Her nan makes a frowny face. "Of course he will. And he'll like you too. You don't need to worry."

Her nan shuffles out and a minute later Sophie hears the sound of the kettle boiling. Her mum and dad will be back soon and this time Matthew will be with them.

She looks down at the T-shirt her mum and dad gave her that

morning. The material is thick and very pink, and written across the front in white plasticky writing are the words *Big Sister*.

She would've preferred a Furby toy. The purple one with the sticky-up white hair like her friend Charlotte got for her birthday.

"You're a big sister now, Sophie," her mum said, handing her the new T-shirt. "It's your job to look after Matthew. You have to promise you'll always be there for him."

"I promise. I pinky promise."

The doorbell chimes its four-note bing bing bing bong. It's hot now, reminding Sophie of her classroom in summer when the air feels thick, like trying to breathe through the gloopy yellow custard they serve with the jam sponge on Tuesdays.

"Sophie, they're here," her nan calls as if Sophie hasn't figured it out for herself.

This is it, she thinks. She's getting a brother. She hopes he's the nice kind. Not the pick-his-nose-and-flick-it-at-her type like some of the boys in her class. Sophie smiles. Maybe she is excited, after all.

As her nan opens the front door, Sophie stands up, moves forward, then back. She perches on the sofa and then tries the armchair. Nothing feels right. In the end she sits back on the carpet and arranges the coloring pens in a neat line.

"In we go," her dad says. "Watch your step now."

"Well, hello. Aren't you a handsome boy," her nan coos.

The door to the front room opens and Matthew is guided into the room with her parents behind him, then her nan. When everyone is in, the grown-ups fan out and stand back.

Matthew looks around at the faces. Sophie thinks he's going to cry and bites her lip as the desire to laugh bubbles inside her. Sophie doesn't want to laugh. She'll get in trouble and might upset her new brother. He is the smallest five-year-old Sophie has ever seen. He looks like a toddler. She remembers that from last time too—the tiny mouse of a boy who didn't speak.

Matthew's T-shirt is too big and hangs off him, like when Sophie borrows one of her mum's old T-shirts for painting. Matthew's T-shirt is blue and has *Little Brother* written on it in the same white writing as hers. He catches Sophie staring and touches the letters.

"Would you like some cake, Matthew?" her nan asks, waving a slice of chocolate Swiss roll in front of him. The heat from the fire has made the icing melt and the sponge look all splodgy.

"Can I have a bit, please?" Sophie asks.

She looks around, but no one seems to hear her.

Sophie's mum, dad, and nan hover on the edges of the room talking about the weather, pretending everything is normal. Sophie picks up a pen, careful to keep the rest of the line in place, and returns to her coloring. So much for exciting. This is boring.

Matthew walks to the fire, each step slower than the last. Then he plonks himself down on the carpet, transfixed by the orange and blue flames shooting straight up behind the metal grille.

Sophie feels the eyes of her parents on them both, like they are in one of those wild-animal documentaries and everyone is waiting to see what she and Matthew will do next.

"Would you like a drink, Matthew?" her dad asks, already making a beeline for the door and probably the tins of beer Sophie saw him stash in her nan's fridge when they dropped her off. He stands by the door, looking expectantly at Matthew.

"Kettle's just boiled," her nan chips in, filling the silence.

"Are you going to say something?" Sophie asks Matthew.

Matthew doesn't move or reply. *It's like he's alone and doesn't know they're there*, Sophie thinks.

"Can he hear us, Mum? Is he deaf? No one told me he was deaf," she says, feeling suddenly annoyed at her parents and this boy. Why was everyone acting different?

"Don't be rude, Sophie. He's just taking it all in," her mum replies, her voice cheery, but Sophie hears a warning in her tone too. "Remember your promise?"

Sophie nods, feeling a lump in her throat. She was only asking a question. Her vision starts to blur but she doesn't want to cry. Her dad will say she's attention-seeking like he always does anytime she gets upset.

Sophie flops onto her belly and pushes the coloring book closer to the fire. She moves the line of pens toward Matthew's reach and then bends her head over the picture of the unicorn, forcing herself to concentrate on the rainbow pattern she's been doing for the mane. It's taking ages but looks really good.

There's a movement beside her but she keeps on coloring. From the kitchen, she hears the pop of a lager can and her dad's long thirsty slurp.

Matthew shuffles his bottom backward, easing himself slowly onto his belly like Sophie. His short, chubby fingers reach out and touch a pen, messing up the line.

A second later he picks up the orange and dabs the nib onto the page, making a tiny orange dot. He stops, as though expecting someone to tell him to stop. Then he leans forward and drags the orange pen back and forth in long scribbles across the top of the picture where Sophie was planning to color a blue sky.

"Well done, Matthew," her mum says. "Great job. Isn't that a great job, Sophie?"

Her picture is completely ruined but Sophie nods and pretends it's OK. He's only five, after all. Her friend Charlotte's little cousin is bad at coloring too.

"Are they flames?" Sophie asks him, tapping her pen on the orange scribble.

He doesn't reply. His face is turned back to the fire, his eyes staring into the flames like it's the best TV show in the whole world.

CHAPTER 10

Thursday, June 13
JENNA

I slip out of the house early before anyone wakes, before Stuart can ask me in a voice groggy with sleep if I'm in a fit state to work. I know the answer, but I also know that work is the only distraction from you. So I might be jumpy, my nerves shot, I might have barely slept, but the hospital is the only place I want to be right now.

Westbury is eerily quiet as I drive through the streets, like the town itself is still tucked up in bed with the duvet pulled over its head. I pass the metal grilles of the shut-up arcades and the motionless rides of the funfair. There are a few runners and dog walkers on the pavements, a delivery van pulled up outside a kebab shop, and a man with a wheelie bin is picking up litter dumped on the beach.

The town has a long pedestrianized high street—a mile-long strip of shops that cuts through the center of Westbury, all the way from the seaside and funfair at one end to the college and train station at the other.

It's a discount-store-and-thrift-shop kind of place. The sort of high street with empty stores that become pop-up shops at Christmas, selling garish festive jumpers and twinkling lights that will break after a day.

The hospital is another mile beyond the college on the way out of town. It's set back from the road behind three huge car parks and gardens with an artificial lake. The buildings are a mix of old and new. The old—two tower blocks in pale gray cement, built in the '60s and hideous—and the new—an entrance, an out-patient area, and A&E, rebuilt just before I started here twelve years ago. The new parts are one-story and built in sandy yellow with large windows.

I'm at my locker, sweating and breathless just before seven a.m. It's not the heat that's making my skin clammy, although the air outside is already insufferable; it's you and the "What's next?" question I can't shake from my mind.

I close my locker and tighten my ponytail.

"Hi, Jenna." Thomas smiles, stepping into the locker room. "I got you a coffee."

"Really? Thanks. You didn't need to do that." I take the coffee and breathe in the earthy bitter smell I love so much.

"I thought you might need it after yesterday."

My mouth drops open a little and for a moment I think Thomas is talking about the doll in my kitchen and I want to ask him how he knows, but then I remember the car park last night and the way you whispered my name. What would've happened if Thomas hadn't come along then?

"Thanks for your help last night."

"Anytime." He smiles. "If you fancy getting a quick sandwich at lunchtime, you know I'm . . ."

"I'd love to but I've got to run into town quickly. Another time?"

"Sure," he says, his smile fading a little. "Well, I'd better get in there."

Thomas strides away and I sink down onto the chair for a moment and sip my coffee. "Game face on, Jenna," I say to myself, smiling a little as I think of Diya.

My first patient is a woman with a broken nose and mild concussion who tripped on a loose paving stone outside one of the supermarkets. Her hands were filled with shopping bags and there was nothing to break her fall.

The next patient is a plumber who dropped a toilet on his foot, then a teenage girl with a severely infected belly button piercing, and then, and then. I move from one triage bed to the next. Focused. Listening. Asking. Examining. The barely slept exhaustion no longer matters. This is what I live for.

The next thing I know it's early afternoon, and aside from the twenty minutes where I rushed into town and back to get Beth's ribbon, I haven't stopped seeing patients. I'm passing by the nurses' station on my way to grab a quick drink of water when the red phone rings. Its ring, like its color, like its position dead center on the wall, screams urgent.

My feet slow, I sidestep to the edge of the corridor and out of the flow of doctors, nurses, porters, and patients. I don't answer it. That's not my job, but I listen as one of the junior nurses picks up.

"Westbury District Hospital, A&E," she says, rattling off the hospital name as easily as she would her own.

There's a pause before she speaks again. "Trauma or medical?"

The nurse hangs up and reaches for the tannoy speaker—a small black microphone with a single-press button, the same type they have in supermarkets when the call goes out for a cleanup in aisle seven.

"Trauma call, adult male, five minutes," she says, her voice clear and loud in the speakers over my head.

The charge nurse leaps up, giving instructions to her team.

"I'm here," I tell her before she pages me.

We gather by the entrance. Diya as lead consultant, then me, then Thomas Carrick. Two nurses—Amie and Callum—join us. The thrill of the unknown, the buzz of the unexpected humming in our veins.

"Hey," Diya says, touching my arm. "You OK?"

The truth pushes down on me for a second before I nod. "Yep, I'm good."

She returns my stare and I know by the look of concern creasing her slender face that she doesn't believe me. I open my mouth to say something, to explain, but stop myself. This isn't the time or the place, and if I start to talk about last night then I will crumble into the quivering mess I feel inside.

Diya gives my arm a quick squeeze before turning to talk to Thomas. She knows me well enough to know not to push me for answers now.

The ambulance pulls up hard. Two paramedics in dark green uniforms rush through the doors with their patient flat out on the stretcher. There's a large red collar securing his neck and obscuring part of his face. It's clear he's in a bad way.

"Let's take him to resus," Diya calls out, and we're all moving through the swing doors away from the cuts and the fevers—the walk-ins—and into the resuscitation bay where we take the worst of the worst injuries and those closest to death.

I walk beside the stretcher, my mind already building a mental picture of my patient. He's around six foot, medium build, and based on the dark hair and smoothness to the skin he's in his mid-twenties. A long scrape covers the half of his face that I can see. It's red, raw, and dotted with specks of black tarmac. There's blood matted in his hair too.

We're about to crowd into the resus bay when Diya's pager beeps. Before she can check it the charge nurse is by our side.

"Unresponsive toddler one minute out," the nurse pants.

Diya nods before looking at me.

"I've got this," I say, and she's gone.

"Listen up," I call as the stretcher is wheeled alongside an empty bed. "Everyone, listen to the handover."

Silence falls and all eyes fall on the female paramedic. "This is Matthew Dover. He was hit by a bus going approximately thirty miles an hour and dragged for around four meters. His left lung sounds clear. There is diminished air entry on the right side. Likely pneumothorax. Patient sustained an injury to his jaw. He managed to give us his name but he is having difficulty speaking."

The picture forms, and like a film I replay the accident. I see the bus striking the patient's right side, forcing him to the ground and dragging him under. I'd bet money on a broken rib being the cause of the collapsed lung.

"OK," I say. "On my word. Ready, steady, slide." And the patient is moved to the bed.

The nurse swaps the neck brace for one of ours. It's smaller, revealing more of my patient's face. A sudden unease tickles the back of my neck but there is no time to question it.

One of the paramedics hands a backpack and umbrella to Callum. "No idea why he thought he'd need an umbrella today," he says, and they share a smile. Callum tucks the patient's belongings to one side, but not before I see it, the black top, the streak of white logo on the side.

My heart starts to pound.

The paramedics step away. Their work is done, and mine has just begun. Callum leaves too. The patient is bad, but not so bad that we need an entire team around us.

Gloves on, I step forward to check the ABCs—airway, breathing, circulation—the three things that will kill him the quickest. I put my stethoscope into my ears and then, just as I'm leaning over his body with the sound of his heartbeat racing in my ears, faces inches apart, our eyes meet.

My hand reels back like I've been burned. I jump away, a gasp of air stuck in my lungs.

"Dr. Lawson?" Thomas says. "Are you all right?"

I nod. I swallow. I carry on. Goose bumps crawl over my skin. It's you, but I carry on.

I place my stethoscope back onto your chest and hear the reduced breath sounds the paramedic mentioned. "Get the portable X-ray," I say. "Circulation—pulse rate and blood pressure both raised." Your heart is working overtime to compensate for your collapsed lung.

I wave my pocket flashlight in front of your eyes. "Sluggish pupil response," I tell the team. "Call CT. Make sure we get the next space." We need to see the internal injuries.

Amie disappears to make the call and Thomas leaves to find the portable X-ray. For a moment it's just me and you.

I look down at my gloved hands. The tremor looks almost violent. I close my fingers into two fists and will it to stop.

You make a noise. If there are words mixed in with the grunted gargle I don't catch them. My feet draw nearer despite the terror gripping every muscle in my body. My heart is beating as fast as yours.

When you stare up at me it is with fearful unblinking eyes. You're scared. The thought causes a bullet of emotion racing through my body. It's anxiety, it's fear, but also, and I can't believe this—there's a tiny thrill charging with it. How does it feel to be scared? To be trapped? To be completely at the mercy of someone else?

The moment passes and Thomas is back, positioning the portable X-ray machine over your chest.

I should page one of the other senior registrars to take over and call DS Church. The thought is there, but I don't move. Instead, the X-ray loads. You have two broken ribs. One bad enough to puncture your right lung, just as I expected.

"Prep for a chest tube," I tell Amie.

"Matthew, my name is Jenna Lawson. I'm a registrar here at Westbury District Hospital," I say like you're any other patient, like you don't know exactly who I am. "Your right lung has collapsed which is why you're having difficulty breathing. We're going to place a tube in your side which will reinflate your lung. You'll feel a sharp pinch but it's important you stay still."

You give a slight nod. I turn to Thomas and motion him forward. "Have you inserted a chest tube before?"

"Only once," he says, his face lighting up. He hides the grin well but it's dancing in his eyes along with surprise.

"You do it and I'll supervise." This is not the time for a teaching moment, but my hands are still shaking.

Thomas works quickly, prodding your side and finding the space to insert the tube that will allow your lung to inflate and take the pressure off your heart.

"CT's ready for him," Amie tells me when the chest tube is in.

"Good job," I tell Thomas, and we're off again, out of resus and toward CT.

There's another "Ready, steady, slide," as we move you onto the CT machine.

"Matthew," Thomas says, "we're going to give you a CT scan to see what's going on inside. A nurse will be right here the whole time and I'll be in the next room. We can hear you so if you need anything just make a noise. OK?"

You lick your lips as if you're going to speak but scrunch your eyes shut instead and give a small nod.

"Stay very still for me and listen to the instructions on the machine," Thomas adds.

I drop into the chair beside the radiographer and watch from behind the glass as you move through the CT machine. It looks like a giant Life Saver, round and white with a hole in the middle that pulls you in inch by inch.

Time drags. There's an empty plastic cup on the desk in front of me, reminding me of my thirst, my tiredness, the ache in my back. My muscles are tense and I'm terrified you're going to get up and hurt me somehow, but you're not. Your injuries are real.

"Can you get the X-rays done on his leg, arm, and jaw?" I ask Thomas as the CT finishes. "I'll review the CT scans." The consultant radiologist on duty will analyze the scans too, but it could be an hour or more before that happens and we don't wait with injuries like yours.

"Gotcha," Thomas says, flashing me a wide grin and we hustle out.

I pull up a stool by a bank of three computers beside the nurses' station and wait for your scans to load. Nurses reach around me and knock my back, but I barely notice. Space is limited and we're always on top of one another.

The first scan appears on the screen. There's blood around your spleen—a wait-and-see injury. Then it's your spine. I stare at it—notch by notch, inch by inch. You're lucky there is no damage.

Just the head CT to go. The screen turns black then the shades of gray appear.

You've got an intracranial hemorrhage on the left side of your brain. I picture the bus again, plowing into you. I picture your legs crumbling, body flying, head smacking the tarmac. It's bad. As bad as it gets. You'll die if we don't act quickly.

A shot of adrenaline hits my body, shaking up my senses better than a hundred cups of coffee. You have been torturing my life for months, and now you need me to save yours.

But what if I don't?

CHAPTER 11

Jenna

The thought is sharp—an electric shock.

You need to be sedated immediately and shipped to intensive care. The longer you are awake, the longer your brain is active and the more damage the bleed will do, until eventually your brain will be starved of oxygen and you'll die.

I stare at the blob of bright white where only gray should be. It's a textbook example of an intracranial hemorrhage. The kind of scan the lecturers put in the PowerPoint slides in year one of medical school. Unmissable. But what if I did miss it? What if I let you die?

The question is so alien it doesn't feel like my own. As though someone else has whispered it so quietly into my ear that it slipped past my eardrum to the place where my own thoughts exist without me noticing.

It can't be my thought, my question. My whole life is about being a doctor. Yes, I live to be in A&E and the unspoken excitement of the emergency, but really it's about the people, it's about helping. Whether it's the plumber with the broken foot or the girl with the piercing infection, whether it's blue lights flashing or the slow steps of someone who's walking through the door themselves, I long to help, to treat, to save. It's what makes me who I am, it's the one thing you haven't stripped from me, so I can't let you die.

But if you live, if things carry on the way they were, how will I survive?

I close my eyes for a moment and try to remember what it felt like to walk down the street unafraid, or to check my e-mails without my heartbeat skyrocketing. The images don't feel real and yet hope still pulls at my chest. I could stop hiding inside our house and take Beth and Archie to the beach and the funfair, to London to ride the open-top buses. We could be a family again.

My head jumps forward two steps from theoretical to practical. I could claim it was a mistake. Human error. It wouldn't be the first time. In my first year of specializing in emergency medicine I missed a postsurgical pulmonary embolism in a young mother of three, and if it wasn't for the quick work of the senior registrar on duty, she'd be dead.

With you, I wouldn't even have to do anything. Your only hope is if I walk into resus right now and tell Thomas about the scans. If I don't, by the time the radiologist calls down to speak to one of the team the damage will already have been done.

Time marches on. I don't slide from the stool and walk away, but I don't go to resus either.

"Jenna," a voice calls from behind me.

I jump, and when I turn the room turns with me in a sickening wave of dizziness.

"Your trauma patient's SATs are dropping."

I almost fall from the stool in my haste to get off, as if my feet don't get the message it's time to move. The resuscitation bay is busy again—Callum is back with Amie and Thomas, and they're all waiting for my command.

"It must be the pneumothorax," I say, scrubbing my hands at the sink and pulling on a pair of gloves. "Let's sedate him."

"Matthew," I say, leaning as close as I can bear, "you're having trouble breathing. I need to sedate you to fix the chest tube in your side."

My hands move, steady and confident now. I find the problem— a kink in the tube inside your chest. I hold the tube in my fingers. My heart is pounding in my ears. I don't breathe. How many more seconds can your heart hold out for before it gives up? Ten? Twenty?

Suddenly Diya is by my side. "Is everything all right?" she asks. "Do you need a hand? Prep another chest tube," she says to Amie.

"No. It's OK. I've got it," I say, forcing my fingers to move, to fix the problem.

Your oxygen levels climb, your SATs normalize. I've saved your life.

Thomas steps forward, less self-assured now than ten minutes ago.

"You did everything right," I tell him, and it's true. "Sometimes this happens."

He nods. "Thanks. The X-rays show a dislocated elbow, a broken femur, and a jaw dislocation at the mandible."

"What about CT?" Diya asks.

I pause for the longest of seconds. Diya's forehead furrows and I can tell she's about to prompt me.

"He has a severe intracranial hemorrhage on the left side," I say.

There. It's done. That's twice now that I've saved your life.

As soon as you're stable, I leave the resus bay and collapse into a chair in the locker room.

"What was that all about?" Diya asks, two steps behind me.

"What?"

"You, just now. You were freaking out in there, Jenna. The others might not have been able to see it, but I could."

"It was . . . nothing. I . . ."

"Jenna, remember who you're talking to here."

I bite down on my lip and nod. "It was him."

"What do you mean?"

"That trauma patient, he's my stalker."

"What?" Diya's mouth drops open, her eyes widen. "Are you sure?"

"Yes."

"Oh my God. Why didn't you say something? You shouldn't have been in there."

"He'd be dead if I hadn't been."

My words hang in the silence between us, and as I watch the emotions play on my best friend's face I see the same thoughts turn over in her mind that I had earlier, and I love her for it.

She reaches over and squeezes my hand. "Go home now. OK? You look exhausted. Are you working this weekend?"

I shake my head.

"Good."

Diya's pager beeps and she stands up. "I'd better get back. Call me anytime, all right?"

"Thanks. And Diya?"

"Yeah?"

"Will you text me later? Tell me what happens to him."

She pauses for a moment before nodding her head. "Sure."

She strides out and the walls seem to close in around me the moment I'm alone again. Am I relieved I didn't kill you? Or disappointed in myself? Did I choose life because of my oath as a doctor, because whether you deserve it or not, I don't know who I'll be if I intentionally let you die? Or is it more simple: Did I just chicken out?

I don't know.

CHAPTER 12

JENNA

"Mummy," Archie shouts, racing across the floor and throwing himself at me as I step through the front door.

He hits me hard and I stagger to keep us upright and wrap my arms around him. My emotions burst out of their hiding place and flood to the surface. Love and joy and guilt, mixing like tie-dye colors.

Stuart walks down the hall with a washing basket full of clean and folded clothes. He grins when he sees me, lifting the basket like a prize. "A man's work is never done."

I laugh as Stuart steps forward to kiss my cheek. "You're amazing," I whisper.

"So true." As Stuart walks up the stairs, Beth runs down them.

"Hi, darling." I smile at my freckle-faced daughter, feeling whole somehow by the presence of my children.

She glances back at the stairs before turning to me. "Did you get the red ribbon?" she asks in a hissed whisper.

"How was your day?" I ask her, pulling her into a reluctant hug.

"Fine. Did you get the ribbon?" She steps away, watching me

accusingly as though she knows the answer is no and she's already planning her outburst.

"It's here." I rummage in my bag and pull out the reel of thick red ribbon I'd dashed into the high street for at lunchtime.

Beth tucks it into her school bag with a mumbled "Thanks," just as Stuart jogs down the stairs.

I'm swept into the kitchen by the tide of my family, my feet moving in slow motion. Everyone is talking at once. Archie is telling me about a game he played at lunchtime. Beth is asking a question about the weekend. It's hard to think straight. In the past twelve hours I've seen dozens of patients, I've saved lives—yours included—I've worked flat out, nonstop, and yet it's these moments with my family that overwhelm me.

"You look"—Stuart tilts his head and frowns for a moment—"wiped out. Did anything happen today?"

I nod.

"What?"

"He came into A&E today," I tell Stuart in a quiet voice. His eyes widen and he opens his mouth to ask another question, but I shake my head, nodding toward the kids.

"Guess what?" Archie says.

"What?" we both ask Archie.

"I completed my merit chart today. I'm the first one in my class to move on to purple charts."

Beth tuts from beside me. "Only because you get extra ones for not wetting yourself," she says, rolling her eyes.

"Beth," Stuart and I chastise together. "That's not nice," I add.

"What? It's the truth." She rolls her eyes again. "Can we watch a film tonight?"

"Well done, Archie. That's great." I smile at my boy and hold out my hand for a high five. "I'm proud of you."

"Not tonight, kiddo," Stuart says. "It's a school night."

Beth groans and her shoulders sag as though her arms have been knocked out of their sockets.

"Mummy, look at the finger dust." Archie jumps up and down in front of me, pointing to the patches of gray dotted across the kitchen. "Isn't it cool?"

"The forensic team came this morning," Stuart adds. "I stayed home for them."

"Thanks for doing that."

"No worries. I've cleaned up most of it, but it's a pain in the—" He catches himself in time and glances at the kids. "A pain to clean."

"Thank you."

"Right. Upstairs, you two, to brush your teeth now, please." Stuart waves his arms in the air, shooing the kids out of the kitchen. "I'll be up to read a chapter of Harry Potter in five."

"Who's taking us to Lacey's party on Saturday? Is it you, Dad?" Beth asks.

"What party? Have we got a present?" I ask. My eyes pull to the calendar, remembering something about a trampoline park.

Beth sighs and Archie jumps up and down in front of me. "It's at Wicked, the new trampoline place. I'm invited too because Lacey's brother said I could come as his friend."

My head pounds. Stuart touches my arm. "It's fine. We've got a present. I thought I'd take them. Get us out of your hair for a few hours," he says as though reading something in my face.

Is it that obvious? And if Stuart can see it, can Beth and Archie?

I force a smile. "Actually I'm not working this weekend. I'd like to come. It sounds like fun. Do they let mummies jump too?"

"Yessss," Archie shouts at the exact same moment Beth huffs a "No way."

"You have to wait in the café," she adds.

"OK then." I smile, pretending not to notice her outright disdain for me.

"Teeth and ready for bed," Stuart says again. "Now, please."

There's a clatter of feet as Beth and Archie storm up the stairs. I listen to their lighthearted bickering over whose turn it is to use the bathroom first and whether Archie is big enough to give Beth a piggyback across the landing. There's a high-pitched giggle from Archie and an almighty thud. He's not.

"Jenna, what happened? Did you call security?" Stuart asks.

I slide onto one of the stools and feel the cry of relief from the muscles in my lower back. "He came in an ambulance. He was hit by a bus."

"Are you sure it was him?"

I picture you staring at me from the corner of the road yesterday and dozens of times before that. I think of the umbrella you had when the ambulance brought you in. A black one with a white logo. "One hundred percent."

"Have you spoken to DS Church?"

"Of course." It was the first thing I did when I left the resus bay, as soon as Diya was gone, when you were waiting for a porter to take you upstairs. DS Church answered on the first ring with her usual brusque "I'm too busy to talk" hello. I tried to be concise, ignoring the quiver in my voice as I told her that I knew not only who you were, but where you were. She made all the right noises and promised to get back to me after she'd looked into it, but I hung up feeling deflated as though I were reporting a lost cat or a stolen bike rather than the name and location of the man who has been relentlessly tormenting me for months.

"Good. They'll arrest the bastard before he does a runner."

I think of the text Diya sent me on my way home. He's out of surgery for the broken leg. Induced coma. Intensive care. Try not to think about it! Call me tomorrow xx

"He's unconscious and in intensive care so he's not going anywhere." There's more I want to tell Stuart. I want to tell him about the power I felt when I stood over you and how close I came to breaking my oath as a doctor, but something stops me, rock-bottom exhaustion probably.

"Daaaddy," Archie and Beth call together.

"I'll be up in one minute," he shouts before coming over to me and sliding his arms around my waist. "Let's open that bottle of champagne that's in the fridge. This feels like something we should be celebrating."

"Does it?" I make a face.

"Jenna." He smiles. "He can't get to you anymore. The only place he'll be going when he gets out of hospital is to prison. Don't you see—the police will know who he is now! We can stay in the house, we can move on with our lives, get back to how it used to be." His face freezes at that last bit, his smile dying a little on his lips. "Like when we were first married," he adds.

"I know what you mean." I smile and wonder if Stuart is right—is this a celebration?

He opens the fridge, the jars in the door rattling with the movement. "Here," he says, ripping off the foil and popping the cork before I can say no. He slides the bottle and two champagne flutes toward me. "I'll be back in five minutes."

I lift the bottle and pour the fizzing liquid into the glasses before resting my head in my hands and breathing in the silence.

Stuart's voice replays in my thoughts. "The only place he'll be going when he gets out of hospital is prison."

If you get better. My heart flutters in my chest—a trapped bird trying to escape. I could've stopped you today. I could've killed you.

CHAPTER 13

SOPHIE

It's late by the time I get home. It's been a full day of clients in the heat followed by a long run.

I'm slipping my key into the apartment door when it's thrown open from the inside, leaving my hand hanging uselessly in the air. Something sinks inside me. I was hoping Nick would be asleep by now. I should've known his protective side would win over his "early to bed, early to rise" style, and he'd wait up for me.

"Hey." I smile, pretending not to notice the anger pouring out of Nick like steam from one of my client's hot tubs.

"Hi," he replies, the one word punched with annoyance. He stands back to let me in and even though I'm heading straight into an almighty fight, I can't help but marvel at the dark floors and the smooth oatmeal-painted walls as I make my way into the kitchen–living room.

I love this apartment. Everything is fresh and new. There are no spores of mold growing in the bathroom, or damp patches on the ceiling, no decade's worth of grime lining the cupboards like the last few places I've lived in. But it's more than that. The apartment block is brand-new and we are the first tenants to live here, and there's something about that fact that makes it feel like this one-bedroom, ninth-floor apartment overlooking the back of Westbury's shopping center is mine, even if we do just rent it.

It was Nick's idea to live together. "We hardly see each other at the moment. If we're living together, then we'll have so much more time to just hang out. And we'll be able to afford somewhere really nice if we combine our incomes," he said six months ago when the contract on my old place came up for renewal.

I wasn't convinced. Nick and I, well, our relationship has always been rocky. We both like our space too much, and I'd only just quit my job at the gym to work with him as a personal trainer. But then he'd showed me this place and the doubts disappeared. It was the kind of flat I'd only ever dreamed of living in, the kind of fresh start our relationship needed, I told myself.

If only sharing our lives was as easy as sharing half the bills.

My legs are aching from my run and I swoop down to touch my toes and stretch my hamstrings. I need to eat and I need to shower, but by the look on Nick's face neither is going to happen anytime soon.

As I straighten up, Nick brushes past me and moves to the window. "Where have you been?"

"I was working and then I went for a run." I drop onto the sofa, my body suddenly weak. Any endorphin boost is being sapped away by Nick's mood. A sudden anxiety twists in my stomach. Why did I stay out so late? I knew it would upset Nick, but I did it anyway.

"Your last client was Greg Leighton and that was over three hours ago. Who have you been with all this time?"

"No one. Greg was late so the session ran over." I choose my

words carefully. Greg is the only male client Nick has ever scheduled for me, and that was only because he double-booked himself
a few months ago. Greg is newly divorced and an outrageous flirt,
but it's harmless and I don't want Nick to catch a whiff of it and
reschedule Greg's sessions with him.

"And then?"

"Then I dropped my bag with the concierge and went for a run."

"And you didn't think to pop up first and tell me? I've been
worried sick about you. I called Greg and made myself sound like
an idiot. I even went out looking for you."

Nick doesn't look worried. He looks mad. Actually, with his
tight red workout vest on, muscular arms folded across his chest,
and his mouth pouting in annoyance, Nick looks just like Desperate Dan, the cowboy oaf in the old *Dandy* comics my nan kept
in the spare room. How have I never noticed the similarities before? Staring at him now it's hard to see the good looks, the kindness and warmth, that I felt so drawn to when I met Nick two
years ago.

"I'm sorry, I didn't think. I told you this morning I was going for
a run and I thought it would be OK." My voice sounds suddenly
small and I catch the flicker of triumph that crosses Nick's face.

"You didn't tell me you were going to be back so late. It's dark
out. How the hell did you run in the dark?" Nick starts to pace
back and forth in front of me. I wonder if this is what it would've
felt like to have been told off by my dad, if he'd ever bothered to
look up from his bottle of whiskey to notice me coming home late.

"It's the only time it's cool. And the entire seafront is lit up like
a Christmas tree," I explain.

"Why was your phone off? I must have called it a hundred
times."

"My battery died." I pull it from my pocket and plug it into the charger by the sofa. I want to remind Nick that it's his fault my battery is flat. If he didn't call me five times a day I'd have a lot more battery, but I keep it in. It's just not worth the hassle.

"How many times do I have to tell you to carry a power pack with you?"

At least another ten. I sigh and pull myself up to standing. "I'm sorry, I forgot. It won't happen again."

"Where are you going now?" Nick stops pacing and steps toward me.

I point at the kitchen. "To get something to eat."

"What are you going to eat?"

"Just a bowl of cereal."

"You're not eating cereal. I'll make you a protein smoothie. You'll need it after your run." He crosses to the kitchen in four long strides and starts pulling out fruit and spinach from the fridge.

Nick's smoothies look like the vomit in *The Exorcist* and taste just as bad. A memory flashes in my head of my old friend Vicky and the two of us eating popcorn on her bedroom floor; hiding our faces behind our pillows every time something scary happened, and giggling like a pair of loons when it did. We must have been twelve or thirteen at the time. It was my first sleepover and I didn't want to tell Vicky how scared I really was.

I shove the memory aside, surprised by its appearance in my thoughts, and I mutter a "Thanks" to Nick. There is no point arguing with him when he's like this. If I was still living on my own I'd open a huge bag of crisps and eat the lot. We don't even keep crisps in the apartment.

My phone lights up and I open Instagram for the hundredth

time today. Another reason for my flat battery. Greg has tagged me in a photo of him posing like a macho man in front of the mirror. He's pouting like a model and there's a cheeky glint in his eye that makes me smile. It's like so many of the photos on my feed, except Greg's is a joke. He's a long way off from losing the dad belly and having a body like Nick's.

"What are you looking at?" Nick asks.

I lift my head to meet his gaze. "Nothing much."

"Are you playing Candy Crush again? You need to give that game a rest."

"No," I reply, shaking my head. "I deleted it." *After you nagged and nagged me to stop playing it.*

I'm about to leave a comment under Greg's photo when the display changes and my phone rings with an incoming call. Trevor's name appears on the screen and I sit bolt upright, staring at his name and what it means that he's calling me.

Mum.

"Are you going to answer that?" Nick snaps, slamming the fridge shut.

Come on, Soph. Answer.

"Hi. Is everything OK?" I ask, pressing the phone to my ear. My insides turn to jelly and I fold my legs close to my body, steeling myself for what is to come. Neither Trevor nor my mum have ever made a secret over how they feel about me and Matthew. If he's calling me, it can only be bad news.

"Sophie. There you are. I've been trying to call." Trevor's voice sparks a thousand memories in my head; like ghosts being released from a box, they fly around my head until my thoughts are spinning.

"I . . . sorry, my phone was off," I say. "Is Mum OK?" *Please, please, please say she is.* My throat starts to ache and the threat of tears throbs behind my eyes.

"She's fine. It's your brother. The police came by earlier."

"What?"

"He was hit by a bus this afternoon. He's in intensive care at Westbury District Hospital."

I close my eyes, shutting out the room. Emotions explode inside me. Relief first—nothing has happened to Mum. Then guilt. Bile rises up to the back of my throat. Matthew was acting weird the last time I saw him. He wanted to talk to me and I wouldn't let him. This is my fault.

"Matthew isn't like you and me, Sophie. He doesn't see the world the same way we do. We need to protect him."

There's a silence on the line and it takes me a moment to realize Trevor is waiting for me to speak. "Is he . . . is he OK?"

"I don't know. It sounds pretty serious. He's in a coma. The police think someone pushed him. They asked me if he was in any kind of trouble—"

"He's not." I jump to Matthew's defense without any thought to what I believe. Same old, same old.

"You would say that, wouldn't you?" Trevor replies with a bitter tone I remember so well. "I told the police that we have nothing to do with Matthew anymore and they should be speaking to you."

From the corner of my eye Nick waves his hands at me, mouthing a "What's going on?" When I don't answer, he switches on the NutriBullet and the apartment is filled with the hum of the rotating blades.

"How did Mum take the news?" I ask when the blender stops.

Now it's Trevor's turn to be silent and I picture him in a tartan dressing gown and matching slippers, sitting in the kitchen of his house, probably drinking a mug of Horlicks. I want to ask where Mum is right now. Is she asleep or sitting beside him? I wish it was her calling me, her voice in my ear instead of just in my thoughts.

"You know how it is, Sophie. She doesn't like to be reminded," Trevor says eventually. "I should go."

He ends the call and I let the emptiness sweep through me. I do know how it is. Mum can't forgive me or Matthew for what happened, and not even being hit by a bus can change her mind.

"Here, drink this." Nick sits down beside me, handing me a glass of green gloop.

I do as I'm told and finish the drink in four long gulps, like it's a bushtucker trial on *I'm a Celebrity*, and will myself not to gag.

"Who was calling you?"

"It was Trevor, my mum's partner. Matthew's been hit by a bus. He's in intensive care." Tears well in my eyes. How could I have let this happen?

"Bloody hell," Nick says, wrapping an arm around me. He pulls me close and I can't stop my body tensing, like there's a pillow over my face and I can't breathe.

"I need to see him." I try to stand but Nick's strength holds me back.

"You can't right now. It's late. They won't let you in. My grand-dad was in intensive care last year, remember? They're really strict with visiting hours."

I sink back. Whether Nick is right or not, I know I'm not going anywhere tonight.

"We'll go together tomorrow or Saturday. You'll need my support. Besides, if he's in a coma, he won't know if you're there or not."

I drop my head into my hands. My ponytail drops forward, the bonds of the extensions tugging at my hairline, and it's all I can do not to rush to the kitchen for a pair of scissors and cut them off.

"This is my fault," I whisper.

"Yeah right. Matthew was a nutjob, Sophie."

I lift my face to look at Nick. "He's not dead," I cry out.

"Fine. Matthew *is* a nutjob. This isn't your fault."

"He's not crazy."

"What is he then? Because he sure ain't normal."

"He's just different. He doesn't feel the need to be a certain way for anyone. He's just himself, all of the time. If he doesn't want to talk, he doesn't. If he doesn't want to be somewhere, he leaves. For the first five years of his life, Matthew was in and out of foster care or being shipped from one relative who didn't want him to another. When he came to live with us, he didn't know what love was, or what was normal or not. My mum coaxed him out of his shell, but . . . after what happened . . ." I sigh, the hurt cutting into my body. "I think it's just easier for him to be the way he is."

"And are you ever going to tell me what exactly did happen?"

"It's not important." It is, but I can't talk about it now. Or ever. Memories push forward, jostling with one another to be free, and I shut them down.

"Whatever you say, babe." Nick cocks an eyebrow. He's pissed I won't tell him, but on this one thing, I don't care.

I'm not sure why I'm trying to defend Matthew. There's a part of me that thinks Nick has a point, especially recently. Matthew has always kept to himself. Taking his photos and working at the restaurant. About once a month, sometimes more but never less, we'd meet for a coffee or he'd offer to cook something for me. I don't know when exactly it changed, but there's been a darkness hovering over Matthew these last few months. He's taken to waiting for me outside the flat or bumping into me on the street. The questions he asks me, the looks he gives, there's an intensity to it, like he's trying to be my protector.

Maybe if I'd tried to understand it instead of avoiding him, he wouldn't be in hospital right now. The thought feels like a physical pinch to my insides.

"Let's go to bed. It's late and we've both got back-to-back clients tomorrow."

I open my mouth to tell him I can't sleep right now, but Nick is already standing, his strong arms pulling me up from the sofa with ease. Instead, I slip into my gleaming white bathroom and stand under the shower until my fingertips wrinkle.

"I'll never give up on him and you shouldn't either."

But you did, Mum.

CHAPTER 14

Saturday, June 15
JENNA

"A re you sure you're OK to take them to the party?" Stuart asks, leaning against the archway into the kitchen with half a sandwich in one hand and a cup of tea in the other. "I'm happy to do it. You didn't sleep last night, did you?"

"I never sleep, but I'm fine," I reply, ignoring the headache pulsing in my temples. "I want to go. Why don't you go out on your bike?"

"Might be a bit hot for a bike ride," he says, more to himself than to me. His eyes draw to his book, facedown on the counter. "Maybe I'll spend some time in the garden. Tie the rosebushes back a bit."

"Why don't you just read instead?" I know full well he'll stop whatever job he's doing five minutes in, and the tools will sit on the lawn until I badger him to put them away before one of the kids starts playing with them.

Stuart hesitates as though he wants to say something more, but I force a bright smile and unbolt the front door before he can. "Come on, kids, let's go jump."

Beth scurries down the stairs wearing black leggings and a cropped T-shirt that shows off her navel. With her hair tied up in a high ponytail and the shimmer of gloss on her lips, she looks tall, slender, and older than her nine years.

"Er . . . where did that T-shirt come from?" I ask.

"Lacey got it for me for my birthday." She shrugs. "I've worn it loads of times and you've never said anything."

I throw a glance at Stuart, pointing to my stomach and raising my eyebrows with a silent *Are we letting her wear that?* question. She looks so grown-up. Have I really been so wrapped up in you not to notice her wearing it before?

"It's what all her friends are wearing." Stuart shrugs. "Besides, it'll be like a sauna in that place."

Another day I'd press the point and make her change, but today I keep it in. I so want things to feel normal again for Beth and Archie. No more checking the doorstep before we go out, no more pulling over to the side of the road to call the police. No more fear.

"Are we going then?" Beth asks, a bright purple gift bag swinging in her hand. Archie is by her side, hopping from foot to foot in the blue and white Westbury football kit we gave him for Christmas. It already looks a little small.

"Yes, let's go," I say, making a silent promise to pay more attention to my children.

Stuart waves us off from the doorstep, one eye already looking at the football scores on his phone and whistling to himself. On Thursday night, with the champagne fizzing in our glasses, we talked for a long time about you. Actually, we talked about what our lives will look like without you in them. His optimism, his rose-tinted view of our future lives, feels as exhausting as my lack of sleep. In the car I let Beth put on a Little Mix album. We drive with the windows down, and both of them singing along to the tunes. Neither picks up their tablet from the pockets in the seat. It feels like a small victory.

"Has that man stopped following you now, Mummy?" Archie asks.

Beth hisses something at him, followed by an "Ouch" from Archie.

"Beth." I frown, catching her eye in the rearview mirror. "It's fine to talk about it. I'm sorry I was trying to keep it from you. It's only because I wanted to protect you."

"So has he?" Beth asks.

I nod. "Yes." For now anyway.

"Why has he stopped?" Archie asks.

"It's complicated," I reply. "The important thing is that he has and I'm going to try and make it up to you. I know this past year has been tough on you both as well."

The next song loads and the singing begins again. I concentrate on the traffic and the people on the streets and wonder if I'll ever stop looking for you.

We take the seafront road. The afternoon sun is still bright in the sky and reflecting on the surface of the water like a thousand shards of mirror. We pass the fairground and the stretch of beach with the yellow sand and brightly painted beach huts. Away from the amusements and the crowds the beach is pebbled and strewn with clumps of dark green seaweed. A memory from last spring surfaces in my thoughts. A family day at the beach and Stuart chasing a squealing Beth and giggling Archie across the beach, seaweed lofted in the air, threatening to drape it over their heads. I smile at the memory.

I can't remember the last time we all laughed with such ease.

The delighted screams of children and adults on roller coasters reach my ears and I watch the Ferris wheel making its slow turn next to the pale wood pier that stretches into the estuary.

The trampoline park is in an industrial estate on the way out of town. It's a huge metal hangar wedged between a kitchen trade warehouse and one of those car dealerships that promises to buy any vehicle.

The kids are bouncing with excitement as we pile out of the car, and I can't help but grin at their giggling. But then, out of nowhere, the spider returns, crawling up my back, the feeling of being watched, eyes on the nape of my neck that burn stronger than the sun's rays. I spin around so fast my loose hair whips the side of my face. My gaze darts in every direction, peering in between the cars and across the road.

Where are you? I want to scream.

I turn back to Beth and Archie and find they're already walking across the car park without me. My sandals flap the pavement as I run to catch up. "Beth, Archie, wait," I shout, my eyes looking ahead to the corner of the building. I can't see what's there.

They stop dead and wait for me to catch up. "Quick, get inside," I hiss, reaching for Archie's hand and pulling him along.

"What's wrong?" Beth asks, throwing a glance behind her.

"Nothing, nothing at all," I say too breathlessly, too panicked. "We're just late. I don't want you to miss the start of the party."

I have to get my children inside and away from you. The thought races through my head over and over until we rush through the doors of the trampoline park and I find myself peering out through the glass, searching for you.

My heart is still pounding as we step through a brightly colored reception area. I'd give anything to be at home with Beth and Archie and Stuart, right now. The doors locked, all of us safe.

Inside, the place is an explosion of color and noise. The heat in here is formidable and hits with a physical shove that sends nausea tumbling in my stomach. Loud music, screams, and shouts bounce off the metal walls. I stare out over the trampolines. At least fifty kids and some adults are jumping from one trampoline to another; others are bouncing themselves into a pit of squishy foam blocks. There's a café to one side that overlooks the jumpers. The place is cramped with sweaty-faced parents and another horde of children hanging impatiently over the barriers, waiting for their slot to jump.

Beth gives a little yelp, jumping up and down before sprinting across the café to her friends.

"Stop, Beth," I call out, but she doesn't hear me.

I push myself in between two tables so fast, a bottle of lemonade knocks to the floor. Someone tuts and I throw them an apologetic smile. I can't let Beth out of my sight.

At the far end of the café there's a group of girls hanging around a table with presents and gift bags piled on it. Stuart is right about the T-shirts. Apart from one girl, who is wearing a Manchester United football kit, the rest are in leggings and cropped T-shirts, just like Beth.

"Jenna, hi," Rachel shouts over the noise, waving a manicured hand in the air.

"Hey." I try to smile. The music is so loud. Every beat of it feels like a punch to the side of my head. I look down to Archie by my side, then back to Beth.

"I'm so pleased Beth and Archie could make it." Her smile is wide, but she keeps looking behind me, like she's waiting for some-one else. The rest of the kids for the party, I guess.

"Archie," a boy calls out, appearing from underneath the gift table. I look down and watch Archie grin from ear to ear and scurry toward the boy.

"Don't go where I can't see you," I shout.

"There's no need to stay," Rachel says. She steps closer and I catch the scent of her sweet perfume. "It's a drop-off party. The party host will be here in a minute and they'll take them off to jump. And I'll be here the whole time."

"Oh. I thought I'd stay."

"Really?" Rachel laughs. "I wouldn't be sitting here if I didn't have to be. You're welcome to, of course, but there's no need. They're perfectly safe here."

"It's not that," I lie. It is exactly that. You're out there. I felt you watching me in the car park. My children aren't safe. Even as the thought presses down on me another is rising up. How can you be out there when you're in hospital?

I feel myself torn. I don't want to leave Beth and Archie, and yet, how can I protect them like this? I have to go to the hospital and check you're still there, then I'll know we're safe.

"I promise, I'll watch them like a hawk," Rachel adds.

"Um . . . OK, thanks," I find myself saying.

"No problem at all. Pickup time is four. Here, let's swap num-bers and then I can let you know if there's a problem."

We type in each other's numbers and then Rachel spins away, throwing herself into a conversation with another parent who's just arrived.

"Beth," I call, waiting for her to untangle herself from her friends. "Will you be OK if I pop out to the shops? I'll be back soon."

"Yeah, fine." She nods distractedly and is already moving back to her friends.

Archie is more than happy to wave me off too, but I don't go. Instead I linger at the edge of the café and watch a teenager with a clipboard talk to the children.

The logical part of my brain knows that you're in hospital and that what I felt outside is a hang-up from the months of torture you've put me through, but until I've seen you lying in a coma with my own eyes, there's no way I'll be able to feel that Beth and Archie are safe.

With a final glance to the party, I turn away and head for the exit. I can be at the hospital in fifteen minutes, and back here again in less than an hour.

I'm walking across the car park when I spot Christie and Niamh. Christie looks different today. Her brown hair is sitting over her shoulders in light curls and there's a splash of gloss on her lips. I see her only when she's on the school run and looking after other people's kids and forget how pretty she is.

"Hi," we say at the same time. My eyes travel around the car park. Did something just move over by my car?

"Are you OK?" Christie asks, frowning as she looks at me.

"Yes, sorry. I was miles away for a second."

"I know the feeling. The swimming lesson ran over. I feel like I've been running around like a headless chicken all day. Are we late?"

"No, they've not started jumping yet."

"Oh great. What are your plans now? Want me to drop the kids home after the party? It's on my way."

"Thanks, but I'm just popping to the hospital quickly. I'll be back in plenty of time."

"There's no such thing as popping anywhere in Saturday traffic." She laughs. "Well, text me if you change your mind. I'm staying to help Rachel set up the party food so I'll be here."

Christie pushes Niamh toward the entrance and we say a quick good-bye.

I feel myself being torn right down the middle as I pull into a line of traffic moving slowly toward town. I don't want to leave Beth and Archie, but I have to know if we're safe. I have to see you for myself.

CHAPTER 15

SOPHIE, *age 9*

Sophie, Sophie, Matthew's locked himself in the toilets," Laura's voice shouts from the ground.

Sophie pretends not to hear. She doesn't like Laura Newman.

She doesn't like Laura's singsong happy voice when she's telling Sophie something that only Laura knows. Sophie also doesn't like the way Laura puts her hand up in class all of the time, even when Mrs. Noakes hasn't asked them anything.

"Why does Laura have to be such a know-it-all?" Charlotte used to whisper to Sophie before Charlotte's mum got a job in Liverpool and they moved away. Now Sophie doesn't have a best friend.

"Did you hear me, Sophie?" Laura calls up.

Sophie opens her eyes and watches the world from upside down. Her head is starting to feel woozy, but in a nice way. Sophie likes to count how many seconds she can hang like this before one of the other kids wants to use the monkey bars. Last week she managed ten minutes. Half of break time just spent swinging upside down.

Sophie focuses her eyes on Laura's bright blond hair and freckly nose and tries a shrug. Inside, her stomach knots and she wishes she could block out the world like Matthew can.

Matthew is always getting into trouble. Last week he stole the football from the older boys and threw it over the fence into someone's garden because they called him names. Sophie grabbed his arm and pulled him into the school before the boys could do anything to hurt him.

Two weeks before that Matthew tried to climb the fence and run home. Mrs. Carlson, the dinner lady, spotted him just as he was going over the top. They got him back, but Sophie's mum was called and she had to take another afternoon off work.

"Where were you, Sophie?" her mum had asked that night. "I thought you were going to watch your brother at break times for me?"

Laura spins away, running back to the big oak tree where her friends are waiting in their stupid little circle.

Mrs. Carlson is making her way toward the climbing frame now. Sophie watches her approach and wishes her nan could be a dinner lady, or work in the kitchens. Sophie and Matthew would be first to get the extra helpings of leftover mash.

"Sophie, dear, Mrs. Noakes wants you," Mrs. Carlson calls out.

Sophie nods, pulling herself up and swinging herself to the ground. Her head rushes with the sudden change in position.

"She's outside the boys' cloakroom."

Sophie runs across the playing field at full speed. She's the fastest girl in the school. Faster than most of the boys too.

"Sophie, Sophie," Laura trills. "Do you want me to come with you?" Laura runs up to Sophie, ponytail swinging, and loops Sophie's arm through hers. "I want to help Matthew."

"OK," Sophie says even though she doesn't want Laura to

come. Laura will laugh and tell everyone Matthew is a baby, and that's the last thing he needs.

Sophie steps into the school and makes her way to the cloakrooms. Stepping in from the bright yellow daylight, she thinks the school feels dark and gloomy.

"Hello, Sophie. Sorry to drag you away from your lunchtime play," Mrs. Noakes says.

"It's fine." Sophie isn't used to teachers apologizing. It's normally Sophie who has to say sorry all of the time.

"I've come to help too, Mrs. Noakes," Laura trills with a big smile that makes Sophie's insides tighten.

"That's very thoughtful of you," Mrs. Noakes says, giving Sophie a kind look. "But I think Sophie can handle this on her own, don't you? Now off you go and play. Sophie will be out in a little while."

Laura sticks out her bottom lip in the babyish way she always does, but she turns and runs off.

"Thank you," Sophie whispers to Mrs. Noakes.

"You're a good girl to look after your brother," Mrs. Noakes says, laying a hand on Sophie's shoulder and guiding her into the boys' cloakroom.

Sophie has never been in here before. It's painted a dull blue and smells funny, like the bottom of the laundry basket. She can hear Matthew crying. He sounds like Lady in *Lady and the Tramp* when she's left in the kitchen by herself.

"I just thought you might have a little luck getting Matthew to open the door for us," Mrs. Noakes says, "before we call your mum." She runs her hand through her short hair and lets it flop back into place. Sophie's dad calls Mrs. Noakes a born-again hippie, but

Sophie isn't sure what that means. Maybe it's something to do with the brightly colored clothes Mrs. Noakes always wears.

"I can do it." She hopes.

Sophie has to fix this. After the time he climbed the fence, she promised her mum she'd try harder to look after Matthew at school, and most of the time she does, but she also loves the monkey bars and Matthew is too young to go on the climbing frame with her.

The thought of her mum's disappointment makes Sophie feel sick.

Sophie knocks on the toilet door. "Matthew, it's me, Sophie," she says, even though she's sure he heard her talking to Mrs. Noakes.

The whimpers soften and Mrs. Noakes gives a big smile before backing away and leaving her alone.

"The bell's going to go soon," Sophie says. "Don't you want to come outside and play with me? We can play hide-and-seek or pretend to be Power Rangers. You like doing that."

Silence.

She inches closer to the door and pokes her foot underneath so Matthew can see it. "Aren't you going to say something?"

Another whimper.

"What's wrong?"

"I want Mummy," he whispers, before unleashing another round of sobs.

"Mummy's at work," Sophie says. "She's going to pick us up from Nan's house later."

"I . . . I want her now."

"Has someone been mean to you?"

Silence.

"Mummy can't leave work all the time, Matthew. She'll get fired." Sophie isn't sure what fired means, but judging by the argument her mum and dad had last week, it's bad. Sophie's mum takes a lot of time off work already for Matthew's speech therapy sessions. She has to work late on Tuesdays and Thursdays to make up hours.

"Come on, Matthew."

There's another silence, followed by the shuffle of feet and the sound of the lock sliding to one side.

She waits for the door to open, but when it doesn't Sophie pushes her way in, feeling suddenly cross at Matthew for the break time she's missed and the letter home that will cause another fight between her mum and dad. Her dad will storm off to the pub and her mum will spend the evening in tears, and Sophie and Matthew won't be allowed to watch TV.

She puts her hands on her hips, about to say something sharp when Matthew launches himself at her, wrapping his arms around her and crying into her waist.

"How's everything in here?" comes Mrs. Noakes's voice. "It's almost time for afternoon registration."

"We're OK," Sophie calls. "Aren't we, Matthew?"

Matthew's fingers dig into her back, squeezing her skin between his thumbs and index fingers. She gasps and pulls away, tears pricking at her eyes. "That hurt," she mouths.

"You didn't play with me." He scrunches his eyes shut, frozen to the spot as though trying to block out the world.

"Please, Matthew. Please. For Mum. Let's just go to class. I'll play with you after school, I promise. Any game you like."

Matthew opens one eye a fraction and stares at Sophie's face with his dark watery eyes.

"Please," she begs again.

He nods and Sophie feels the knots in her tummy unwind.

It's only when she takes a seat for afternoon registration that she feels the throb of pain in the middle of her back from where Matthew pinched her.

On the way out from school that afternoon, Matthew slides his hand into Sophie's. She sees Laura look their way and then turn, whispering something to Alison Browning. The pair glance again and giggle to each other. Sophie wants to pull her hand away but that would upset Matthew.

When she sees her nan waiting for them Sophie breaks into a run, pulling Matthew with her. She wants to tell her nan how much her back is still hurting from Matthew's pinch, but she's scared of getting into trouble for not playing with Matthew, and she doesn't want her mum and dad to argue anymore.

"He needs taking in hand," her dad is always saying. "You're too soft on the boy."

"How would you know? You're always down the pub," her mum replies. "What Matthew needs is our unconditional love. He didn't have the same start in life. We need to be patient. Even your nine-year-old daughter understands that concept. Why can't you?"

Sophie buries her face in her nan's clothes and breathes in the smell of freshly baked cookies, and promises herself she'll try harder with Matthew and keep her mum and dad happy.

CHAPTER 16

JENNA

Christie is right—traffic is slow and it takes forty-five minutes to snail-crawl my way across town to the hospital. Air-conditioning blasts my face, making my skin dry and shivery, but keeps the exhaustion from sweeping over me at least.

My stomach is a tight jumble of nerves that will never unravel itself as I think of Beth and Archie, and you, and everything that has happened.

The staff car park is quiet and I find a space near the entrance. It's Saturday. All nonessentials have shut down for the weekend, as if medicine can ever be nine-to-five. When I'm parked, I send a text to Christie asking if she minds collecting the kids for me, after all. It'll be easier to drive straight home and meet her there than battle the traffic again, and I don't want to be late to collect Beth and Archie. Christie replies a second later with a thumbs-up and I feel instantly better knowing that she is with them.

As I make my way toward the entrance I spot Thomas running across the car park.

"Hey," I say.

"Jenna, hi," he replies with a breathless gasp, jogging over to me.

"You look like you've run a marathon," I say, taking in the gleam of sweat on his face.

"I feel like I have. I overslept for my shift. What are you doing here? You're not working today."

"I'm visiting someone."

"Ah, I see. I'd better run. See you Monday."

I watch Thomas jog away. For a moment I wonder how he knows when I'm working. I shake my head and let the thought drop. I'm being paranoid. When I was in my specialist training years, I always knew which registrars and consultants were on duty with me.

Intensive care is on the fourth floor in the old part of the hospital, where the walls have cracked in places, showing the layers of paint and the years of touch-ups. I take the stairs two at a time and reach the double doors into the ward just as a man is being buzzed through.

The air is cool, one of the only floors in the old building to have air-conditioning and temperature-controlled bays. I walk with purpose to the large whiteboard by the nurses' station to find your name. The board is a mess, almost unreadable to those who aren't familiar with it. Dark smudges cover the board where one patient has been rubbed out in a hurry before another has been written over the top. There are rows of initials and abbreviations adding to the mess, but it doesn't take me long to find you.

Bed 6, bay B. Matthew Dover is written in small scrawling writing.

I weave past an empty hospital bed and a postbox-red resuscitation trolley and reach bay B. The area is larger than the triage spaces in A&E—one bed for our every two. But like A&E, there are no personal TVs, no extra comforts on this ward. Just machines and monitors and alarms.

There are six beds in the bay. Six patients, six people unconscious, six ventilators making their push-pull shhh of air in and out of lungs. But it's the bed in the far corner that I focus on. Bed 6.

I force myself to shuffle forward. One step, ten steps, and I'm standing over you.

The scrape along your cheek is now a dark red, but the black specks of tarmac have been cleaned away. There's a purple bruise forming along your jaw where the dislocation occurred. Your entire right arm and leg are wrapped in pure white plaster that hasn't had a chance to get dirty yet. I wonder with sickening hope if it ever will.

Up close you are more attractive than I thought. Broad shouldered, dark hair, and a tanned face with a bit of stubble.

What possessed you to do this? Why would an attractive man in his twenties stalk and terrorize me? I scrub up well enough for a woman in her forties when I have the energy, which is rare, but I'm nothing special.

You're smart too. All of your horrible gifts have been left without a single identifiable image on the CCTV camera, no fingerprints. You are cautious and meticulous. A ghost on the streets, appearing and disappearing just as fast. But why? Who the hell are you, Matthew Dover?

I focus on the wires trailing out of you—from your fingers, from your chest, from your head, snaking down your body and all the way into the machines keeping you alive. How easy it would be to flick those switches to off. The thought makes my fingers itch, my pulse skittish.

I pluck your chart from the end of the bed and flick through the notes, anything to occupy my hands. I discover your age—twenty-five; your address—134 Long Road West; and that forty-eight hours after being wheeled into A&E the swelling in your brain has yet to subside enough to risk waking you from your coma.

An induced coma is not like an ordinary coma. You can't hear me, you aren't dreaming or fighting your way back to consciousness. Your body has been pumped with a cocktail of sedatives, which have deactivated your brain. Everything your body needs to stay alive—cardiac rhythm, blood pressure, and breathing—is being maintained by machines.

Total shutdown. It's the only way your brain has a chance at healing itself. This isn't an episode of *Grey's Anatomy*. In real life, patients don't get whizzed into open-brain surgery every five minutes, and they don't wake up from surgery the next day feeling fine. There is so much more wait-and-see in medicine than most people realize.

I slide the chart back into place at the end of your bed and open the bedside cabinet. My eyes remain on you as if any second now you'll wake up and stop me. You won't. You can't. Inside the cabinet is your backpack, the one you wear slung over one shoulder. It didn't fare much better than you in the accident. One of the straps is ripped and there's a tear in the fabric down the middle.

In the main compartment there's a uniform. A white top and blue check bottoms. Whiffs of onion and garlic drift from the bag. Are you a chef in town? Did you see me in a restaurant once? Is that how we met? It makes no difference—the how, the why—but still I wish I knew. I wish I could pinpoint the exact moment when everything changed for the both of us.

I check the front pocket next, pulling out a set of door keys and an iPhone. It's smashed in the top corner and there's a long sharp crack down the side. The screen is black, but from a flat battery or the impact of the bus I don't know.

A loud urgent alarm beeps from somewhere on the bay. Two nurses rush in. I stuff your backpack into the cupboard and glance toward the noise, but it's not the commotion my eyes are drawn to, it's the couple holding hands in the middle of the floor. The woman is staring right at you.

She's tall and in her mid to late twenties, but looks girlish in a T-shirt and sports leggings that cling to her slender legs. Her skin is pale and flawless and her hair is long and dyed an icy gray.

The man beside her is wearing denim shorts and a T-shirt that shows off his muscular frame. He has a tanned face and brown hair styled in a gelled quiff.

The boyfriend starts to move, tugging the woman with him so quick that she stumbles and he has to pull her upright before shooting her a worried glance. As they draw nearer to you, the woman's face drains of color. Her mouth goes slack, dropping open, and her already large eyes are wide with shock or fear, I'm not sure which.

CHAPTER 17

SOPHIE

The hospital is busier than I expected and we have to push our way through meandering visitors to reach intensive care.

My heart is thundering in my head like the bass line to one of my running tracks. I should've come yesterday. I should've canceled some clients like I wanted to, but Nick hates it when we do that. Even this morning would've been better, but I had to wait for Nick to finish the boot camp fitness class he runs in the nearby park. Now it feels like I'm late, like I shouldn't be here at all.

A nurse shows us where to go and Nick grabs my hand, squeezing it tight before yanking me forward. He gives me a look, a silent warning to get a move on, to get this over with, but I'm jittery, unable to move.

This morning Nick suggested we go to the gym after visiting Matthew and work on our weight training. "As long as your legs aren't hurting too much from that long run," he added. They were, but I could tell by Nick's tone that he was still angry. The weight training will be my punishment for coming home late.

An alarm starts beeping from the bed near the door as we enter the bay. Two nurses rush by us.

My mind blanks. I can't think. I can't be here. Nick keeps pulling me and I let him, my eyes fixing on the bed in the corner and Matthew's lifeless body. I don't know what I was expecting him to look like, but it isn't this. His face is all banged up. There's a horrible red mark covering one cheek, and he has one arm and one leg in plaster. His skin is a ghostly white and if it wasn't for the beep, beep, shhhh of the machine beside him, I'd think he was dead.

"It's OK, Sophie," Nick whispers from beside me.

I nod and move the final few steps without being pulled. My gaze is no longer on Matthew, but the woman standing beside him with the dark red hair. She looks . . . she looks so much like Mum that for one crazy moment the world around me disappears and she is all I see. I feel gut-punched, the air forced out of my lungs, and I have to concentrate really hard on keeping my expression neutral and not blurting something stupid out.

Get it together, Soph.

This woman isn't Mum. She just looks like Mum used to look fifteen years ago, but skinnier. There's something fragile about her too, as though the slightest nudge will send her shattering to the floor.

As we reach the bed, I try to wriggle my hand away from Nick. Our palms are sweating and my fingers are starting to hurt from Nick's grasp, but he doesn't let go.

"Hello," I say.

"Hi," the woman replies. "Are you here to see . . ." She pauses, glancing at the bed for a moment. "Matthew?"

"I'm his sister—Sophie."

Nick clears his throat. "And I'm Nick. Sophie's boyfriend. How do you know Matthew?" There's an amused smile tugging at Nick's lips and I can see the thoughts rolling through his mind. He thinks this woman is Matthew's girlfriend.

"I'm Jenna Lawson. I'm the A&E doctor who treated Matthew on Thursday."

Nick clicks his fingers. "Yes, that's where I know you from."

"Excuse me?" Jenna says.

"I thought I recognized you from somewhere. I never forget a face. I had appendicitis last year," he says as though trying to prompt Jenna's memory. "I walked into A&E clutching my stomach, thinking I was going to die, and you guys wheeled me straight up to a ward and into surgery."

Jenna gives an apologetic look. It's clear she doesn't remember Nick. "We see a lot of faces in A&E. A lot of appendicitis too."

"Of course." Nick shrugs.

"Do you know what happened?" I ask. "The police said he was hit by a bus." And they don't think it was an accident. I forgot to tell Nick the other night, but if I say anything now, he'll think I was hiding it from him.

"That's all I know, I'm afraid. I'm not his doctor anymore but I can find someone to talk you through his injuries."

"Thanks."

Nick's hand tightens around mine and I have to bite the inside of my lip to stop myself yelling out.

"Can't you just tell us?" Nick asks, glancing at his watch. "Since you treated him."

Jenna looks to me and I nod. "Please."

"Your brother was brought into A&E on Thursday afternoon.

He had a dislocated jaw and elbow, a broken leg, and a pneumo-thorax." Jenna's voice changes. She sounds so sure of herself, but she's talking fast and I struggle to keep up.

"What does that mean?" Nick cuts in, and for the first time I'm glad he's here. I would never have asked.

"One of his ribs broke and punctured his lung, causing it to collapse. We were able to fit a chest tube that reinflated it. He also had a bleed in his brain from a head injury, which is why he's in intensive care."

"Is he in one of those vegetative states?" I turn to stare at Mat-thew, my vision blurring. He looks smaller, like the little boy he used to be. I think of the nights we spent with my duvet pulled over our heads and a flashlight on, Matthew crying at the sound of Mum and Dad's shouts, and me telling him silly stories about flying dogs to make him laugh, pretending I wasn't just as sad and scared as he was.

Guilt worms in the pit of my stomach. Is there something I could've done to stop this?

Jenna shakes her head. "No. He's in a medically induced coma, which means we're giving him a drug that is keeping his body and his brain shut down to allow his brain time to heal. Until the swelling reduces we won't know what, if any, brain damage there might be."

"Can he hear us? Should I talk to him?"

"No one really knows. You should talk to him if you want to."

"I don't know what to say." I look to Jenna as my breath catches in my throat and I can't breathe properly over the emotions raging through my body. I wish I was anywhere but here right now.

From across the bay the alarm stops and quiet settles over the room again. I listen to the thud, thud, beep, shh, thud, thud, beep, shh of the machines that are keeping my brother alive.

I wonder if I should take his hand. We've never been touchy siblings. Hellos and good-byes have always been accompanied with a wave, never a kiss, never a hug, and in the end I decide it would be too weird to touch him now.

If I were alone right now, without Nick or the doctor beside me, I'd ask him, "Aren't you going to say something?"

How many times have I asked him that exact six-word question? Hundreds. Thousands probably. It became a joke between us before everything changed. He never answered me, but sometimes he'd raise an eyebrow as if he was asking me a question back. *What do you want me to say?*

I stare at Matthew's face, searching for any sign of a twitch but there's nothing.

"He's taking it all in, that's all."

I try to imagine Mum's face when the police told her about Matthew. Does she really not care? My eyes draw back to Jenna and suddenly all I want to do is cry and ask Jenna if Matthew is going to be OK. But Jenna is concentrating on her phone and there's a deep frown creasing her forehead.

"I'm sorry," she says, standing up and shoving her things into her bag. "I need to leave. Your brother is in the best possible hands, Sophie."

"Thank you."

I watch Jenna hurry out of the ward and think again about Mum. A lifetime of hurt washes over me. The pain is as real as a physical cut, but worse. Cuts heal. When will I?

CHAPTER 18

JENNA

I jab at the button beside the lift two then three times and wait.
Nothing happens. I stare at my phone, rereading the text from
Christie.

Hi Jenna, Niamh has just been sick. I'm taking her home so I won't
be able to drop Beth and Archie back at the end of the party. I know
you said you were planning to make it back anyway so hopefully
this won't be a problem. Sorry xx

Shit! It *is* a problem. A big one. I didn't hear the two missed
calls from Christie or see the message until just now, and it's nearly
four p.m.

The lift is taking too long and so I leap down the stairs and
check the time on my phone again. I need to be at the trampoline
park in ten minutes. Images strobe in my mind—the sweaty, red
faces of my children. Tearful Archie, and Beth stoic for the sake of
her brother, but just as upset.

I should never have left them. I should have stayed and watched
them have their fun, but Christie was there and said she could drive

them home, and I had to come to the hospital. I had to know my children were safe from you.

And they are.

By the time I'm out of the hospital I'm running, my phone pressed to my face, the hum of ringing in my ear.

"Hello?" Rachel answers on the third ring. I can hear the noise of the kids shouting in the background.

"Hi, Rachel, it's Jenna. I've just seen a text from Christie saying she can't drop my kids home. I'm on my way, but I'm going to be ten minutes late." If I'm lucky. "Do you mind waiting?"

There's a pause. I hear her breath rattle in the microphone. "Normally it wouldn't be a problem of course, but we're off to a family dinner straight after the party and we're cutting it a bit fine. I didn't know Christie was taking them home. I thought you said you were coming back."

"I was, but then I bumped into Christie in the car park. Didn't she say anything to you?" I ask as I reach my car and throw open the driver's door.

"No, she didn't. I guess I could drop them home instead if that works. It's on our way to the restaurant."

"Er . . . are you sure you don't mind? I'm so sorry about this. Their dad, Stuart, is home."

"It's fine," Rachel says. Her voice is neutral. There's no clipped annoyance, but none of the breezy "I wouldn't be here either if I didn't have to be" humor from earlier.

"I'm 24 Park Avenue."

"I know," she replies.

"Thank you, and I'm sorry again."

The guilt is a jagged rock in my stomach as I drive home and park outside the house just as Rachel is shepherding Beth and Archie out the back of her shiny silver Audi. I give the horn a light tap and wave, forcing a smile.

"I'm so sorry," I say again as I dash over to them.

"It's really no problem."

"Would you like to come in for a cuppa?" I ask. It's the last thing I want to do but I feel like I have to offer, to make the effort to seem like a normal mum instead of one who leaves her children at a party then doesn't pick them up.

"That's really kind but we've got our dinner to get to."

"Sorry, yes, you did tell me that."

We stand awkwardly for a moment and I feel Rachel staring at me. Pitying me, it feels like. Then she steps around the car and opens the driver's door.

"Well, anytime I can help with Tracey, please just ask," I call after her.

"It's Lacey," Beth hisses from beside me. I glance down at my daughter. Her face is shining red from jumping, but it's her eyes that startle me. They are narrowed and fierce and directed straight at me in a *how dare you?* kind of way.

"Take care of yourself, Jenna," Rachel calls, giving a quick wave before sliding back into her car. I watch her pull away, taking the speed bump in the road too fast. Did I imagine it, or was there a knowing in her voice just then? I picture Rachel and Christie huddled around the table in the café. How quickly would their chitchat about husbands and kids have veered into gossip?

"Did you hear about Beth's mum? She's got a stalker. Can you believe it?"

"No wonder she looked so dreadful on the school run this week."

My face smarts thinking of what they might have said, but then I force it away. Christie wouldn't gossip about me. She's too nice.

"How was the party?" I ask, looking between Beth and Archie as I open the front door.

"Great," Archie replies with a grin. "I bumped my head and had to have an ice pack," he tells me, beaming with pride as he points to a purplish bruise on his cheek.

"Oh, you poor baby. Did it hurt?" I reach out and pull his body close to my side as the guilt jabs again. I should've been there.

"Only for a minute. Christie looked after me. She said I'd have a shiner in the morning. What's a shiner?"

"It's a bruise around the eye." I stare at Archie for a moment, looking beyond the smile and the bright eyes for any sign of sadness, but all I see is the chocolaty ice cream ring around his mouth and a boy who's had a fun time.

Beth gives a loud sigh, kicking off her shoes in the hall and leaving them scattered in the place they fall. When she speaks her voice is snappish. "It was great until you forgot to pick us up."

"I didn't forget," I say, nudging her shoes to one side with my foot. One battle at a time. "And I am sorry."

"No you're not." She launches herself up the stairs, her feet stomping harder with every step.

"Hey, what's the commotion?" Stuart asks, appearing from the kitchen. His hair is disheveled, his face sleepy and bronzed from the sun.

"It's nothing," I reply.

"Mummy forgot to pick us up," Archie crows as he jumps into Stuart's arms.

"Hey, kiddo, had a good time?" Stuart asks, flashing me a quizzical look.

"I didn't forget. Christie was going to drop them home, but Niamh got sick and she had to rush off. I couldn't get back in time so Lacey's mum, Rachel, dropped them home."

"That was nice of her. I thought you were going to stay at the party?"

"It was a drop-off thing. No one was staying."

"I hit my head," Archie says. "Can I have a drink?"

"What do you need to say?" Stuart tips Archie upside down and tickles his belly as he walks to the kitchen.

"Please, please," Archie cries out in between his giggles.

I reach into my bag for my phone to reply to Christie's text. My finger catches on something sharp and I feel the sting of blood. I pull out my hand and suck the thin cut on my index finger before looking more carefully inside my bag. It's then that I see the smashed screen of your iPhone and your door keys resting on top of my diary. I had them in my hands when Sophie arrived and must have dumped them in my bag without realizing.

"Are you going to check on Beth?" Stuart calls out.

I nod, leaving my bag by the door and walking up the stairs.

Beth's curtains are still drawn from last night and she's lying on her bed. The air is stuffy and hot. I remember painting her bedroom one day when she was at school—a birthday surprise. The walls are white except one which is a bright turquoise. Fairy-light stars dangle over her bookshelves, and on the floor beneath the piles of clothes, books, pens, notebooks, teddies, and toys is a black-and-white zebra-pattern rug.

She loved it. Promised to keep it tidy too, which lasted all of a day before the mess started creeping out like a fungus that wouldn't stop growing. Every now and again I make her tidy up, dust and vacuum, but it never lasts long.

I inch forward, stepping on a plastic bird that chirps at me with an irritating song.

"Beth?"

"What?" she asks, her voice muffled. Accusing.

"I wanted to see if you're OK." I sit on the mattress beside her body and place a hand on her back. Her skin is smooth and hot.

"Where were you?" she asks.

"Didn't Christie tell you? She was going to drop you home, but then Niamh was sick—"

"She puked after, like, ten minutes, Mum. And Christie said she called you to tell you and that you'd be back in time."

"I'm really really sorry. I didn't get the message right away."

Silence.

"Beth?"

"S'kay."

"I should've checked my phone earlier. You have every right to be mad at me."

"I'm not mad, it's just . . ." She pauses, turning onto her back and staring up at the ceiling.

"You can tell me, Beth. I won't be cross."

"It was embarrassing." She shrugs. "All of my friends have mums who are there all of the time. Dad's great, but I want you to take us places more, and not leave us there."

Her words slice through me. Easy tears build behind my eyes. "But you know I'm—"

"A doctor and you have to save people." Her tone makes it sound bad somehow, and the guilt returns.

She turns away to the wall and I lie down beside her, wrapping her into my arms and letting the silent tears drop from my eyes. Everything would be so much easier if I could get just one night's sleep. Just one full night. Eight hours straight, like Stuart, eleven, like Archie. Hell, I'd take anything that would make me a better mother to the one I feel right now.

"Do you want to go to the park for an ice cream?" I ask. "Or we could play Monopoly?"

"Can I play too?" Archie shouts from the hall. "Can we play aliens?" he adds, wandering into Beth's room. "You can be the mummy who is secretly an alien out to destroy earth, and me and Beth discover the truth and have to save everyone."

"I'm tired," Beth replies. "Can I watch something?"

"Can I watch something too, Mummy?" Archie adds, his game forgotten in favor of TV.

"Of course."

The kids race downstairs and spend the afternoon slumped on the sofa, lost in their latest cartoon obsession. Cheesy high-pitched voices screech from the TV. I hover nearby and tidy up toys and clothes that have been dropped and forgotten this week.

A while later Stuart pours me a glass of wine and steers me into the garden. "Sit here. Enjoy the sunshine and this," he says, handing me the glass. I take a sip and then another. The cold zest of the wine coats my thoughts. I feel myself unravel.

It's early evening but the heat wave is still in full swing, the sun showing no sign of setting. The breeze from the sea is weak, pushing the air but not cooling it.

"Are you OK? You haven't seemed yourself since . . . Thursday." He means since you came into A&E. Stuart sits beside me with his own glass of wine.

Am I OK? *No*, is my first thought. *I'm not OK. I'm anything but OK.* "I . . . went to see him today." I take another sip of wine and swallow back the lump in my throat.

"What? Jenna! Why the hell would you do that? Leave it to the police. Let them deal with it."

"Because when we got to the trampoline park this afternoon I was convinced someone was watching us. I didn't know if I was losing my mind or if he was still out there and I was terrified he'd do something to the kids. You know the e-mails he sends are always about them. I had to make sure he was still in hospital and the kids were safe."

"And is he?" Stuart's tone softens.

I nod.

"Was he awake? Did you talk to him?"

The question turns my stomach with a sickening unease. "Of course not. I'd never . . . I . . . I couldn't do that. He was still in a coma."

"He can't get to you or us anymore, Jenna. You realize that, don't you?"

"Yes, of course, but—" I pause. How can I explain how I feel when I don't even understand it myself? "I can't switch it off. I can't wrap my head around why he was doing this to me. Why me? Why him?"

"What about going to see someone?" Stuart asks softly.

"Like who? A therapist?"

"I was thinking a GP to start with, but yes, a therapist too. You've been through a lot."

"I don't need medication. I need answers." The moment the words leave my mouth, I realize they're true. The anxiety, the panic, the fear, that you've pumped into my body day after day, week

after week, isn't going anywhere. Instead, it's morphing into something else—a burning desire to understand why this has happened
to me, to understand you and what I did to make you feel so much
hate toward me.

"I wasn't suggesting you do," he says, taking my hand. "Of course
it's going to take some time," he says. "But you have to find a way
to deal with it for Beth and Archie as well as yourself. There was no
one there today. You're safe and so are the kids. It's just like we talked
about the other night. We don't have to run away. We can stay in
our beautiful home and get back to normal."

Normal? I don't know what normal looks like anymore.

"I'll run the kids a bath," I say after a pause. "They need it after
all that jumping."

"You sit here. Let me do it."

I think of closing my eyes and snoozing in the sunshine. It's a
tempting thought, but I push myself up from the chair before it can
settle over me. "It's fine. I want to do it," I reply, thinking of the
anger in Beth's eyes when she looked at me and my promise earlier to pay more attention to her, to both of them, which already
feels broken beyond repair.

CHAPTER 19

Sunday, June 16
JENNA

I sleep for four hours and when I jolt awake my eyes feel sticky and my mouth paper dry. It's not nearly enough sleep to catch up on what I need, but it's the most I've had in weeks. Stuart is beside me, a lump of duvet. He won't move now until his alarm chimes at seven a.m. How does he do that? Sleep so easily, so well?

I shouldn't have drunk the second glass of white wine with dinner.

Thinking of dinner reminds me of Stuart's joke. Archie asked what the capital of Argentina was and Stuart reached for his phone to look it up just as I said, "Buenos Aires."

"There you go, Archie, your mother—the human Google." He grinned and so did Beth and Archie. "If only she could get Google Maps installed too, then she wouldn't be late collecting you from places."

Archie howled with laughter and Beth sniggered, and I knew he was joking and so I laughed along, but his comment stung. It reminded me of the little digs we used to fire at each other.

Stuart didn't understand why I went to see you. How could he?

In all of your e-mails, it's always been about me and Beth and Archie. Never Stuart.

I think of the way Sophie looked at you today and try to imagine you as a brother, but the image doesn't fit. My older brother, Nathan, is a doctor too. He travels from country to country, offering help where it is most needed, but he would fly straight back here in a heartbeat if I asked him to. You can't be like that. In my head you've always been a deranged member of society, living in the shadows. No friends, no life. You can't be kind and funny and help your sister anytime she asks, and then do what you've been doing to me.

My head starts to spin. Images of the resus bay crowd my thoughts. I swallow back the rising bile. My fingers twitch as though they're still inside you, holding the pinched chest tube. What would have happened if Diya hadn't returned?

For the first time in years I think about taking a sleeping tablet, but they never work and I always end up feeling worse the next day. Instead I slip out of bed, shutting the bedroom door behind me and walking quietly to the living room.

I find an old episode of *Grey's Anatomy* on the TV and watch it for a while, marveling at the amount of sex the characters seem to have at work. I rarely get time to pee most days.

The characters on the screen blur before my eyes. My mind drifts. I know your name now. Matthew Dover. And I have your phone, I remember suddenly.

My bag is where I left it by the front door and I dig out your phone, turning it over in my hands. The screen on the top-right-hand side is covered with a thousand cracks like a network of blood vessels, and there's a dent in the back. I didn't mean to take it, but now that I have, the need to see what's on it is fierce.

I plug your phone in to my charger and two minutes later it lights up with the Apple sign. I snatch it up and for a split second I falter. What the hell am I doing? A hot rage bursts out of somewhere inside me. This is nothing compared to everything you've done to me. I have a right to find out who you are, and if there is evidence on this phone, then I'm going to make damn sure the police get hold of it.

The lock screen loads. Your wallpaper is a gray tabby cat sitting on a window ledge. The top of the cat's head is distorted and stretched by the cracks in the screen. I stare at the photo for a long time. You have a cat. A cat you love enough to take photos of and keep as wallpaper on your phone. It's a "round-peg, square-hole" piece of knowledge that I don't know what to do with.

I hold my breath and press the home button. The screen turns black and four rows of white dots appear, demanding a password or touch ID, neither of which I have. I connect the dots in a square just on the off chance, but your phone buzzes—an angry bee. I've got the code wrong.

The only person who can unlock your phone is you.

Then a thought hits me like an alarm chiming in my head. I sit up straighter. I don't actually need you to unlock your phone. I just need your thumbprint.

CHAPTER 20

SOPHIE, *age 11*

Sophie flops on her bed, stares at the textured swirls of plaster on her ceiling, and chews at the edge of a hangnail. She is so bored right now. She wishes her nan still cooked a big roast dinner on a Sunday and followed it with a Sara Lee chocolate cake and double cream. Even watching her nan's old black-and-white films would be better than this.

Outside, the day is gray and there is a drizzle in the air. It's too cold to play in the garden and all of her toys are babyish and dumb, like her mum thinks she's still eight or something. Sophie keeps wanting to say to her, *You know I'm eleven now, right?*

Being grounded sucks. She's not even allowed to watch TV and now she's missing the *Dawson's Creek* omnibus. It's Matthew's fault she was grounded, not hers. He was the one who wanted to watch *Jaws*. She wasn't even bothered, but her mum and dad had been arguing in their bedroom again and Matthew had seen it in the *TV Guide* and begged and begged. She only wanted to shut him up and make him happy.

But the film had been way scarier than Sophie thought it was going to be. And Matthew had freaked out and started screaming. Sophie turned off the TV as fast as she could and tried to cuddle him, but he kept screaming and doing that thing where he screws his eyes up really tight.

"Matthew?" her mum had called, rushing into the room and to Matthew's side while her dad stayed in the doorway with his arms folded. "What's wrong?"

"We were watching *Jaws*. And we both got scared," Sophie tried to explain.

Her dad laughed and for a moment Sophie thought she wasn't going to be in trouble, after all.

But then her mum shouted at him. "For God's sake. This isn't funny."

"What? You never watched something you weren't supposed to when you were their age?"

"Of course I did, but not something this scary, and this situation is very different."

Sophie stared at her feet, feeling really bad. "Sorry."

"It's not me you need to apologize to," her mum snapped, rubbing Matthew's back.

Sophie wanted to tell her mum that Matthew begged Sophie to let him watch it, but she knew it wouldn't make a difference.

"I'm sorry, Matthew," she said. "I didn't know it was going to be so scary."

"It's not good enough, young lady," her mum replied. "I want you to promise me you'll never do anything like this again. You're grounded. No TV. No going out. No friends. No phone calls."

Hot tears dripped from her eyes. *I only did it because you were arguing again*, Sophie wanted to shout.

It was only TV Sophie cared about. She didn't have any friends to knock for her or call for a chat. The girls in her class are OK, apart from Laura Newman, but Sophie always feels like they're talking about her whenever she leaves the room, and she knows they all have sleepovers at the weekends without her.

She doesn't care though. In a few months she'll be at high school and making new friends.

Sophie drags herself off the bed and wanders out of her bedroom, looking for something to do. Her mum is in the bathroom on her hands and knees, scrubbing the floor with vigorous back-and-forth motions. Sophie stands in the doorway, wondering if her mum is still mad at her. If Sophie tells her mum she's bored, she might stop cleaning and play a game. Then again, her mum might make her help.

"Where's Dad?" Sophie asks instead, lifting a finger to her mouth, biting at a jagged nail.

"Out." There's an edge to her mum's voice, but Sophie doesn't know if it's Sophie or her dad her mum is mad at. "And don't bite your nails. I don't know where this habit has come from. You used to have such lovely nails."

"Is Nan still poorly?" Sophie asks.

Her mum sits up, pressing a hand to the small of her back. "I'm afraid so. I'll call her later and see if she's up for a short visit one day next week. I know you miss her and she misses you too. Are you bored?"

Sophie shrugs. "Sort of."

Her mum pulls an *I told you so* face. "Hopefully you'll think twice before letting Matthew watch scary films with you. Why don't you go play together for a while? Get the games out of the cupboard?"

Sophie thinks for a moment. The Game of Life is a her favorite, but Matthew always gets upset when he loses and she ends up making rubbish decisions so he can win. "Can we make cupcakes?"

"You and Matthew?"

"Yeah. We'll do the mixing and tell you when they're ready to go in the oven."

"And you'll help Matthew? No taking over. Show him what to do and give him a chance."

"I know. I will."

Her mum smiles. "OK then. But you're tidying it up too?"

"Deal."

Sophie heads downstairs to the living room. Matthew's Lego is spread across the floor in a jumble of primary-colored bricks, and there's a big house-like structure in the middle, which is actually pretty cool. Her old baby dolls are stacked up beside it and she wonders what game he's playing.

Maybe after they've made cakes they can play with the Lego together, Sophie thinks, feeling bad about the film. She should have turned it off the moment he got scared. Matthew is really sensitive. He still cries at night if her dad turns his light off before he's asleep, and he still wets the bed.

"Matthew?"

Sophie heads into the kitchen, expecting to find him coloring at the table but he's not. The back door is open and there's cold air blowing through the house.

"Matthew?" she calls again when she reaches the back door.

She sees him then, sitting on the lawn with his back to the house, legs crossed like he's sitting in assembly. He's not wearing a coat and must be freezing. She calls his name a third time, but either the wind snatches her voice or he isn't listening. He does that a lot—shuts out the world, like he can switch his ears off and not hear things.

Sophie shoves her feet into her trainers and hurries outside. The wind pushes against her, cold like a fridge. As she draws nearer she can see little swirls of smoke blowing out from something in front of Matthew.

"Matthew, what are you doing?"

He doesn't move or flinch. Sophie keeps walking until she's almost standing over him and can see the source of the smoke. It's a fire, like a mini bonfire, with sticks and screwed-up bits of paper. There's writing on the paper and Sophie can see a photograph of a shark. He's burning his book about sharks, she realizes with a sudden panic. Starting a fire is really wrong. Matthew must know that. Is she going to get in trouble for this too?

The front door bangs, the noise bouncing out to them. Her dad's voice bellows, "Hello?"

Sophie grabs Matthew's arm and tries to pull him up but he won't budge, he won't even look at her. "Matthew?" she hisses. "Dad's home. You're going to get in trouble. Please get up now. Mum and Dad will really argue if they see this."

Her throat hurts, like she's ill but she's not. She wants to cry. She wants to run up to her bedroom and pretend she doesn't know Matthew is out here.

A gust of wind pushes her again. It hits the fire too and Sophie hopes it will blow it out. Instead the flames leap up, like they're trying to chase the wind. One of the sticks in the stack moves and the flames jump closer to Matthew. The fire doesn't look so little anymore.

"Why is the back door open with the heating on?" her dad shouts out to them.

She turns, panic gripping hold of her. Her dad's face is red and his eyes look weird. "Matthew started a fire," she says quickly. "I was trying to stop him."

Her dad swears and runs toward them. "Get away from that, Matthew. It's going to burn you." He steps up behind Matthew and tucks his arms around Matthew's waist before scooping him up. Matthew lets out a piercing scream and kicks out with his legs.

"Stop it, Matthew," her dad shouts, dropping him to ground as Matthew's foot lands between her dad's legs. Her dad yells in pain and at the same time his hand flies through the air, smacking Matthew on the leg.

A weird silence falls over them. Matthew stops screaming, but he pants as he stares hard at her dad.

Then Sophie's mum appears, rushing straight to Matthew and cradling him in her arms. "What do you think you're doing?" she screams at Sophie's dad as he stomps on the flames until they're gone.

"He set a fire. Look at this mess. What if he'd done this inside, eh? The whole house would be up in flames by now."

"Shouting and hitting him isn't going to solve anything," she says, her voice angrier than Sophie has ever heard it before.

"He caught me in the balls, Sarah. I didn't mean to hit him."

"But you did because you're drunk. You're always drunk. Just get out. Drink yourself into an early grave somewhere else."

Sophie waits for her dad to laugh or shout something back. Instead he strides away without another word.

CHAPTER 21

Monday, June 17

JENNA

It's a quiet day for once in A&E. A slow current of patients pulls me through the morning. My thoughts feel coated in gloop. I can't concentrate. I work on autopilot, treating patients without thinking, then having to double back and check them all over again, doubting myself.

There is no game face today, no way to switch off my thoughts from you. For five whole days, five wonderful days, there have been no dismembered dolls left on my doorstep, no shattered glass, no cruel taunts e-mailed to me. And yet I can't unwind. I can't shake you from my thoughts.

By lunchtime my head is pounding and the fluorescent strips of light on the ceiling are hurting my eyes. All I want to do is crawl onto one of the beds and close my eyes. I must look as bad as I feel because without asking, Thomas acts like my shadow, helping me with my patients, fetching me cups of coffee, and guiding me to where I need to be.

We see a man limp in with a pulled groin muscle. I tell him to rest and take ibuprofen. Then it's a woman with a rash on her arm that is barely visible by the time I see her. She thinks it's meningitis. I tell her to take an antihistamine and consider changing her brand of suntan lotion.

My next patient is a fifty-five-year-old male presenting with a sum total of a runny nose and a headache. I get it. People use A&E when they can't get an appointment with their doctor. It's part of the job and something that is unlikely to change. I've never let it get to me before. But something about the weasel-like man with his oval glasses crawls under my skin. I check his vitals for any sign that this is more than just a cold. It isn't. I give him two painkillers and a cup of water before going to check on another patient. Twenty minutes later I return to the man with the runny nose.

"Mr. Shorter," I say, walking to his bed. "How are you feeling now?"

He touches the tip of his red nose, sniffs dramatically, and closes his eyes for a moment as though the effort required to reply is insurmountable. "Better, I think," he says with a long sigh. "The medication you gave me seems to be working. I can probably go home now." He checks his watch and nods, agreeing with himself. "The golf starts on the telly in half an hour."

A wave of frustration crashes over me and the words fire out before I can stop them. "So it's fine for you to waste our time, but not for us to waste yours?"

Mr. Shorter jerks his head back, cowering a little as though I'm wielding the mother of all needles and want to inject it into his eyeball.

I take a step closer, a "why the hell not?" feeling pumping through my body, finally wiping away the sludge from my thoughts. "You do realize that people die here, Mr. Shorter? Elderly people, mothers, fathers, children, even. Many would be alive today if the doctors had seen them just ten minutes earlier, but we don't because we're wasting our time on people like you."

This is an exaggeration and it isn't. If someone comes to A&E seriously ill, they'll be pushed to the top of the line and people like Mr. Shorter will have to wait. But for all the people who come to A&E when they don't need to, there are just as many who stay home when they are desperately ill because the wait times will be so long or because they don't want to be a burden to the NHS.

"I . . . I . . . I'm ill," he splutters. "The medicine you gave me worked, that's why I'm feeling better."

I sense someone behind me and a hand rests on my shoulder. I turn to see Diya, her face full of concern, and even though I know I've gone too far I can't seem to stop myself. "I gave you aspirin, Mr. Shorter. It's available from most shops and costs less than a chocolate bar. You've wasted your own time, you've wasted a bed, you've wasted the nurses' time, and you've wasted mine."

"That's enough, Dr. Lawson," Diya says, her voice low but filled with authority.

I shrug Diya away, aware of Thomas's eyes on me. His face is a mix of alarm and something else. Awe, maybe. It's not often we stand up to the time-wasters, but right now I don't care what anyone thinks.

I feel caged in, trapped. I have to get away before I do something worse than shouting at a patient. I spin on my heels and stride away, out of A&E and through the warren of corridors until I'm locked inside the last cubicle in the toilets and wishing I was the type of person who could lash out, kick at the door until my foot hurts, and feel better.

My pager beeps ten minutes later. Two sharp beeps that vibrate against my hip bone. My hand moves, curling around the black matchbox shape on my hip. The movement is automatic, like reaching to scratch an itch, but it's not an emergency. I'm being summoned.

THE MEDICAL DIRECTOR's office is small. No bigger than a treatment area. There is a desk and a computer instead of a bed; paperwork instead of medical supplies; two framed photographs of Westbury hanging on the wall instead of wires and monitors.

Nancy Macpherson, the A&E medical director, appears in the doorway, smoothing down the silk of her red blouse and offering a tight smile. She sits behind her desk, the chair creaking from her weight. The assessment runs through my head before I can stop it. Obese female, midfifties, presenting signs of high blood pressure and possible early diabetes based on the empty tins of fizzy drinks I spy in the wastepaper bin.

"I'm sorry." I blurt out the apology before Nancy can say anything. "I shouldn't have let that patient get to me. He was wasting our time." The anger has yet to dissolve and it's there in my tone. I grit my teeth and will myself to calm down. This isn't me.

"I agree with you, Jenna." Nancy drinks from an open a can of Coke on her desk.

"But?" I prompt.

She dabs her mouth before she speaks. "But there are ways of handling it, as you know."

"Everything I told him was true."

"Yes, but the way you said it is not how we operate here. We've spoken to Mr. Shorter and appeased the situation. I don't think he'll be making a complaint." Nancy's words suck the anger right out of me.

"I'm sorry," I say again, my tone softer this time. "It's just . . . I let it get to me today."

"You've been through an awful lot in the past year and I hope you've found the hospital has done its best to support you."

"I have. And you should know that the police know who my stalker is now. He can't get to me anymore, so the harassment is over. I'm ready to focus on my job." I stop myself from saying any more and hope Nancy doesn't ask any questions about you. I doubt she would be pleased to learn that I treated you.

"I know."

"You do?"

"Yes, and while I'm relieved to hear it, my concern is that to-day's outburst indicates that you are under an undue amount of stress. I'd like to refer you to occupational health to see if there is anything we can do to help you."

I nod. "OK. Thank you."

"Also, how would you feel about taking some time off? It's not a suspension," she's quick to say. "But I do think you would bene-fit from a break from work. Just for a week or so. Spend it with your children and enjoy this glorious weather."

"I think that's a bit extreme." I try to wrap my head around what Nancy is saying. What would my week even look like with-out work, without the buzz, the distraction?

"Are you aware that your colleagues are concerned about you?"

"No. Who?"

"It doesn't matter who, Jenna. I'm trying to make you see that today was not an isolated incident. You haven't been yourself for some time."

My face flushes hot. The skin on my neck and chest burns too. I don't know what to say.

"Have you spoken to anyone about what's been happening to you?"

"I've spoken to the police." It's not what she means and we both know it.

"There are victim support agencies out there who can help you."

"I know." And I do. But I hate the word victim. I know it's what I am, what you've made me, but I hate it.

We sit in silence for a moment but in the end I relent. What choice do I have? "There's still an hour left on my shift. Do you want me to—"

She shakes her head. "Go home now. You'll get a call from someone on the occupational health team within the next week. Why don't we arrange to meet again in a week's time and see how you're feeling? Of course, I'm at the end of the phone anytime, if you need me."

There is nothing left but to agree. A numbness takes over as I slip out of her office and head for my locker. I don't know if I'm angry or relieved.

All I know for sure is that this is your fault. Totally and completely. I hate you for what you've stolen from me. I hate you for shrinking me down into a fearful, timid creature I don't recognize.

CHAPTER 22

JENNA

As I collect my bag from my locker I check the time. It's four p.m. Stuart will be at his desk now, using the final hours of quiet on the building site to complete paperwork. What will he make of my leave? I can't get my head around it. Have people really been so concerned about my abilities as a doctor that they've spoken to Nancy behind my back? Who would do that?

Beth and Archie will be playing in the garden at Christie's house. I imagine the surprise on their faces when I collect them early. I wonder if they'll be happy to see me or annoyed I'm interrupting their fun. In my current state it's hard not to think that they'd be better off with Christie than with me, their own mother. The guilt lodges in the pit of my stomach, digging in its spikes.

They've watched their mother disappear over the last year.

It's that final thought that makes me weave through the patients and visitors milling by the main entrance, grab a can of Red Bull from the shop, and make my way up the four flights of stairs to intensive care. I can't move on, I can't feel safe until you're dead or in prison. I have to know who you are and why you chose me. I have to make sure it never happens again.

I'm going to open your phone and see what's on it.

Back in intensive care I keep my head down, walking straight to bay B, but you're not there. I make my way back to the whiteboard and find you in bay F.

It's the same as the other areas, but smaller. Only three beds, and a nurse at a desk stationed by the door. I reach into my bag and feel for your phone, my hand closing around it.

The nurse looks up at me with a questioning smile. She's wearing a pale blue tunic and there's a fob watch hanging from her breast pocket. Her hair is brown with bold chunks of blond streaked through it, and styled in a high bun.

"Can I help you?" she asks.

"Hi, I'm Jenna Lawson. I'm a doctor in A&E. I just came to check on one of my patients. It was touch and go for a while and I wanted to see how he was getting on."

"Sure," she says. "Who are you looking for?"

I glance at the beds. One is a boy in his late teens with a bald head and a body so thin that I can see the shape of his skull where his cheeks have sunken in. Cancer, I guess. Bed 2 is a woman about my age. Unconscious and on a ventilator. Bed 3 is you.

"Matthew Dover." I nod toward you and that's when I see why you've been moved. The ventilator is gone. Your body is still wired to the machines, but you're breathing on your own, which means you're no longer in an induced coma.

A stone drops in my stomach, the sudden rush of emotion burning on my face. My grip on your phone tightens until the sharp crack digs into my palm. Red Bull and stomach acid scorch the back of my throat and for a horrifying second I think I'm going to be sick.

Fight or flight? The desire to run is overwhelming.

"He's not awake yet. They only brought him in here a little while ago, but you're welcome to sit with him for a minute."

"Thanks."

I walk forward on legs that don't want to carry me and make a fuss of moving the visitor's chair, positioning myself halfway down your body, my back to the nurse. The urge to look at you builds until I stop resisting.

The graze on your face is no longer the raw angry red it was on my first visit. Now it's one long scab which must be itching like hell. There's more color to your skin. You look peaceful. Asleep. You are asleep, I remind myself.

You're wearing a hospital gown, loose around your chest where the wires wriggle their way to the machines. Your arms are lying by your sides over a tucked bedsheet and I shift closer, my hands trembling with fear and caffeine.

I watch your monitor and your slow steady heartbeat, the opposite of my own. I risk a look behind me to the nurse. Her head is bent over a chart by the patient with the hollowed cheeks.

Now is my chance.

Your phone feels damp as I unpeel it from my hand. There's a deep red groove across my palm from where the crack has pressed against it. My skin crawls—beetles scurrying over my body—as I reach out and touch your hand. Your skin is dry but warm, and as I unfurl your fingers your hand twitches in mine.

I stop, not daring to breathe. My whole body is tense. I'm ready to run. I glance at your face—your eyes are still closed—

then the monitor. Your heartbeat is steady. It was nothing. An involuntary spasm.

When I move again it's not slow and steady, but quick. Your thumb is out and I press it against the home button.

Your phone springs to life. I've done it. I've actually unlocked your phone. A dozen different apps appear on the screen and behind them is another photo of your cat.

The photos icon is at the top of the screen and it takes three jabs of my finger on the cracked area for the folder to open.

Tiny images appear before my eyes. I click on the last photo you took and the same gray tabby cat fills the screen. I swipe left. More cat photos. Then food, delicately placed on plates. Then a road. A blur of cars. A bin overflowing with litter. A dead seagull. The sky. A tree. On and on they go. Hundreds of images of nothing.

Swipe swipe swipe.

And then it's photos of your sister, her eyes fixed on the camera. Dozens of them. She looks worried. Then there's more of Sophie, walking away this time. Then a house with a big driveway. And finally I see what I'm looking for.

Me.

My face from behind the windscreen waiting at the traffic lights on Wednesday. The photo is blurry and I'm out of focus but it's definitely me. If I zoom in I can see a smudge of Beth's red hair in the backseat.

You bastard.

This is the proof I wanted to find. This is the evidence that will convict you. I keep swiping through more photos of me in the car. I see myself staring at the traffic lights and then the horror when I spot you.

There are hundreds of photos here. More nonsense ones of nothing in particular. Then it's a busy street and a woman who at first I think is me, but it's not. This woman has blond hair and long legs and I recognize her instantly. It's Rachel. Lacey's mum.

My heartbeat quickens. I scroll through more photos of Rachel. Some of the photos are zoomed in on her face and others are more focused on the background and the busy street, but it's definitely her. Does she know you? Are you friends with Rachel? I turn the question in my thoughts, trying to see how someone like you, a monster, can be friends with a school mum. It doesn't fit, but then what does that mean? Are you stalking her too? Is she the next woman you're lining up to prey on?

There's a sudden change in the air around me. A tickling of hair on the back of my neck. My eyes drag upward from your phone to your arm, your shoulder, the graze. Your eyes are still closed but your face is pinched in concentration and when I look at the monitor I see your pulse is racing as fast as my mine now.

Oh God. You're waking up. Even as the thought looms in my head, your hand shoots out from the side of the bed and grabs my wrist.

I gasp and try to shout but fear has stolen my voice. I twist my arm away but your grip is an iron vise.

I look up and your eyes stare straight into mine—two piercing black holes of hate.

CHAPTER 23

JENNA

You make a noise, a low, gargling doglike growl that chills me to my core.

The phone drops from my hand, hitting the floor by my feet. I yank my arm again and this time your grip loosens and I shrug myself free. I hold my wrist close to my body and lean back out of reach.

"What do you want from me?" I ask, suddenly finding a voice I didn't know I had.

Your eyelids flutter. Your arm flops back to your side and your pulse slows.

I drag in a ragged breath, trying to process what just happened. I leap out of my chair, suddenly aware that you might wake up again, and glance quickly around me. The nurse is still busy taking observations and I pick up your phone. I don't know what to do now. All the evidence the police need to convict you is right here.

Should I hand it to DS Church myself? Or leave it for them to find?

You groan as though you're in pain and the sound makes me

want to scream. I wipe my fingerprints from your phone and stuff it back into your backpack. Better DS Church doesn't know I've had it.

I glare at you a final time before I leave. You're lying there like nothing happened. But it did. I touch my fingers to the red welts appearing on my wrists as if proving it to myself. At the last second I dig out my own phone from my bag and snap a photo of you.

My body is cloaked in a film of sweat as I stagger from the bay. The nurse gives me a cheery "See ya," and I manage a wave, but inside the panic is still raging.

I call DS Church the moment I'm out of the ward. The tremor in my hands travels to my body, and as the phone starts to ring in my ear I sink down and sit on the top step of the stairwell. I'm so tired.

DS Church answers with a brusque "Hello."

"DS Church, it's Jenna Lawson."

"Hello, Jenna. How can I help you?"

I realize I'm stuck. I can't tell her what you just did to me. She'll ask why I was visiting you. I can't tell her about the photos on your phone either. My knowledge of police procedures stems from watching old episodes of *The Bill* with Nathan when we were kids, and the occasional TV drama, but I'm sure that if DS Church discovers I've had your phone in my possession for two days it would make any evidence on it inadmissible, and I can't let that happen.

"Jenna?" the detective prompts.

"Sorry. I . . . I thought you should know—Matthew Dover— my stalker, he's awake. I was visiting another patient in intensive care." I tack on the lie but by the silence that follows I'm sure the detective sees straight through it. I shouldn't have called.

"Right. Well, thank you for letting me know," she says. "We are liaising very closely with the hospital staff and the moment Mr. Dover is well enough to be questioned we will visit him."

"What about his belongings? The last time I saw him he was taking photos of me. There might be evidence on his phone that will prove he's been stalking me."

"And when was the last time you saw him? Before the hospital, I mean," she says.

"Oh . . ." I think for a moment. So much has happened and I don't have time to rake through it all. I should be collecting the kids and taking them home for dinner. "On my way to school with the kids on . . . what day was it." I've lost all track of time. "Wednesday. I logged it with the station like you told me to. Have you found his phone?" I ask again.

"I visited Mr. Dover this morning. As I'm sure you're aware, he was in no state to be questioned. We're still looking for his phone. It wasn't with his belongings when I looked this morning. We'll be following up with local businesses near the scene to see if anyone handed one in."

It was with him, I want to shout, but I had it.

"I saw it in his backpack," I splutter. "Just now."

Another silence, this one longer. When the detective speaks, her voice is clipped and edged with warning. "I'm advising you not to visit Mr. Dover again, Jenna," she says. "It could damage your case."

"I didn't mean to. It just happened." I feel like a scolded child.

"I'll check his backpack myself tomorrow. Did you look through the phone or touch it in any way?"

"No," I say quickly. "Did the forensic team find prints at our house?" Now it's my turn to change the subject.

"We're still processing the evidence."

There's noise in the background and someone calls the detective's name. She says a hurried good-bye before adding a final warning to stay away from you.

I slump my head into my hands and wonder what I'm doing. I thought I wanted answers, as if there can be any excuse, any reason, why you've made my life a living hell. All I've found are more questions.

CHAPTER 24

SOPHIE

My trainers hit the pavement in time with the beat of the Black Eyed Peas thrumming in my ears and for the first time in days I feel utterly free. It's just me now, the beach to my left, the funfair behind me. There's a slight breeze blowing from the sea, making the humidity almost bearable.

Nick has clients until early evening and thinks I'm at home catching up on a Netflix series I lost interest in weeks ago. I could've told him I was going for a run, that I was going to see Matthew. I could've told him that I was stopping at McDonald's for a Big Mac on the way home. He wouldn't have stopped me, but it's not worth the dozen questions he'll ask, and it's definitely not worth the disapproving look that he gets whenever I eat something he doesn't like—those narrowed eyes and pursed lips—and how no matter what our plans are for the next day, they always become about hitting the gym.

I know he cares about me. He wants me to be healthy and he worries about me when I'm not at home. There's a part of me that craves that worry. It's been so long since anyone cared enough to get angry with me about anything, but there's another part of me that wishes that things were different.

My entire adult life has been about trying to forget the past and start again, as though a new flat, a new job, new hair, can make a new me. But there are certain things I can't escape. Like how much I love to eat junk food, and how I've never been able to stand up for myself. And then there're the memories that seep into my thoughts and shake me up when I least expect it. There's nothing I can do to erase them. But the biggest thing I can't escape, the thing that seems to always drag me back, is Matthew.

I've never been the sister to him that Mum wanted me to be, no matter how hard I've tried. I couldn't stop what happened twelve years ago, just like I couldn't stop him being hit by a bus. Nick says I shouldn't blame myself, but how can I not?

"Matthew has never been loved like you have, Sophie. He doesn't know how to love either. We have to teach him. We have to show him that no matter what, we are his family and we love him."

But he took our love, drank it back like Dad used to drink that first can of beer in the evening—guzzling and greedy—only stopping when there was nothing left. And then he destroyed it all.

The thought comes out of nowhere and I choke on the air dragging into my lungs. Do I really mean that?

I turn along a side road. The breeze doesn't stretch this far up, and as I leave the shady pavement and turn along another road, the air suddenly thickens, like a ton of corn flour has been added to the day, like I could slice the air with a knife.

My thoughts turn to the police detective who came to see me yesterday, just as I was walking out the door to meet a client. Nick was at the gym and it was just me and this woman—DS Church—asking me question after question about Matthew. "Can you tell me the names of any of your brother's friends? Who did he spend time with? What kind of life did he live? Was he in any kind of trouble?"

I told her the truth. Matthew doesn't have any friends, or much of a life either. He is either out taking photos, at work at the restaurant, or at home. "He hung out with me a bit and Nick, that's my boyfriend, but they didn't always get on, so mainly it was just me."

My heartbeat quickens, messing up my breathing. I wish I hadn't mentioned Nick. The detective wanted to know why they didn't like each other and I didn't know how to explain that it feels like neither of them want to share me.

I slow down a fraction and find my stride again, focusing on the movement of my arms and lengthening each breath in. I dart between two lanes of slow-moving traffic and feel the exhaust fumes scratching the back of my throat. The grass verges are yellow and scuffed with dry, dusty earth. I can't remember the last time it rained.

The entrance to the hospital is just ahead and as I slow to a walk and catch my breath I see the doctor we met—Jenna. Her hair is tied back in a loose ponytail and her head is bent, eyes fixed on the ground. But it's her, and as I watch her move, a cold brushes over my skin despite the heat and the perspiration from my run. She really does look like Mum.

"Jenna?" I call out before I can stop myself.

She looks up and there's a brief moment where I can tell from the confusion on her face that she can't place me. It's enough to release a burst of anxiety, like a firework inside me, and I wonder what the hell I'm doing. Jenna is not my mum. She's a doctor. She sees hundreds of patients and their relatives every week; why do I think she's going to want to talk to me? A fierce hate burns through me. *You idiot, Soph.*

But then recognition sparks and she smiles a little. "Sophie, hi. How are you?"

"I'm fine, thanks. Sorry, I just saw you and I wanted to ask something, but it doesn't matter. I'm sorry. I didn't mean to trouble you."

"It's no trouble. What did you want to ask?"

"I just . . . I wanted to know what you thought about Matthew's injuries? It was all such a shock to see him on Saturday and I don't think I really took it in. Do you think he's going to get better?"

"I really don't know. I'm not his doctor anymore and I don't know what his prognosis is—"

"Of course. I shouldn't have bothered you." I feel like an idiot again and wish I could rewind my day by five minutes and not shout out to her. I should be visiting Matthew right now, not standing here talking to Jenna.

"It's OK. You don't have to keep apologizing."

"Sorry—" I shake my head. "It's a habit." We share a smile and I don't feel so bad now.

"I'm sure you must be worried about your brother. I was just up in intensive care actually," she says, and something in her face changes. She looks so pale in the sunlight, highlighting the dark circles under her eyes. "Matthew has been brought out of the induced coma. They wouldn't do that if there wasn't significant improvement with his brain injury. Have you seen Matthew's doctor in intensive care?"

I nod, thinking of the portly Dr. Daghestani, who came to check on Matthew on Saturday just as Nick wanted to leave. "Yes, but I didn't really understand what he was telling me. And he was in such a rush that I didn't feel I could ask him stuff."

"What kind of stuff?"

"Like, will he remember things, from the past, I mean?" In the distance, a siren whoops. The sound hits me hard, like it always does. A memory slips out of its hiding place. Giant orange life-of-their-own flames, smoke as black as coal, and the police officer holding me back.

"Every brain injury is different," Jenna says, her voice cutting through the images clogging up my head. "And I'm not an expert, but I think it's going to be a case of wait-and-see. The drugs they've given him need to leave his system, so it could be a while before they can assess his cognitive function."

"Of course. I'm sor—I mean, thank you." We smile again at my slip.

"It's really no trouble, Sophie."

Jenna walks away in the direction of the car park and I move too, forcing myself toward the hospital and Matthew's bedside.

The siren blasts again from somewhere on the road and I hear the policeman's voice in my head. *"Where was your brother when the fire started, Sophie?"*

AN HOUR LATER I unlock the door to the apartment and head straight toward the bathroom for a shower, almost missing Nick sitting silently on the sofa.

"Where have you been?" Nick drags out each word as he stands.

"Hi. I just went for another run." I take in the set of his jaw, the quiet fury, and a fear sweeps through me. *You weren't supposed to be here.*

"In this heat. Of course you did." Nick swallows, his Adam's apple jutting out with the movement.

"I thought you were working until seven." It's a stupid thing to say, like I was trying to hide stuff from him. I am, but I don't want Nick to think that.

"I would've been," he hisses, "but then the police came to see me. Apparently someone told them that I don't get on with Matthew and so they wanted to know where I was on Thursday afternoon. They think I pushed him under the bus. I tried to call you but once again you didn't pick up."

"My phone was on silent. I was visiting Matthew. I'm sorry," I say. "What did you tell them?"

Nick rubs his hands over his face before looking up at me. "I panicked and just wanted them to go away, so I told them I was home with you."

"But you weren't." I keep my voice even while inside a storm rages. *What the hell did you say that for?* I want to scream.

"I know that, Sophie, but I didn't think." Nick moves toward me. "Can you tell them we were here together going through the rota?"

My head jerks up and down in a fast nod as Nick reaches out and pulls me into his arms. I've never seen Nick scared before. There's danger to it I don't want to think about. "Of course I will."

You coward, Soph.

"Good. Now, I've got to get back to work," he says, his anger vanishing. "I'm going out with some friends later and won't be back until late," he calls over his shoulder as he walks to the front door.

I don't shout after him. I don't ask whom he's seeing. I don't ask him where he really was on Thursday. Nick is the one who likes to ask the questions, not me. But it's not the questions that worry me. It's the answers.

I'm shaking all over by the time I step into the bathroom. I stand under the spray of the power shower, but for the first time there is no joy at being in this apartment. All I feel is trapped again in a life I don't want.

CHAPTER 25

JENNA

My head is spinning when I drive out of the hospital. The photos of me and the ones of Rachel flash in my thoughts and every time they do I feel your hand grabbing me. All I want to do is collect Beth and Archie and take them home, bolt the door, and never leave again.

Beth and Archie. My babies. I promised them I'd do better, but things feel more out of control than before.

I draw in a long breath and try to steady my thoughts. As I head to Christie's house I start to think about the time off I've been given. We could take a holiday, somewhere warm with a pool and a sun lounger. I picture the children playing in the water for hours on end, and Stuart and me drinking ice-cold beer and reading books in the sun. We haven't been on holiday since before you. Stuart landed a big project last August—109 houses in a new complex on the outskirts of town—and we couldn't get away, but maybe now we can.

By the time I'm parked outside Christie's house, a fragile peace has settled inside me.

Christie is laughing as she opens the door. Her face is flushed and her eyes are sparkling with amusement. "Jenna, hi." The laughter stops and she throws a glance back to the kitchen. "I wasn't expecting to see you. Stuart's already here."

"Is he?"

"He said he was collecting the kids today. Come on in."

Christie's house is a three-bed semidetached in a sprawling '70s housing estate where every house looks the same. Her kitchen is a chaotic collection of paintings on the fridge and photos Blu-Tacked to the wall. There's a sticker chart behind the door with the names of all of the children she cares for.

"Hi," I say to Stuart. He's in his work clothes—a dusty gray polo shirt and khaki shorts. He looks rugged and tanned and very comfortable in Christie's kitchen with a cup of tea in his hands. I always assumed he collected and dropped off in the same rush of "Hi, how are you?" and a flurry of thank-yous like I do. Does he always stop for a drink?

"Hey, what are you doing here?" he asks, leaning forward to kiss my cheek.

"I thought I was picking the kids up today." I frown and glance between them, feeling like an outsider. I'm sure I'm supposed to be collecting them today. I always collect them when my shift finishes at five.

"Saturday you forget them and today you try and collect them when you don't need to." Stuart laughs and so does Christie.

"Hey, that's not fair," Christie says, throwing a tea towel at him. "Saturday was my fault, not Jenna's."

I give Christie a grateful smile and force away the feeling that Stuart's words are another dig.

Archie rushes into the kitchen, followed by Beth and Niamh

and another boy I don't know. "Can we have a snack please, Christie?" Archie asks, looking to the others with a wide grin that makes me think they've put him up to asking.

Christie laughs and pulls out a biscuit tin. "How can I resist such starving baby birds, eh?"

The four children leap forward in a scramble of hands and the kitchen fills with the noise of riffling biscuits. Archie pulls his hand free first, lofting two and a half custard creams and grinning triumphantly.

"Just take one please, Archie," I say. "You'll be eating dinner soon."

"Let them be." Stuart grins. "They're having fun."

A frisson of annoyance winds through me. It was him who didn't like how many snacks Beth and Archie ate at Christie's, but actually doing something about it would ruin his best-dad-in-the-world routine.

"Cup of tea?" Christie raises the kettle at me before filling it with water.

"Coffee, if you've got it, please. Are you sure we're not disturbing you?" I want to leave, but with Stuart still drinking his tea, I can't exactly round up Beth and Archie and walk out the door.

"Not at all. Jason won't be home for a while yet and it's nice to have some adult conversation." She flicks a switch on the kettle and turns back to me. "Stuart just told me about your stalker being in hospital. That's good news."

"I guess." I shoot Stuart a look and wonder why it bothers me so much that he's been talking about me.

"You don't sound convinced. It's over, isn't it?" she asks. The question is for me, but she's looking at Stuart.

"There's still a long way to go. Convicting people for harassment is notoriously hard and even with a conviction there's no telling if he'll actually be sent to prison. He could get a suspended sentence and carry on doing it."

"But there'll be a restraining order," Stuart pipes up.

"Which something like fifty percent of people break." My statistic and gloom hang in the air for a minute as Christie slides a mug of coffee across the counter toward me.

"Just try and take care of yourself anyway," Christie says, eyeing me carefully.

"I will. In fact, I've taken some time off."

"Have you?" Stuart fixes me with a quizzical stare. "Why?"

"Because I need a break. I thought we could take the kids out of school and go on a last-minute holiday somewhere."

Stuart shakes his head, looking pained. "Jenna, I can't take time off now. We're right in the middle of having the plans for the site reassessed. Some nosy resident is claiming our houses are taller than we have planning permission for. It's all rubbish but there is no way I can leave right now. You know this is the biggest project I've ever handled."

I take a sip of coffee to hide my disappointment. It's watery and turns my stomach but I drink it anyway. "Oh well. It'll still be nice to spend some time with the kids. I'll take them to school and pick them up for the rest of the week," I say, turning to Christie.

There's a flash of disappointment on her face and she glances at Stuart for a second before it's gone and she's smiling at me again. "No problem. If you need me though, you know where I am."

We leave soon after that, the kids moaning about being in the middle of a game and Stuart suddenly quiet. At home I make chicken fajitas and we eat them on a blanket in the garden, and I tell Beth and Archie about my time off. It's easy to make it sound fun after a glass of wine.

"Do we get a week off from school then?" Beth asks hopefully.

"No, but we'll do lots of fun things after school, I promise."

"What kinds of things?" Archie asks with a mouthful of food.

"Don't speak with your mouth full," Stuart says.

"Bike rides and a trip to the funfair one day. Whatever you like."

Beth's smile buoys me on and even I'm convinced it's a good idea.

Later, Stuart gets the truth. My face burns hot at the thought of a colleague raising concerns about my abilities as a doctor to Nancy. It had to be someone who doesn't know me that well or they'd have spoken to me first, surely?

"So they're making you take the time off?" he asks. "Can they do that?"

"I guess so." My head sinks into the pillow and already I feel half-asleep.

Stuart slides into bed beside me and instantly his breathing slows. I wait for sleep to take me too, but it doesn't. I lie in the dark and think about you and all the things I now know.

CHAPTER 26

Sophie, *age 13*

M atthew?" Sophie calls out as she unlocks the front door. Matthew's head pokes out from the kitchen at the end of the narrow hall. He raises his eyebrows but says nothing.

"I've got two friends from school coming over for a bit. Don't . . ." *be weird*, is what she wants to say. *Don't stare at them without saying anything.* The words stick in her throat. ". . . tell Mum," she mutters instead.

Sophie's mum has never said she can't have friends over after school, but she never said Sophie could either, and it's not worth the hassle to find out. Sophie promised her mum she would come straight home from high school to keep an eye on Matthew, and she is—she's just brought some friends too. It's only fair. Everyone else in her year gets to go into town or to the park after school.

Matthew nods and when the doorbell rings a moment later, he disappears upstairs.

A flurry of nerves dances in Sophie's stomach as she opens the door. High school is so much better than her old school, apart from all the homework, but it's still taken Sophie ages to make a proper friend like Vicky. But now Felicity—Flick as she likes to be called—has joined them and Sophie always feels like she needs to prove herself, like she's not good enough for them.

"Hey, come in," Sophie says. "Want a snack? There's some Wagon Wheels and crisps."

"Sure." Flick shrugs, sharing a look with Vicky that Sophie doesn't understand. Are they mocking her because their houses are much nicer than hers? She pushes the thought away and wishes she could relax.

"Have you got MTV?" Vicky asks, munching on a chocolate biscuit and opening up the cupboard with baked beans and tinned tomatoes in it. Vicky wrinkles up her nose and shuts the cupboard with a slap of her hand.

"Nah." Sophie sighs like it's the worst thing ever. She'd die before she tells Vicky and Flick this, but the few times she's watched MTV at their houses, she thought it was kind of boring. "I've got the new *Now!* CD in my room though."

"OK," Flick says with a long yawn that makes Vicky smirk.

When Sophie opens the kitchen door to show them upstairs, Matthew is standing there, leaning against the wall and watching them through the crack.

"Hey." Sophie smiles and hopes he catches the silent plea in her eyes to actually speak and be normal.

Sophie turns, looking between her friends and Matthew. "This is my brother, Matthew."

"Hi," Flick says with a bored wave.

"Hi." Vicky repeats Flick's action.

Matthew doesn't reply. He just stares in the way he does. Sophie is used to it, but she knows how odd it is and wishes he would go away.

"What year are you in?" Vicky asks him.

No response.

Sophie feels her face turn red and bites at one of her nails. "He's in year five. Come on. Let's go up to my room." Sophie nudges Matthew out of the doorway and the three of them run upstairs.

The moment Sophie closes her bedroom door, Flick bursts out laughing. "Your brother is a freak. I mean, seriously, hello? What's his deal?"

"He's just shy," Sophie says, wishing the heat in her face would go away. She turns on the CD player and presses play. The stupid machine whirs but doesn't start.

"He was like this," Vicky adds, pulling a wide-eyed face and gawking at Flick until they're both laughing. Sophie laughs too, ignoring the dread in the pit of her stomach and wishing the first song would hurry up and load.

Sophie smacks the side of the CD player and jabs play again.

"Such a creep." Flick giggles, raising her voice another notch.

A floorboard creaks from the landing outside Sophie's room, making her friends scream before collapsing into more laughter. "Is he going to kill us with a carving knife?" Vicky hisses.

The beat of the first song bursts into the room, finally drowning out her friends' voices.

"What time is your mum coming home?" Vicky asks.

"Not till six."

"You're soooo lucky," Flick chips in. "I never get the house to myself. Almost makes me wish my parents were separated too."

Sophie grins, but she doesn't feel lucky. Most of the time she still can't get her head around the fact that her dad doesn't live with them anymore. She hardly ever gets to see him. With her nan dying last year and her mum now working so much, it feels like it's just her and Matthew most of the time. She still misses her nan so much.

"Got any cigarettes?" Flick shouts over the music. She leans against the window ledge and looks so expectant that Sophie feels herself die inside.

"I've just run out," Sophie lies, regretting it instantly.

"Do you smoke then?" Flick asks. There's something smug about her smile that makes Sophie feel uneasy.

Sophie shrugs. "Not much, but, you know, sometimes."

"I'd better get home anyway." Flick stands and opens the door, making a show of peeking into the hall first for Matthew.

"Me too," Vicky says, switching off Sophie's CD player and plunging the house into silence. "Hate that song."

"I thought you liked it," Sophie says. "You played it nonstop last summer, remember?"

"Yeah, well, that was before."

Before Flick came along, Sophie thinks to herself.

"Hey." Sophie reaches out and grabs Vicky's arm. From downstairs, Sophie hears Flick open the front door. "We are still friends, aren't we?"

"Of course we are." Vicky laughs before racing down the stairs to catch up with Flick.

So why doesn't it feel like it? She imagined the three of them hanging out on her bed, talking about which boys they fancied and playing truth or dare. But nothing has gone right.

Sophie waves good-bye at the front door and tries not to listen to Flick and Vicky's laughter carrying down the road. After tidying up the chocolate wrappers in the kitchen, Sophie goes to find Matthew. She hopes he's not upset about Flick's stupid comment.

Matthew is in his room, slouched on his bed, and staring at

nothing. The window is open and the room smells of the sickly sweet flower air freshener her mum keeps in the bathroom. There's another smell underneath and it takes Sophie a moment to realize what it is. Smoke.

Sophie eyes the bowl of blackened paper by the window. A box of matches sits beside the bowl.

"I was trying to make some paper look old for my history homework," Matthew mumbles.

Sophie isn't sure she believes him. "Don't tell Mum, OK? She'll get mad."

He nods.

"You use black tea or coffee and pour it onto the paper. When it dries it looks like old parchment or something," she says, trying to read his face.

"Wanna play a game of rummy?"

Sophie pauses at the door and smiles a little. Matthew might be her brother rather than her friend, but at least hanging out with him is easy. She doesn't have to constantly worry about what he's thinking. "Sure, if you don't mind losing."

"As if."

"I'll go get the cards." Sophie tucks the matches in her pocket and takes the bowl to the kitchen to tidy away. If her mum finds it in Matthew's room she'll freak out and no doubt it will be Sophie that gets the blame.

CHAPTER 27

Tuesday, June 18
JENNA

Bright morning sunlight pours through the bifold doors, highlighting every smear and smudge on the glass and the remnants of the gray fingerprint dust on the cupboards. I stare out into the garden, my eyes pulling like they always do to the bare patch of lawn in the shape of a *J*. We've reseeded but it's been too dry for the grass to regrow and it's a constant reminder of the terror you've wielded over me.

"So you're taking us to school today and picking us up?" Archie singsongs as he dances around me.

I look down at him and feel my head spinning from the circular motion of his movements. Last night, I managed three hours of sleep before I was shaken awake by a dream of sitting beside you in the hospital, your arm grabbing me, hurting me.

"Yes." I smile, wishing his joy was infectious. "Sit down and eat your breakfast please, Archie."

"And tomorrow?" he asks, continuing his circle, just a bit slower now.

"Yep." I close my eyes, fighting a sudden nausea.

"And the day after that."

"She said all week, Archie," Beth hollers from the living room.

"Thank you, Beth." I open my eyes and focus them on Archie. "Baby, would you please stop walking around me?" I take a step toward the counter and busy myself washing up a cup that could easily go in the dishwasher.

"And we're going on a bike ride after school?" he asks, still skittering like a puppy at my legs.

The nausea builds and with it the frustration. "Archie," I snap. "Will you sit down and eat your breakfast?"

A silence falls over the kitchen, my outburst too loud, too extreme. I should have asked again.

Archie's little feet grind to a halt. His big brown eyes fill with lip-wobbling tears. "I want Daddy," he croaks.

The guilt balloons up. Hurt pulls at my chest—not my own hurt, but Archie's, and the knowledge it's me who's caused it. "I'm sorry. Archie, I'm sorry for shouting. I did ask you twice already to stop walking around me. It was making me feel ill."

I crouch down and scoop him into my arms, lifting him up and holding him close to me. A second passes and then I feel his body relax against me and his arms stretch around my neck. It's so easy to forget he's only six years old; he's only just started eating with a knife and fork, only just learning to join his writing, to add up and take away.

"Sorry," I whisper in his ear.

"Maybe we should go to Christie's if you're sick," Beth says quietly, appearing in the doorway.

I try to laugh at Beth's remark and ignore the question in my head that asks if she's right. And now it's not even eight in the morning and I already feel fraught, snappish. How am I going to get through the day?

"Come on, let's have breakfast and get ready for school. And yes, we are going on a bike ride later. We'll go anywhere you like."

"Really?" they both chime, like I'm offering them a two-week holiday to Disneyland. My own life has shrunk so much because of you, but I don't think I've ever stopped to think how much smaller the children's world has become.

I think the fresh air will do me good as we leave the house and walk to school, but I'm wrong. The day is so humid, not fresh at all. We're not even at the end of the road before my T-shirt is clinging to my back.

There's talk of a storm that will finish the heat wave, but the sky is still cyan blue, the sun impossibly bright. An end seems impossible.

Beth and Archie bounce down the road, side by side, jabbering to each other about which route they want to take for our bike ride later. I half listen and half look for you, a habit I can't seem to break.

When we reach the school playground it's already buzzing with the noise of adults chatting and laughing. Flashes of green uniforms catch constantly in the corners of my vision as the smaller kids charge through the groups of parents and strollers.

Happy screams mingle with sad ones—a child with a grazed knee, a toddler who doesn't want to sit in the stroller and is bucking against the straps. I close my eyes for a second, trying to block it all out, but without my sight, my hearing intensifies until the screams are punching into my eardrums.

I force my eyes open and find Beth staring at me.

"OK?" I ask.

She nods. "Are you?" The way she narrows her eyes is just like Stuart and I'm not sure whether to laugh or cry.

"Of course. Just hot," I smile, fanning the air around my face.

"Beth," a girl cries out from across the playground. Beth turns and shoots off toward a petite girl with silky blond hair that I recognize from the party. Is she Lacey? I search the faces for Rachel.

The bell rattles at last, the screams die away, and order assembles in the playground. Even the toddler stops crying.

I say a hurried good-bye to Archie and Beth before pushing through the crowd to find Rachel. I knock against someone's shoulder and hear a tut followed by a whispered comment. My eyes dart from one face to another as I offer an apologetic smile.

I normally hurry like this, squeezing through the other parents to get out of the gates first, but usually my head is leaping ahead, thinking of work and the patients I will treat. I feel hollow when I think of the week ahead.

I still can't believe someone I work with would speak to Nancy about me behind my back. Was it one person? Or two or three? Was I making mistakes? Was someone covering for me and I didn't know? I can't believe that's true. I was tired, sure, but I was focused too. Working was the only time I could escape thoughts of you.

At the roadside, I pretend to check something on my phone while watching for Rachel. I wish I'd spent more time studying the photos on your phone now. I try to remember the details of the photos, the sports kit she was wearing in one of them and the street she was on with the trees and cars and people in the background.

I spot Rachel in a group of five women. Their heads are bent close as they talk to one another. Christie is among them. As I approach the group, Rachel slides on a pair of sunglasses and starts walking in the opposite direction.

I call out to her, hurrying to close the gap between us. She glances around, a smile already on her face. When she sees me it falters. I guess I didn't make a great impression at the party.

"Hi," I say. "Sorry to grab you like this, but have you got a minute?"

She looks at her watch—a sleek, rose gold Fitbit that matches the color of her gym vest. "Sure. I've got a fitness class in ten minutes though."

"No problem. I can walk with you."

There's a brief pause where her head tilts to one side as if she's assessing me. I wish I could see her eyes behind her sunglasses. "Sure."

We fall into step together and move away from the parked cars and other parents. Her strides are long and quick and I feel myself hurrying to keep up.

"What's up?" Rachel glances my way and when I look at her, it's my own drawn face that reflects back from her sunglasses.

I take a deep breath. "Thanks again for driving the kids home from the party on Saturday."

"It's totally fine. Honestly, don't even think about it." She flashes me a smile of bright white teeth.

There's something so light about Rachel—an air of bubbly perfection that adds to my own feelings of exhaustion.

We fall into silence; the only noise is the flapping of my flip-flops on the pavement. Rachel is waiting for me to say more, but I'm not sure how to start.

"My gym is just up here," she says, pointing to a shiny glass structure on the corner of the main road that leads into town. I'm running out of time.

"I wanted to speak to you because . . ." I swallow, wishing there was an easy way to explain this. "I've found some photos of you."

She stops dead and spins toward me so fast that for a second it seems like she's going to grab me. "What? Where?" She pulls off her sunglasses and stares at me with alarm.

"On my stalker's phone. Do you know a man named Matthew Dover?" I ask before I lose my nerve.

She narrows her eyes, her lips pinching together before she shakes her head. "No."

"For almost a year he's been stalking me."

"I'm so sorry. A few of the mums were talking about it in the playground a while ago. What you've been through is horrendous."

"Thanks," I reply, gritting my teeth against the feeling of annoyance now pulsing through me. The teachers know about you, so does Christie, and whoever else Stuart's told. I shouldn't be surprised parents are talking about me.

"But what's this got to do with photos of me?"

"Matthew Dover is in hospital. I was able to look through his phone and I found dozens of photos of me and you." The words spill out in a rush. "Are you sure you don't know him? I've got a photo of him."

I dig in my bag and pull out my phone. "Here."

Rachel leans closer. She starts to shake her head before she even looks at you. "Never seen him," she says, slipping her sunglasses back on, but not before I see something flicker in her eyes. Was it recognition? Panic?

"Are you sure?"

"One hundred percent. Does that mean he's following me too then? Am I in danger?"

"He's in hospital. He can't get to us."

"That's a relief." She presses her hand to her forehead before smoothing out the top of her already perfect ponytail.

"You should still go to the police and report the harassment though. It will strengthen our case against him if you do. There'll be more of a chance he'll go to prison."

"But I haven't been harassed, have I? You're telling me about some photos some guy has on his phone of me, but that's all I know about it. No offense, Jenna, but they'll laugh me out of the police station."

She's right, I realize, swallowing down the emotion threatening to burst out. But I can't just walk away from this. There's something not quite right about Rachel's reaction. "If you're worried about saying something, if he's threatened you—"

"I don't know what you're talking about." She laughs, but it's not the same pally humor I've heard before.

Rachel starts to walk again. Slowly at first, then her pace picks up. "Maybe you've got me mixed up with someone else?"

"I don't think so. Have you had any strange cards through your letterbox? Or anything weird left for you?"

Just for a second Rachel's feet stall. Then she's off again. "No, nothing."

"He can't hurt you," I call after her as I hurry to catch up, wondering if she's listened to a word I've said. "He was hit by a bus. He can't hurt you. You don't need to pretend." My throat feels tight. I'm not sure which one of us I'm trying to convince.

"I would know if I was being stalked, right?"

I think of the fear, the spider on my back. "I did, but—"

"And the first I've heard about it is from you. So it's much more likely that you're wrong, not me."

Rachel reaches the gym and pulls open the door, releasing a gush of cool air.

"Please," I beg now. "If we could just talk for another few minutes."

"There's no need to talk anymore," she says, already stepping through the door. "I'm so sorry for what you've been through, I really am, but I've never heard of this guy, I'm not being stalked by anyone, I've not had a single gift left on my doorstep, no vandalism in the garden. Nothing."

"How did you know about the damage in our garden?" I ask.

She pauses for a second before she replies. "I think Christie told me." And with that she disappears into the gym.

I turn around, trudging back the way I came. My mind turns over everything Rachel told me. She said Christie told her about the *J* you scorched into our lawn, but I'm sure I didn't tell Christie about it. I wonder if Stuart did. Or even Archie.

Still, there's something about Rachel that isn't sitting right. The way she reacted when I said your name, and then saying she didn't recognize you before she even looked at the photo. Am I reading too much into this?

CHAPTER 28

SOPHIE

I'm stretched out on the sofa, lost in Kim Kardashian's latest Insta-gram frenzy, when my phone rings with an unknown number.

"Hello?"

"Good morning. Is this Sophie Dover?" My volume is still high from listening to music on my last run and the thick Glaswegian accent is loud in my ears.

"Yes."

"I'm Lynsey Dunsby, a neurologist at Westbury District Hospital. I'm calling to let you know that your brother, Matthew, is awake and asking for you."

"Oh my God." I sit up, covering my mouth with my hands. My thoughts jumble with the emotions tearing through me. Matthew's OK. He remembers me. "Should I come in now?"

"If you can then that would be helpful. There is still significant swelling in Matthew's brain, which is causing him some cognitive impairments. Right now, Matthew is having trouble forming some speech and is easily confused. He appears to have moments of understanding and was able to ask for you, but there are also times when he doesn't know his own name. Until the swelling is completely gone we won't know what lasting effects there will be, nor the impact on his day-to-day life.

"He has been moved to my care in the brain injury unit, and I think it would aid his recovery to spend time with someone he is close to."

"I'll come now. I can be there in thirty minutes."

We say good-bye and I leap into action, grabbing my bag and heading for the door. The moment I'm moving I feel more in control. The relief that Matthew is OK is palpable, but so is something else curdling with it, and I can't pretend it isn't there anymore. Dread.

I'm almost at the lifts when Nick calls. He'll want to know what exercise plan I've developed for the session with the new mums later. I stare at his name on the screen and all I see is the quiet rage, the disapproval, the constant need to know where I am, and suddenly I can't answer.

I switch off my phone and stuff it in my bag. All morning I've been waiting for DS Church to get in touch and ask me if I was with Nick the afternoon Matthew was hit by the bus. When she does, I don't know what I'm going to say.

Things are getting out of control. Last night Nick accused me of cheating on him because I didn't want to have sex. "Even when you're here, you're not here," he said to me. "It feels like you're keeping things from me. What's going on?

"Nothing," I replied.

"Are you sleeping with someone else?"

"Of course not. I'm just tired."

He turned to face the window, a bulk of anger simmering beside me, and I wished I'd given him what he wanted.

THE BRAIN INJURY unit is tucked at the end of a corridor on the ground floor. I press the buzzer and peer through the glass-windowed doors. Inside, it looks more like a hotel than a hospital.

The door unlocks and I walk into a wide lobby with a nurses' station that could easily be mistaken for a check-in desk if it wasn't for the nurse in a pale blue uniform standing behind it.

"Sophie Dover?" he asks.

I nod.

"Would you mind waiting here for a moment?" He points to four chairs positioned around a glass coffee table. The nurse is short and his hair is dark brown, shaved at the sides and a curly mop on top. "Dr. Dunsby has asked to talk to you before you see Matthew."

"Oh. I didn't know that." I sink into one of the chairs, feeling stupid.

I wonder how much Matthew remembers.

"There's something we need to talk about," he'd said to me that day we met on the street.

I think back to the last time I saw him. The darkness burning in his eyes. His almost self-righteous air. As though he believed that all his checking up on me, his keeping tabs on me, was actually a way of helping. He didn't like Nick. He didn't like the way I was living my life. I'm sure that's what he wanted to talk about.

I should've done more to listen to him, but it didn't feel like Matthew was trying to help. It felt like Matthew was clinging on to the past, and he wanted me to cling on to it with him.

My mind draws to a sudden stop and I realize I've been thinking about Matthew in the past tense. For all I know, he remembers everything, and the moment I walk through the door in a minute, he's going to start on again about Mum and me and everything I don't want to think about.

I really hope that doesn't happen. Matthew is my brother and I want him to be OK, but maybe it would be better if he didn't remember anything. Ctrl-alt-delete on a shitty start to life and everything that followed. *He can have the ultimate fresh start*, I think with a pang of jealousy.

It's ten minutes before a woman appears. "Sophie? I'm Lynsey Dunsby, we spoke on the phone. Thank you for waiting." The neurologist's accent is less pronounced in person, but there's a no-nonsense headmistress feel to her which makes me wish I wasn't wearing my gym clothes.

"Let's go to my office."

I follow Dr. Dunsby through the ward. It looks nothing like the rest of the hospital. There's a door open into an empty room and I catch sight of a small kitchen area.

"We strive to create a home environment wherever we can; it helps with the rehabilitation," she explains. "Many of our patients have to learn basic skills again, like how to hold a knife and fork."

She leads me into a small office and sitting down behind a tidy desk. "I won't keep you long. Please sit down. I like to talk to family members before they visit because brain injury recovery is very unpredictable and it can often be a case of one step forward, two back.

"Please don't be disheartened today when you see your brother. His head injury was very severe and he's already made immense progress to be out of the coma. It's important you don't upset him or ask questions that might confuse him. Recovery of memory after a brain injury is very fragile. It could be days or weeks before a patient with Matthew's type of brain injury remembers anything. And there is of course the chance that many memories may be lost forever. Do you have any questions before you see Matthew?"

Dozens, I think before shaking my head.

"OK then. Come this way." She stands and leads me down another corridor.

Matthew's room is like a bedroom from an Ikea catalog, not that different from my own. The furniture is functional but nice too. There's a lamp on a bedside table giving a dim buttery yellow glow, an empty bookshelf, and two leather armchairs. A small flat-screen TV is fixed to the wall.

The bed is the only giveaway to the real purpose of the room. It's a hospital bed with bars on the sides and hydraulics underneath to move it up and down. That, and the red alarm cord hanging down beside it. A sudden urge to yank the cord, sound the alarm, and escape pushes through me.

"I'll leave you to it," Dr. Dunsby says. "I think it would be best to keep the visit short today. Just five or ten minutes will be enough for Matthew." She closes the door behind her and then it's just the two of us.

I turn to Matthew, taking in the change in him. There are no wires or machines now, but his arm and leg are still in plaster, his left eye is swollen, and there's a dark scab running the length of his face.

For a moment I don't know what to say or do.

"Don't be angry with him, Sophie. He loves you. He just doesn't know how to show it."

"Hey," he says in a voice deeper than I remember.

"Hi." I perch on the edge of the armchair by the bed and chew at the side of a jagged fingernail. I pull my hand away. It's been years since I bit my nails. "How are you feeling?"

Matthew frowns then. He moves his lips as though testing the word before he speaks. "Tired." After a pause, he asks, "What happened?"

"You were hit by a bus." Dr. Dunsby's warning plays in my mind and I leave out the part about being pushed.

"I remember someone telling me that. The police were here. They kept asking questions about . . . about—" The next words are mumbled, gibberish nonsense.

"What do you remember?"

"Random stuff. Dad's dead, right?"

I nod. "He died eight years ago. Liver cirrhosis—the booze finally killed him just like Mum said it would."

I want to ask if he remembers the funeral and Mum and Trevor sitting in the front row across from us, unable to show us an ounce of forgiveness even on the day we were saying good-bye to our dad.

"You moved out?" Matthew says.

A jab of guilt gets me right between the ribs. "I'd signed the lease on a bedsit before Dad died. I offered to stay while you finished college, but you wanted to quit anyway and get a job. You found an apprenticeship at the restaurant you still work at now."

"Mum doesn't speak to us anymore," he says.

I shake my head.

"Will you see if she'll come visit me?" he asks, his eyes pleading with me like he's eight and I'm eleven again.

"I'll try," I tell him, unsure if I mean it. The thought of seeing Mum fills me with a twisted mix of emotions, like tangled Christmas tree lights I'll never be able to unravel.

Matthew closes his eyes and for a moment I think he's fallen asleep. I stand up and start to move noiselessly toward the door.

"Sophie?"

I turn and his face when he looks at me is so scared, so like that little boy who first came to live with us, that I feel a pang of sadness in my chest so fierce it takes my breath away.

"Yeah?"

"There's a big gap in my head. I know there's stuff I can't remember. It's just gone." There's a slur to his words, as though he's drunk. "It's all gone."

"They said it would take a couple of days, and besides, you know who I am, right?"

Matthew nods, then winces. "Do I have a cat?"

"A cat? No." I shake my head. "So you don't remember anything from before the accident? You were acting a bit strange."

"Was I?" He rubs his hand across the top of his head as though he's just this second banged it, and looks as though he might cry. "It's OK."

"It's not OK," he says in a voice so laced with fury that I take a sudden step back. "It's . . . NOT . . . OK," he repeats, louder this time, his eyes squeezing shut. "There is something I have to remember. It's important. I know it is. I HAVE TO GET OUT OF HERE." His shouts bounce from the walls and when he looks at me, his eyes are dark and angry. Memories force themselves into my head.

The night air filled with smoke.

The neighbors staring.

The flashing lights, the sirens.

And Matthew looking at me just like he is now.

From in front of me, Matthew pulls at the blanket covering his body. His good leg kicks out, tangling him further, and he bangs his fists against the bed. "I HAVE TO GET OUT OF HERE."

I reach for the red cord, but before I can pull it the door flies open and the nurse from the front desk appears and is across the room in a second, pressing a firm hand on Matthew's shoulder.

"Matthew, you need to calm down. Everything is all right. You've had a brain injury and you need to rest."

My feet are rooted to the spot. I want to leave. Should I though?

"Sophie?" Dr. Dunsby touches my shoulder and I jump.

Matthew's eyes are still shut tight and he's thrashing against the mattress despite the nurse by his side.

"Agitation is very common in recovering patients," she says in a quiet voice, guiding me from the room.

"Should I go now then?"

"Yes," she says. "But please come back. It really will help him to see a familiar face. Are there any other family members or people he's close to who can visit?" she asks, raising her voice to be heard over Matthew's shouts.

I shake my head. "It's just the two of us now."

She smiles sadly and gives my arm a gentle squeeze. "Come back tomorrow."

I nod and try not to listen to Matthew's shouts chasing me out of the ward.

"SOPHIE, SOPHIE, SOPHIE."

I move fast, my stride lengthening until I'm almost jogging toward the exit. When I'm outside, in the ruthless heat, I break into a run. Seeing the darkness in Matthew after all this time has shaken me to my core. All I want to do is outrun Matthew's shouts echoing in my mind and the memories of the fire. Flames bigger than I could ever have imagined.

CHAPTER 29

Jenna

The kitchen got the biggest clean of its life today. I even took everything out of the cupboards and cleaned inside them. I scrubbed dried spots of pasta sauce off the skirting board, and glitter that has been stuck to the floor tiles since Christmas. And for the first time in as long as I can remember it wasn't you consuming my thoughts. It was Rachel.

I haven't been able to get our talk out of my head. There was something off about the whole thing. I'm sure her face changed when I mentioned your name and yet she said she didn't know you.

I've watched patients look me in the eye and lie about what happened to them—the door they walked into that doesn't explain the two-day-old bruising on their arms; the sixty-year-old man with chest pain and heart palpitations who's lying about the Viagra he bought on the Internet; the sixteen-year-old whose mum is by her side and swears she's not sexually active. Some doctors call it a sixth sense, others think they read body language—imperceptible twitches, things no one else would notice. Me, I call it bullshit radar, and over the years mine has become pretty good. And something about Rachel's reaction this morning isn't sitting right.

When my lower back is screaming in protest and there's nowhere else left to clean, I stand back to survey my handiwork. Every surface gleams and the air is heavy with the smell of lemon-scented cleaner. I check the time. It's two p.m. There's still an hour before I have to collect Beth and Archie from school.

I reach for my phone and call Rachel's mobile. I'm not sure what I hope she's going to say that she wouldn't tell me this morning, but I have to try.

The phone rings three times before she answers with a tentative "Hello?"

"Hi, Rachel, it's Jenna. I just wanted to apologize for ambushing you this morning," I say, launching in before she has a chance to stop me. "I know it must have been a shock to hear about the photos Matthew Dover has taken of you, but I wondered, now that you've had some time to think about it, if you've remembered anything else?"

"No, I haven't," she replies in a hissed whisper. "There's someone at the door, I have to go."

She hangs up without a good-bye, leaving me staring at my phone in disbelief. I call her again, but this time it rings and rings before a recorded voice asks me to leave a message. "Rachel, please call me back," I beg. "It's important we speak. Thanks."

I sit at the kitchen counter and stare at my silent phone for ten minutes. Why doesn't she want to talk to me? Is she hiding something? A nervous energy shoots through my blood. A part of me knows I should leave it now, your months of torture have made me paranoid, but another part of me, a stronger part, is egging me on to keep going. You're awake now. How long will it be before you recover? And then what? It will be months before there's a trial and a chance you'll be sent to prison. If Rachel knows something about you, if you were harassing her as well, then I have to know. I have to do everything I can to make sure you never come near me or my children again.

I dig in my bag for the PTA information sheets Rachel gave me last week. I'm sure I haven't thrown them away. I find them in a side pocket, screwed up and torn at the edges, but otherwise fine. The first is a pleading letter, urging parents to join, and the second is a list of all of the PTA members, their names, addresses, and phone numbers. Don't these people care about their privacy?

Rachel's home line rings five times before she answers it. "Hello?"

"Hi, it's Jenna. I really—"

The line cuts dead. What the hell?

I dial the number again and this time it rings only twice. "Hello?" a man's voice barks in my ear.

"Hi, I'm Jenna, a friend of Rachel's. Is she there, please?"

"Hang on," he replies before there's muffled noise. I imagine him covering the microphone and calling for Rachel.

"Er . . . she's . . . just popped out," he says a moment later. "Can you call back another time?"

"Of course."

Popped out? She was there sixty seconds ago.

When my phone vibrates on the counter I snatch it up, but it's not Rachel, it's Diya.

"Hi, hon," she says, her voice loud over the noise of the clattering cups I can hear in the background.

"Hey. You sound like you're in Costa."

She laughs. "Only a true caffeine addict like you could tell in two seconds flat which café I'm in just from the sound of the coffee machine."

"Busted." I laugh.

"How are you doing? Some kid threw up all over my shoes today and it made me think of you."

"Ah, I'm touched," I joke.

"I was thinking of you lying in the sun, reading a good book, and drinking wine. Please tell me that's what you're doing right now?"

"Not quite. I did give the kitchen its first spring clean in ten years though."

Diya's laugh rings in my ears and I grin, a weight lifting from my thoughts. "That is so typical of you. I should've known you wouldn't put your feet up. How are you? Are you sleeping better?"

"A bit." A tiny tiny bit. I don't like lying to Diya, but I don't want to ruin our chat with the state of my insomnia.

"That's great. Oh, it's my turn to order. Call me tomorrow, OK?"

"Sure."

"Oh . . . a soya caramel latte, please," I hear her say. "Better go. Love ya."

The silent kitchen wraps itself around me and I stifle a long yawn. Talking to Diya has pulled me back to reality and my face burns at the number of times I've just tried to talk to Rachel. I'll apologize next time I see her.

I check the time. I have ten minutes until I need to collect the kids. I leap up to get the bikes out of the shed and check the tires aren't flat, but as I move, my arm knocks my bag, toppling it to the floor and scattering the contents across the tiles.

As I reach down to scoop everything back in, I see a set of door keys I don't recognize. It's as I'm laying them out in the palm of my hand that I remember they're yours. There's a Yale front-door key, a small locker key, another Yale key, and a dead bolt key.

Should I return them to your bag, risk you seeing me, grabbing me? No. I can't do that. I never want to see you again. Maybe I should throw them away. Forget I ever had them, forget that I read your address on your hospital notes and know where you live. I like that thought better, but still my heart is pounding in my chest and I don't know why. There's a whisper of an idea forming, but I block it out and focus on getting ready for the bike ride.

CHAPTER 30

Wednesday, June 19

To: Jenna.Lawson@westburydistrict.org.uk
From: Guesswhosback@mailpalz.co.uk
Subject: Have you

MISSED ME?

CHAPTER 31

JENNA

The e-mail arrives just as I'm climbing into the car after dropping Beth and Archie at school. I read the four words and the fear returns so fast it's like it never left me. Every muscle in my body tenses and even though I know you're not here, I can't stop myself from peering out of the windscreen, my eyes darting in every direction.

A group of mums with strollers wanders slowly by, and a white Land Rover pulls up by the school gates just long enough for three children to clamber out and run toward the school.

My hands shake as I call DS Church.

"Hi, Jenna," she says before I can get my greeting out.

"I just got another e-mail," I blurt.

"I assume you mean the same style you received before?"

"Yes. Exactly the same."

"Is this the first one you've had since Matthew Dover was brought into hospital?"

"Yes."

"Has there been anything else happening? Any other dolls or someone following you?"

"No, of course not. I would've said. It's him though. It has to be. I told you he still had his phone. Have you spoken to him?"

DS Church sighs and I feel her annoyance in the pause before she speaks. Am I being a nuisance? Is she tired of my calls? I bite back the desire to apologize. Whether she's had enough of me or not, she needs to take this new e-mail seriously. "My colleague and I were able to speak to Mr. Dover yesterday," she says. "But it's early days in his recovery and our investigation of him, Jenna. I need to ask you to be patient. I'll be in touch when we make progress."

If *you make progress*, I find myself wanting to retort.

I think of all the hours DS Church and I have spent together, me in the squeaky office chair with the broken wheel that sits beside her desk. Hours and hours of time away from the hospital, away from Beth and Archie, giving statements about melted dolls and being followed. Everything I said was typed up and given to me to read and sign.

I thought I trusted DS Church to stop you, but now I'm not so sure.

"Will you send me the e-mail you received and I'll pass it on to cyber analysis?"

"Yes. I'll do it now."

"Is there anything else?"

The nightmare I had last night rushes into my thoughts. I'd almost forgotten it, but now it feels so real that I want to tell DS Church how I was chased through Westbury town center, running for my life. I want to tell her how I kept shouting for help, but no one came. And when I finally stopped I was by a busy road with buses zooming by and you were at my side. You put your hands around my neck and I couldn't breathe and then you let go and I was falling into the road.

"Jenna?" DS Church prompts with another frustrated sigh.

"No, there's nothing else."

With that she says good-bye, leaving me gritting my teeth against the scream fighting to get out.

It's starting again and no one is doing anything to stop you.

I thump my fist against the steering wheel. I thought if the police could just find you then everything would be OK, but it's not.

The need to do something gnaws at my insides. I call Rachel's mobile and leave another message begging her to call me. "I've got an update from the police. You'll want to hear it," I lie, hoping it will be enough to convince her to return my call.

I reach into my bag and pull out your keys and tap your address into Google Maps. It's an eighteen-minute drive.

Your keys jingle in my palm and I realize how much my hands are still shaking. I have a sudden desire to drive home and bolt the door behind me, but that's exactly what you want me to do, and so I swallow the fear, clench my hands into two tight fists until the shaking stops, and drive across town. I won't let you keep doing this to me.

I START LOOKING for your house at the wrong end of the mile-long terrace road, the end nearest to town with TO LET signs in every other front garden and lawns left to overgrow. They remind me of the student houses I lived in years ago.

I keep driving, all the way to the other end, where the small front gardens are neat and lacy net curtains hang in the windows.

It's 9:20 in the morning and the street is empty. I park your keys in my hand, and walk straight to your front door like I'm supposed to be here. *I'm doing nothing wrong*, I try to tell myself over the furious beating of my heart in my chest. If anyone asks, I'll say I'm a friend, here to feed your cat.

I find the right key and let myself in and try to ignore the furious beating of my heart in my chest and the doubt now circling like vultures in my thoughts.

The smell of garlic hits me as I step in and close the door behind me. No going back now. I stand for a second. My breath is coming in short gasps as the reality of what I'm doing hits me.

"Hello?" My voice is weak. I'm in your house. I've walked through the front door just as you did mine. But what if you live with someone? What if there's someone else here?

"Hello?" I try again, forcing a strength into my voice that I don't feel.

Time ticks by. A minute of silence, then another just to be sure before I dare to move.

Your house is nothing like I imagined. I was expecting an empty flat, a mattress on the floor, empty takeaway cartons, but it's not like that at all.

Canvas prints hang on the walls. Not personalized ones, but the cheap kind from discount shops—a stretch of exotic beach in the living room, a café scene in the kitchen, like you've tried to make the place look homey on a budget.

The kitchen is straight ahead at the end of the hall and I head there first. The sides are clear of plates and cups, the black worktop is clean. I stare at a row of cookbooks and try to imagine you cooking the delicate meals I saw in the photos on your phone.

The living room is at the front of the house and is as tidy as the kitchen. There's a bookcase, a squishy blue sofa and matching armchair, and a small flat-screen TV that looks too square compared to the huge rectangular one that sits in our living room.

I step over to the bookcase with its Harry Potter collection taking pride of place. Below them is a photo in a silver frame. It's you and Sophie as young teenagers sitting on a park bench on either side of a woman with thick auburn hair. The woman's smile is wide, her mouth open as though the photographer has captured the split second before she started laughing.

"Oh my God." My voice startles me and I jump, spinning to check behind me. I swallow hard and turn back to the photo and the woman who looks just like me. It's the shade of our hair, but also the shape of our faces—the angular nose. It's your mother, isn't it? I can see the resemblance to Sophie now too. My chest tightens like I'm being squeezed by an invisible force. It's hard to breathe. Is this the reason for everything you've done to me?

I think of the months of stalking and the gifts—burned dolls wearing miniature versions of my clothes, dead flowers, broken glass. Why would me looking like your mum make you want to do these things to me?

I turn my gaze to Sophie. She looks a little older than you in the photo, with hair the same color as her mum's and a smile that matches perfectly. You, on the other hand, are the odd one out. Tall, with gangly limbs protruding from an oversized T-shirt. Greasy dark hair. Eyes staring at the camera, but no smile.

Who are you?

The desire to turn and flee hurtles through me and I move quickly back toward the front door. Only at the last second do I stop and force myself to climb up the narrow staircase, pulse racing harder than before as I imagine all the things I might find.

The walls are spinning by the time I reach the top. I'm desperate to grab the banister for support but I don't want to leave any fingerprints. There are no pictures on the walls up here, just tired carpet and four doorways.

The first room is a plain white bathroom with a shower over a bath and a shower curtain with dancing penguins in top hats on it. The second room is empty aside from a deflated blow-up mattress and a pillow. Then there's another bedroom, this one small and filled with boxes of cookbooks and college notebooks.

I inch toward the fourth room at the front of the house and kick the door open with my foot. It creaks as it flies open into a room with the curtains drawn. For a moment I just stand and stare, unable to breathe, gasp, move at the sheer horror of what I'm seeing.

Strips of sunlight creep in at the edges of the windows where the curtains don't reach, casting a dim light across the room. Every inch of wall is covered with photographs. Hundreds of them stuck side by side from the skirting boards all the way to the ceiling.

A nausea twists in my stomach, and even though I want to run now, I keep walking further into the room. I step to the wall opposite your bed and stare openmouthed at the photographs. Some are old, curling at the edges. Others are newer and stuck on top. One photo has at least three more peeking out underneath it.

They are just like the photos on your phone. A collage of nothing in particular and placed in no order as far as I can tell. There's a photo of a tree stuck next to one of a car. Then a bin. Then a crowd of shoppers in Westbury. A wilting Christmas tree. The gray cat. And faces. So many people. All of them are looking away from the camera, no doubt unaware they've even been captured by you.

I realize how easy it must be for you to take these photos unnoticed. It's not like you're standing with an old-fashioned camera and a zoom lens. Nearly everyone walks around with their phones in front of their faces. You can snap away without anyone ever knowing.

There are photos of Sophie spanning across every wall. In some she has black hair, in others red or blond. Short in some, long in others. Sometimes she's looking right at the lens and other times she's on the street, another unwitting face.

I am on this wall too, stuck in among the medley. There's one of me leaving the hospital. Another with the children walking out of school. There are half a dozen of our house too. There are close-ups of our doorstep, and the horrible dolls you've left for us.

All the photos of me and the children are recent. Taken in the last few months. I look for older photos, ones from when you started last July but they must be buried beneath the others.

Rachel is on this wall too. There aren't nearly as many of her as of me, but it's enough. There's a side profile of her taken from across the street and she's smiling at someone out of shot. She's wearing skinny jeans and a T-shirt. No coat, so it must've been taken recently too.

I reach out and pull the photo of Rachel from the wall. It holds fast for a second before I feel the glue give way and then it's in my hands. I turn it over, but there's no writing. Just the dried remains of glue, like the white sticks the kids use for their crafts.

I spin around and stare at the walls until they blur before my eyes. Here it is. Conclusive proof of who you are and what you've been doing. Why haven't the police searched your house and found this?

My knees buckle and I double over, swallowing three times in quick succession, holding back the sudden desire to throw up.

I'm moving slowly toward the stairs when the doorbell trills, shattering the quiet of the house.

I freeze.

What if it's DS Church? How will I explain why I'm here to her? I'm trespassing. And worse than that, I'm interfering in my own harassment case.

I hold my breath, the silence ringing in my ears. They'll go away in a minute. I just have to wait them out.

The doorbell rings again. It seems louder this time, more impatient.

Then it's a knock—a tap, tap, tap on the wood, followed by the clatter of metal and the letterbox flap opening.

A man's voice calls through the house. "I know you're in there."

CHAPTER 32

JENNA

For a heart-stopping moment I think it's you at the door and the fear comes crashing back through my blood. Then I almost laugh out loud at the absurdity of it. It can't be you. You're in hospital. It has to be someone who saw me come in. A delivery driver or a neighbor. The thought does nothing to quell the fear. What was I thinking coming here?

"Who's there?" the voice calls again.

I consider staying silent or trying to find a way out the back, but then the doorbell keeps ringing and the voice is shouting at me and I know it's no use and so I hurry downstairs to open the door. A short man with gray hair on the sides, bald on top, and a red face is standing outside your door.

"Hello," I say, catching my breath and shutting your front door behind me so we're both squeezed on the doorstep.

He narrows his eyes. "Are you a friend of Matthew's? I'm his neighbor."

"Um mm," I reply, nodding slightly.

"Oh, do you work together at the restaurant?" The man's demeanor softens.

I make another noncommittal noise.

"Is Matthew all right? I've not seen hide nor hair of him since last Wednesday and he normally drops leftover food over to me at the weekend." The man stops to draw in a rasping breath and I take my chance to speak.

"Matthew was in an accident. He's in hospital. I . . . I thought I'd come and feed his cat," I stammer, realizing too late that I didn't see any sign of a cat in your house.

Confusion darkens the man's face and I know I've said the wrong thing. "Mr. Barnaby isn't Matthew's cat, he's mine. Was the accident at work? Is he OK?"

"He was hit by a bus."

"Oh my! How terrible. Is he going to be OK?"

"I don't know yet. I'm sorry."

Your neighbor leans a shaking arm against the wall. His face has turned a deeper shade of red and suddenly I don't like how he's sweating, even in this heat.

"What's your name?" I ask.

"Bernie. Bernie Schwartz."

"How are you feeling right now, Bernie? Perhaps we ought to get you back home and have a sit-down for a moment."

"It's just this weather. At my age it's a bloody nuisance."

I take Bernie's arm and we walk slowly down your garden path and up his. Bernie's house is a replica of yours, with everything flipped the other way around—stairs on the left, living room on the right—and full of clutter. There are old photos in brown wood frames covering every surface. A cuckoo clock hangs above a fireplace. Swallows have been carved into the wood and pinecone-like spindles dangle down.

Bernie is unsteady on his feet as he eases himself into an arm-chair by the window, which overlooks the street. No wonder he saw me.

"Let me get you a glass of water." I move quickly to the kitchen and find a glass in the cabinet. "Have you been feeling unwell at all?"

"Just the usual heat issues. A bit of dizziness, that's all," he replies, taking the glass from me with a nod of thanks.

"May I feel your pulse for a moment, please?"

If Bernie thinks it's odd that a woman he doesn't know wants to check his heart rate he doesn't say anything. "Be my guest."

His pulse is fast, like he's been running up and down the stairs for twenty minutes instead of sitting in a chair watching the world go by.

"Any shortness of breath?" I ask.

"A little at night. It's the humidity. It was the same when I was stationed in Africa with the army." He lifts a shaking hand and points to a row of photos on the mantel. "Best years of my life, they were."

"What about pain in your arms?"

"Well, I pulled a muscle in my left arm mowing the grass the other day."

"Can you describe the pain for me?"

"It's an ache. I've pulled enough muscles in my time."

"Bernie," I say. "I believe you're having a heart attack. I'm going to call an ambulance to take you to hospital. They'll run some tests to confirm it. Have you got any aspirin in the house?"

He shakes his head, amused rather than frightened. "Oh, my

dear girl, your generation do know how to overreact, don't you? It's the heat. As soon as the weather breaks I'll be fine again. If I was having a heart attack, believe me, I would be the first to know."

He really wouldn't. Heart attacks can be sneaky and slow and just as deadly as the chest-gripping fast ones portrayed on TV.

"Well, just to be on the safe side," I say, reaching for my phone, "I'm going to call an ambulance."

I spend a few minutes on the phone and give my name, too focused on Bernie and his condition to realize I should've lied. There's a trail now. A note on a file that shows I've been here, but I can't worry about that now.

I find some aspirin in a drawer in the kitchen. They'll thin his blood and will help to limit the damage to his heart. When I return, Mr. Barnaby saunters into the living room; his purr is like the small motor of an engine. He brushes his body up against me and I stroke his silky back.

"He's missing Matthew," Bernie says as the cat curls up on his lap. "I've never seen a boy fuss so much over an animal before. I told him to get his own damn cat but he didn't want to upset Mr. Barnaby. You think you're the lord of the street, don't you, puss?"

"Have you lived next door to Matthew for long?" I ask, moving to the window to watch for the ambulance.

"Oh yes. Years and years. Matthew moved here, oh, about seven years ago. I remember because it was quite soon after we moved in here. He keeps to himself and doesn't say much. My late wife, Doreen, would've described him as a loner. You know the type? Living on the fringes of society rather than part of it, but he's harmless."

No he's not, I shout in my head.

"I'm forever telling him to get out more and get a girlfriend," Bernie says. "He works funny hours at the restaurant though and such a shy one. He did have a girlfriend for a while. I saw her coming and going. He didn't mention her and I never asked, but one day she stopped visiting. She was a bit old for him, I thought."

"What did she look like?" I ask, trying to sound casual, as though it's a normal question to ask.

"Blond. Pretty for her age."

The flashing blue lights of the ambulance pulse through the window, stopping me from asking more questions.

"They're here, Bernie. I'm going to open the door for them. Is there anyone I can call for you?" I ask.

"My son lives in a village five miles away, but there's no need to trouble him. He'll be at work now. I really don't want to be any bother."

"Still, perhaps you could tell me how I can reach him, just in case."

Bernie points to a phone book. "His name's Sam. He's a PE teacher at a high school. He always dreamed of being a professional tennis player, but it didn't work out."

I lead the paramedics into the living room and update them quickly on Bernie's condition. They fit an ECG and watch the output for a few minutes, talking in low voices to each other. It's only when Bernie is strapped to the stretcher that he bites his lips and starts to look hopelessly around the room.

"Will you call Sam?" he asks.

"I'll do it right now," I tell him.

"And put three scoops of food down for Mr. Barnaby too."

"Of course."

I watch the ambulance pull away, flashing lights but no siren. I call Bernie's son and explain what's happened. Then I search through the cupboards and find Mr. Barnaby's food, adding an extra scoop on top of the three, just in case.

Out in the sunlight, I stare up at your house. Images of your bedroom flash in my mind. I touch the photo of Rachel in my pocket. I took it to show her proof of what you've been doing, but now I wonder if there is any need to show her.

Bernie's words replay in my mind. *"He did have a girlfriend for a while . . . blond. Pretty for her age."*

Was it Rachel he saw? She is blond and pretty, and much older than Matthew. Did you and Rachel have an affair? It would explain her reaction when I asked about you and why she's been avoiding me for days.

I throw your keys into my glove compartment, and as I drive home my head spins with everything I've learned in the last few hours, and the more I think about Rachel and you, the more I feel as though I'm trying to answer questions that have no answers.

CHAPTER 33

SOPHIE, *age 15*

B ut why?" Sophie shouts, traipsing after her mum, who is carrying a pile of folded washing up the stairs. "Why can't I go out? All my friends are going."

Her mum opens the airing cupboard, places the stack of towels inside, and closes it again before answering. "I've told you, you're too young to go to a nightclub."

"They don't serve alcohol, Mum. It's a special night for our age group. You have to be fifteen or sixteen to get in."

"They might not serve it but someone will bring some. I wasn't born yesterday. And it's a school night too. What time did you say it finished? Eleven thirty?"

"Yes, but Vicky's dad is going to collect us," Sophie adds quickly.

"You won't be home until midnight. It's too late." Her mum shakes her head and moves to her bedroom with another pile of washing, Sophie following close behind.

"Please, Mum. Please." Sophie clasps her hands together and feels the tears welling in her eyes. "It's really important."

"I'm sorry, Sophie. I know you want to go, but it's not the end of the world."

Panic pulls at Sophie's chest. She has to go to the disco. Flick and Vicky are going and if she doesn't go they'll probably ditch her completely. She knows they've been hanging out together when she's not been there, which is totally unfair because she and Vicky were friends before Flick came along. And Reece is going to the disco too. He told Graham, who told Vicky, who told Sophie, that he thinks Sophie is fit. But Sophie knows Flick likes Reece too, and if Sophie isn't at the disco then Reece will definitely get off with Flick instead.

Her mum sighs and sits on the bed. "Look, it isn't just that I don't think you're old enough, or that it's too late, it's Matthew. I need you to watch him on Thursday because I'm going out for dinner with Trevor. I'm meeting his children for the first time."

Trevor. Why is everything suddenly about Trevor? Sophie wants to scream. Her mum started dating him only a few months ago and now he's here every weekend, taking them out to the park and acting like he's their dad.

"So what Trevor wants is more important than me now?" Sophie huffs, knowing she's being unfair but saying it anyway.

"No, that's not true at all. And I really don't understand what you've got against Trevor. He has been nothing but nice to you and Matthew. Only last month he gave you both cameras from the old stock in his shop. He didn't have to do that. He could've sold them instead.

"Trevor is the first man that I have met since your dad left five years ago, and I think it's OK for me to want to be happy. Your father certainly didn't waste any time seeing those trollops from the pub."

But her dad didn't make them spend time with his girlfriends, Sophie thinks, with a stab of bitterness.

"Trevor has invited us all for Sunday lunch too," her mum continues. "He's cooking roast lamb, and I want you to be nice to him. He has a lovely big house on a much nicer road than this one, and you might as well know that he's asked me if we'd all like to come live with him."

"What? No way," Sophie cries out. "I'm not living with him. What about his own kids?"

"They're much older than you. They have their own houses. And please keep your voice down. I haven't said anything to Matthew yet. I'm going to talk to him about it after Sunday's lunch so don't tell him. Matthew is doing so well now and I think a change might do him good."

"If Matthew is doing so well then why can't you get a babysitter for him or leave him on his own? He is twelve."

"You know why," her mum says, lowering her voice. "Matthew's moods may have evened out, but he still needs us around him. I don't want to introduce him to a total stranger to babysit at the moment."

Sophie looks to the open doorway to check Matthew isn't there.

"But he's not a little kid anymore. When I was twelve I was at home by myself, looking after both of us."

"I know that." Her mum reaches out and squeezes Sophie's hand. "You're a good girl. I'm sorry you've had to grow up faster than you should've. If your nan hadn't passed away and your dad hadn't left when he did, then it would have been easier."

He didn't leave, you kicked him out, Sophie thinks, feeling annoyed at her mum for being so blind. Her dad isn't perfect. He drinks a lot and burns the food he cooks for them, when he remembers to buy food and turn up to collect them, that is. But he's still *her* dad.

"In a few years' time you'll be able to go out all the time," her mum says. "Right now I need you at home. Matthew needs you."

"Why don't you get him some help then? Take him to a shrink if he's got problems." Sophie sighs, biting at one of her fingernails. She knows she's lost. There is no way her mum is going to change her mind about the disco. Her life is over.

"He does have help. He goes to a counselor every week. He has done for many years now."

"Has he?"

Her mum nods.

Something clicks in Sophie's head. All those speech therapy sessions her mum took Matthew to when he was younger that Sophie never questioned. Except now Sophie thinks about it, why did Matthew even need them? He's always been quiet, but when he does speak there's no lisp or anything.

"Although, I've got to say," her mum continues, "the camera Trevor gave him has been the best therapy I've seen. Matthew is really taking an interest in the world around him now he's taking photos."

Sophie thinks of the things Matthew burns in his room when her mum is at work. Last week Sophie caught him burning some of the photos he'd taken. When she'd asked, Matthew had said they weren't good enough, but they all looked the same to Sophie. She wonders what her mum would think about Matthew if she knew the truth.

"I know it's hard being your age," her mum says, taking Sophie's hand again. "I promise you, it will get easier. I'm never going to stop loving you or being here for you and Matthew."

Sophie sinks into her mum's embrace and wishes things were easier now.

CHAPTER 34

Thursday, June 20
JENNA

My mobile rings first thing, just as Stuart and I are in the middle of a whispered fight. It started with Stuart forgetting to put the dishwasher on last night and has mutated into something else entirely, and so I ignore my phone and let it buzz unanswered on the worktop.

"Just take a damn sleeping pill, Jenna. You can't go on like this."

"It won't help," I hiss back, shoving a bowl into the already full dishwasher. "If you ever listened to me, you'd know that." I step to the doorway and shout upstairs. "Beth, Archie, we're leaving in five minutes. Don't forget to brush your teeth."

"You need to sleep," Stuart says again. "You stay up all night watching TV and then pump yourself with caffeine. I just don't get it! The harassment is over. The police know who this guy is, and the moment he's well enough, they'll arrest him. You need to let it go now."

"Let it go, right, because it's that easy. Why didn't I think of that?" Sarcasm drips from my voice as I slam the dishwasher shut. "And it's not over." I can't believe Stuart is being so relaxed about this. It was the same last night when I showed him the e-mail you sent.

"You can't let one e-mail rattle you like this. He can't get to you now."

It's more than the e-mail. It's the way you grabbed me in intensive care, it's the look of hate in your eyes, it's an entire wall of photos in your bedroom, but I can't tell Stuart any of that. I can't admit that I've been to your house. He wouldn't understand.

"Life would be so much easier if I could pretend that everything is happy and wonderful all of the time, like you do, but I can't. I'm not built that way. I need to know what's going on and I won't feel safe until I have answers." A lump digs in my throat and when my phone starts ringing again, I spin away from Stuart and answer it. "Hello?"

"Jenna, it's DS Church. Are you available this morning for me to pop round? I have an update on your case I'd like to discuss."

My stomach flips. Does she know I was at your house? Has she been there too? Has she seen your bedroom? "What is it?"

"I'd prefer to talk about it in person. I can be with you in twenty minutes."

I hear myself agree and say a cheery good-bye and all the while the panic is crowding me and I'm sure she's going to tell me they're dropping the case and it's all my fault for snooping in your bag and going to your house.

"It must be good news," Stuart says. He gives an eager smile, our argument forgotten, and I fight the urge to roll my eyes like Beth.

"She said she had an update on the case," I reply, gritting my teeth and running a cloth over the breakfast counter. Any gleam from my spring clean has disappeared. "She didn't say whether it was good or bad."

"I'll drop the kids to school and pop back," Stuart says. "Billy can keep the site going for an hour this morning for me."

"Thanks, but I'll do it. You go to work. I'll call you and let you know what she says."

"I'm doing it," he replies, shouting for the kids to get a move on before I can argue anymore.

"Fine then," I snap, regretting my tone the moment it's out. It's not Stuart's fault that I'm freaking out about seeing DS Church, and it's not his fault that I'm desperate to do the school run so I can see Rachel. I tried to call her again last night, but each time it went straight to voice mail. I don't care if she's had an affair with you. I don't care if she's sleeping with half of Westbury; I have to find out what she knows about you.

Exactly twenty minutes later the door knocker raps twice—short and sharp—and like a prod to the small of his back Stuart is up from the sofa.

I stay in the living room, but stand as DS Church walks in. She's wearing a white shirt and trouser suit and must be roasting beneath her jacket. Her face looks hot under subtle makeup and her dark hair is shorter than the last time I saw her, highlighting her oval face and long neck. She looks professional and calm next to my denim shorts and T-shirt, hair unwashed and pulled back. I wish I'd made more effort now. This is the first time DS Church has been to the house and I feel exposed under her gaze.

"Jenna," DS Church says. "Good to see you again. Thank you for making the time to see me." She shakes my hand, quick and firm, before pointing to the sofa opposite the one I'm standing next to. "May I?"

"Of course. Please do."

"Would you like a cup of tea or coffee?" Stuart asks from the doorway. He claps his hands together as he speaks and seems as nervous as I feel. I guess he wants this all to be over as much as I do.

My anger toward him fizzles out and I motion for him to sit down beside me.

"No thank you," DS Church replies. She pauses as Stuart sits and takes my hand.

DS Church sits on the edge of the cushion, leaning forward, a notebook unopened in her hands.

"Have you found something out about the man who's been stalking my wife?" Stuart asks as though I'm not in the room. "Have you arrested him? What's he said?"

"We've been looking into Matthew Dover's background," DS Church says, her expression unreadable. "DC Briggs and myself spoke with Mr. Dover on Tuesday, however he wasn't able to answer any questions due to the nature of his injuries, and has been deemed unfit for questioning. We are in close contact with the neurologist in charge of Mr. Dover's case, and will try again when he's able. In the meantime we've been speaking to his employer, and last night we received Matthew's shift patterns for the last six months."

I sit forward, unpeeling my hand from Stuart's. Where is this going?

"I've compared the times you reported seeing him against the times we know he was working and there are some inconsistencies."

"What do you mean?" I ask.

"Matthew Dover was at work on some of the occasions that you have recorded being followed or when items have been left on your doorstep."

I swallow hard, the enormity of her words crushing me.

"That's not possible." Stuart looks between us, a confused smile pulling on his lips.

"He . . . he must've have slipped out or been on a break," I say.

"According to his employer, Mr. Dover would not have been able to leave the premises during his shifts and hasn't missed a shift for as long as his employer can remember. I spoke to several of his coworkers as well and they describe Matthew as reliable and hardworking."

DS Church's words hang in the silence before she continues. "You weren't able to get a photo of your stalker, were you?" Her tone is soft but probing, scratching beneath my skin.

I shake my head. "But it's him. How else do you explain the fact that the stalking completely stopped the moment he was admitted to hospital? And now that he's awake, I'm suddenly getting e-mails again."

"You have said in your statements that you only ever saw him for very brief moments of time and often at a distance. On several occasions you reported seeing a figure in the shadows. Is it possible you're mistaken about the identity of your stalker?"

My jaw clenches and I bite back a sarcastic retort. "Pardon?"

"I'm asking how certain you are that Matthew Dover is your stalker. Could it be that he looks similar?"

"No," I cry out. "I know it's him. I'm one hundred percent certain."

And I am. It's not just the photos of me on your phone and in your house—the proof I know exists—or the umbrella you had when they brought you in, the same one I've seen dozens of times on the CCTV footage; it's your face. I knew who you were the moment I saw you properly in A&E. I've seen you waiting outside the hospital for me, and on the school run. I've seen you at the weekends, watching me from the trees when I've taken Beth and Archie to the playground. I've seen you in my nightmares too. It's you, but how can I explain that to DS Church?

"Have you found his phone?" I ask. "And what about his house? Have you searched it?"

"Unfortunately, we were unable to locate a phone in Mr. Dover's possession, and in light of the conflicting information from Mr. Dover's employer, my superiors have not given us authority to enter Mr. Dover's property at this time."

"What?" I splutter. "But it's him. I know it's him, and . . . and I know his phone is in his bag. I saw it. I'm sure there must be proof on it."

Stuart places a hand on my leg. I know he's trying to calm me down, but his touch only increases the frustration raging through my body.

"Did you find any fingerprints in the house?" Stuart asks.

"The forensic team have finished analyzing the evidence collected last week," DS Church says, directing her answer to Stuart and ignoring my outburst. "There are several fingerprints we've yet to identify—"

"So they could be Matthew's," I cut in.

"We have Mr. Dover's prints on file, and they're not his."

"Does that mean he has a criminal record?" Stuart asks, and I sense that we are both trying to grab hold of any whisper of hope. "Has he done this type of thing before?"

"No, it doesn't mean that at all. There are a number of reasons fingerprints can be on the police database. In this case, his employer was burgled some years ago and staff members had their prints taken for comparison."

"So where does this leave us then?" I ask.

"I understand how frustrated you must be feeling, Jenna. But we are still investigating your case."

I don't know what that means, but I find myself nodding. Nothing makes sense. I know it's you doing this to me. Why can't they see it? I bite down on the inside of my cheek, stopping my confession from screaming out. *I went to his house. There are dozens of photos of me and my children on his bedroom walls.*

DS Church drops her gaze and opens her notebook. "There is one other thing I would like to discuss. The road traffic accident involving Mr. Dover is being treated as suspicious. We have a witness who believes he saw Mr. Dover being pushed into the path of the bus. We've been unable to locate any CCTV footage of the accident itself, but we are reviewing all dashcams and CCTV cameras from shops in the surrounding areas."

"What's that got to do with us?" Stuart asks.

"Jenna, could you confirm your whereabouts on Thursday the thirteenth of June at approximately one thirty-five p.m., please?"

Stuart laughs. A snorting guffaw of a noise. "You can't be serious?"

DS Church doesn't reply. Her focus is on me and I feel my cheeks flush under her gaze. She can't really think I had something to do with this, can she?

"I was at work on Thursday," I reply, fighting to keep my voice even. "I did a twelve-hour shift, seven a.m. to seven p.m. And I was in A&E when Matthew Dover was brought in. I saved his life. Twice, in fact. Do you really think I'd go to the effort to push him in front of a bus only to save his life thirty minutes later?"

"You didn't leave the hospital at any point during your shift?" DS Church asks, ignoring my question.

"There is no time to eat or sit down, let alone swan into town and hang around waiting to push people in front of buses."

She fixes me with a look and I wish I could stuff the snarkiness of my comment back into my mouth. "Thank you for answering my question. We'll be verifying your information with the hospital."

"Verify away," I say, my jaw so tight that pain stretches all the way to the top of my head.

"Have you been to visit Mr. Dover since we last spoke?"

"No."

She waits then as if her silence will make me fill in the gaps and it does. "I've taken some holiday," I add. "I've not been near the hospital for three days."

"Good," she says. "Thank you for your time, Jenna." DS Church stands and strides to the door. "I'll see myself out."

The door opens and shuts with a bang that shudders through the house. I lean my head back against the cushions and close my eyes, gaining a second of relief from the ache, like two thumbs pressing into my temples.

Stuart leaps up the moment the silence settles over the house. "Are you going to tell me what the hell is going on here?" He spins to look at me, eyes wide and flashing with confusion and anger.

"What do you mean?"

"You just lied to a police officer, Jenna."

CHAPTER 35

Stuart's words hang between us as I wonder how much to tell him. "I don't know what you're talking about." I head to the kitchen. My stomach is queasy from the three cups of coffee I've already drunk, but I flick the kettle for a fourth anyway.

"Jenna." Stuart takes my arm and turns me toward him. "I was sitting right there and you lied."

"No I didn't."

"You just told DS Church that you didn't leave the hospital at all on Thursday, but you did. You went into town to get Beth's ribbon, remember? I wasn't supposed to know about it, but Beth begged me to remind you on Wednesday night and I saw you give it to her on Thursday when you came home."

"Oh . . . I forgot, that's all." It's the truth, I did forget, but it feels like a lie on my lips, and from the expression on Stuart's face he thinks so too.

"And what was that comment about his phone? How are you so convinced there's evidence on it?"

I sigh and slump onto the stool. I don't have the energy to lie. "I took his phone."

"What?" Stuart stares at me, his face incredulous.

"I didn't mean to. I found it in his bag when I went to visit him, then I left in a hurry and I must've put it into my bag by accident. I looked through it, that's all. I saw photos of me on it and so I know it's him, and the police will too once they look at it properly. I can't understand why they've not seen it yet. I put it back on Monday."

"But they're saying he was working—"

"This guy"—I shake my head, trying to slow down my words—"is not an idiot. He's smart. He never leaves fingerprints. We've never seen his face on any CCTV footage. He never stays long enough for me to take a photo of him. He's had us and the police chasing our own shadows for months now. Is it really so hard to believe that he might have duped his boss somehow too?"

Stuart considers my comment, sweeping a hand through his hair and tugging at the tangles before pushing it behind his ears. "You're right. Of course. But why didn't you tell DS Church this?"

"Because if she finds out then the phone will be inadmissible as evidence. They'll say I tampered with it or loaded the photos on myself. She can't know, Stuart. We just have to hope she finds it soon. I know he's got it because he e-mailed me yesterday."

"Bloody hell, Jenna. I can't believe all this. You have to let the police handle it from now on, OK?"

I nod, swallowing back the rest of my confession. It's my fault the police didn't take your phone into custody when they first visited you on Monday. And if they find it now, they'll surely be suspicious that it wasn't there to start with.

The fluttering bird in my chest returns. I can feel my grip on the situation slipping away. It feels like only a matter of time before DS Church discovers the full extent of my interfering or realizes I was in town at the time Matthew was hit by the bus, but even that isn't as bad as the knowledge that you are worming your way out of what you've done to me. And if you think I'm going to let that happen, you're very very wrong.

Stuart slips onto the stool beside me and even though we're the only ones in the house, he lowers his voice before he asks: "Did you do it?"

"Do what?"

He raises his eyebrows. "Did you push him?"

I laugh. It's not funny. Nothing is funny anymore, but still I laugh. "I wish I had."

"I'd have done it," Stuart says, and now it's my turn to raise my eyebrows. "I mean it. If I'd been with you and you'd pointed him out to me, I'd have pushed him under that bus in a heartbeat if it meant I'd get my wife back and all of this would be over, but I'm not sure it will be, will it?"

Tears prod behind my eyes.

Stuart reaches his arms around me. "I need you back, Jenna. The kids do too. We can't carry on like this. I think . . . I think everything that has happened over the last year has damaged you. I'm glad the hospital have made you take time off. You need it."

Stuart's lips find mine and I let myself fall into his embrace.

CHAPTER 36

Sophie

I step outside the hospital entrance, away from the smokers wearing patient gowns that flap around their bare thighs, and tip my head to the sun. I stand with my eyes closed like that until all I can see is a dazzling white behind my eyelids and the tops of my cheeks burn. I wish I could erase the last fifteen minutes. Hell, I'd go for the last twelve years while I'm at it.

A shiver travels over my body, despite the ninety-one-degree heat. Matthew was angry today. Every question, every word, was snapped. He asked about the fire and the truth lodged in my throat.

"What do you remember?" I asked instead.

"I'm trying so hard," he said, rubbing his head. "All I know is that there was one and it was bad."

I could feel the color drain from my face and a tremor take hold of my legs, and even though his memories were coming back and I knew he'd remember soon, I couldn't bring myself to tell him. "That's pretty much it."

"No it isn't," he yelled. "Why are you lying to me? Tell me what happened? Was it my fault?"

The same nurse as last time rushed in, saving me from finding the words to reply. I wish I could tell him to stop trying. I wish I could tell him that there is nothing but pain in his past, and mine, and the only way to survive it is to look forward. But I'm not sure I believe that anymore.

A shadow blocks the sun from my eyes and I open them, jumping as Nick's face looms over me.

"Nick, what are you doing here?" My heart is a hammer, a pulsing beat. It's Matthew all over again, turning up in places he has no reason to be.

"Waiting for you." His smile is wide but there's something not quite right about it.

"How did you know I was here?"

Nick shrugs. "Lucky guess."

"Nick, you did not come to the hospital in the middle of the afternoon because you thought I might be here."

"All right, all right." He holds up his hands. "I paired our iPhones in the Find My app. It shows me your location."

"What? You've been spying on me." I step back, anger and hurt battling for space inside my body. Nick's hand whips out and takes my elbow, moving me close again.

"I only did it the other night when you were in the shower. You know how worried I was about you when you were out running. I didn't know where you were or what you were doing. And you never tell me where you are half the time. This way, I'll always know and I won't need to worry."

"Nick, you can't put a tracker on me. I'm not a dog."

He laughs for a moment before glancing at my face, his expression turning serious. "It's not a big deal. Don't make more of it than it is, OK? Part of our jobs is to go meet people in their homes and while most people are normal, there are a few crackers out there and this way if anything happens to you then I'll know where you are and can come rescue you."

"I don't need rescuing." *I need space*, I add in my head. I can't believe Nick has done this.

"Look," he says, steering me away from a group of nurses walking toward us. "If you're not cheating on me then you've got nothing to hide, have you? And so it doesn't matter if I know where you are."

"I'm not cheating on you."

"There you go then. So it doesn't matter."

I glance at Nick from the corner of my eye as we walk toward the car park. He's smiling. He's feeling good. He knows he's won. And it hits me—a smack to the back of my head—I'm dating a man exactly like my brother. I can't believe I've never seen it before. Sure, they have different ways of showing it, but both of them cross the line when it comes to being protective over me. Both of them have dark moods that scare me to my core. Both of them want to control me.

The more I think about it, the more the world around me seems to shrink. Am I really that messed up?

"Come on, let's pop into Waitrose and get some food. Neither of us have clients until tomorrow."

I had other plans, I want to scream at Nick. I was going to run until I was too tired to think, but I'm too much of a coward to say anything. Instead I try to convince myself that what Nick has done is no big deal. So what if he can see where I am? I can always turn my phone off if I really want to.

"And next time you decide to visit Matthew, tell me, OK? I want to come with you and be there for you."

We reach Nick's black VW Golf and he opens the passenger door for me. Just as I'm about to climb in, he pushes the door against me, trapping me between the door and the car. I can't get in and I can't move away. "Oh, I forgot to ask you," Nick says, his voice casual. "Have you spoken to that detective yet?"

I shake my head. "No, not yet. Can you move, please? The door is hurting me."

He pulls it back a fraction but not enough for me to move. "They want me to go down to the station tomorrow to answer more questions. They've got me on CCTV in town just before it happened."

"But you said you were at home?"

"I know," he says, and for the first time I see the panic settling over him.

"I'm going to have to backtrack on that. I'll say I forgot that I popped out. Where were you? Can we say we met up?"

"What? Nick? If they've got you on camera then you can't lie."

"I know, I know." His free hand smashes against the roof of the car. I feel the vibration of it against my back and try to shrink away from him, but I'm still stuck.

"I'll say whatever you want me to say," I whisper. "We'll work it out."

Nick pulls back the door and nods. "You're right. We'll work it out." He leans forward, pressing his lips against mine and I try not to flinch.

I climb into the car and stuff my hands under my thighs as the urge to bite my nails builds inside me. All I can think about is the window—the gap in time that I have right now which is shrinking by the day. Matthew is remembering more and more. Soon he'll remember everything, and I don't want to be around him when he realizes the truth about the fire, about everything. Right now he's stuck in hospital and if I leave, there's nothing he can do to stop me.

Then there's Nick. I can't pretend things are normal between us anymore. How long before he starts wanting to know where I am and what I'm doing every second of the day? Before he crushes me with his need to protect me?

I have to get away.

This won't be like the last times. This can't be another change of job and hairstyle. I have to go deeper than that if I want a real fresh start away from Matthew and Nick and the memories. And the only way I can do it is if I stop running from what happened twelve years ago.

"What are you thinking about?" Nick asks, breaking the silence in the car.

"Nothing."

"You must be thinking about something, Sophie."

I shrug. "I was thinking about Matthew, I guess."

He huffs and I can tell it was the wrong answer. The need to escape builds inside me until I have to bite my lip to stop the scream from coming out.

CHAPTER 37

JENNA

The colors of daytime TV flick in front of my eyes. I'm staring at the screen but not watching. The sound is down low, almost on mute. My head feels heavy and keeps drooping down, but I know it's useless trying to sleep.

I'm too fidgety, my thoughts restless.

My phone trills from the space on the sofa beside me and I pounce on it, hoping it's Rachel, but it's not. It's DS Church. I stare at her name and even though my finger hovers over the accept button, I let it ring out just as I did when a hospital number flashed on the screen earlier today, and then Nancy tried to call. I know I should've answered, but I can't think about going back to work right now.

The ringtone stops. DS Church's name disappears from the screen. She can't possibly have anything else to update me on from this morning, which means she's got more questions, and I'm not sure I want to answer them right now.

She thinks I had something to do with your accident. How long before she finds out I was in town the same afternoon? I should come clean and tell her I forgot that I was there, but even in my head it sounds suspicious, and I can hear her question in my thoughts. *So you never normally leave the hospital during your shifts, but on the day your stalker was pushed in front of the bus, you did leave the hospital, you were in the area, and you had nothing to do with it?*

Credits roll up the TV screen. Whatever was on has finished. There's not long before I need to collect Beth and Archie from school, but I can't sit here any longer. I jump up from the sofa and slip on my sandals. Rachel might be able to ignore my calls but she can't ignore me in person. She's my connection to you. I find her address on the PTA handout she gave me and type it into Google Maps as I'm walking out the door, keys in hand, toward my car.

My mind is focused on my phone and on what I want to say to Rachel, but still I sense a change around me. A whisper of alarm that I'm not alone on the road. I barely have time to register the footsteps behind me when a force hits my back—two hands and the weight of someone shoving me hard.

I'm thrown forward, my balance gone. A scream lodges in my throat, but no sound comes out.

I hit the pavement. Knees first, then my hands. Momentum keeps me going and one elbow hits the ground, then my shoulder, and finally my head. A thump against my skull, enough to hurt but not enough to do any real damage.

I lie still for a second, maybe two, as my brain tries to catch up. There's a part of me that wonders if it was an accident—did I walk into the path of cyclist? But even as the thought turns in my mind, I know that's not what happened. I was pushed and it was no accident.

Panic grips my chest and I gasp. I'm being mugged.

I turn and scramble backward, but there's no one there and my bag is gone. The street is empty. I pull myself up and stare down the road, then I run across to the park and peer through the entrance, searching for any sign of who pushed me. The only person I see is a man walking with his back to me, heading toward the boating lake, but he's far away and I'm not sure if he could've run that distance in the time it took me to get up. I stare at him for a while longer, and for a split second I feel like there's something familiar about the way he's walking, but the thought disappears before I can grab hold of it.

I walk slowly back to where I fell and pick up my phone and car keys from where they flew out of my hands. My phone is undamaged, and so am I, for the most part. I gingerly prod at the small lump on the side of my head. It hurts but not badly. One of my knees is prickled with blood and there's a small cut on my hand where I landed on a small rock, but I'm OK. Shaken, but OK.

Then the feeling comes over me—the spider. I'm being watched. Adrenaline explodes inside me and I jump into my car and drive away as fast as I can, only stopping when I park outside Rachel's house.

Months of fear rage to the surface, reminding me I'm not safe, I'll never be safe until you're dead or in prison.

My heart pounds so fast in my chest that my head starts to spin. My breathing comes in quick pants. I try to process what just happened. Someone pushed me to the ground and stole my bag. But you're in hospital. It wasn't you.

A thought begins to unfold in my mind as though it's wrapped up in a dozen layers of tissue paper and I have to keep tearing and tearing at it. Then it's there, pushing through the panic and I gasp. What if you're not working alone? What if someone is helping you?

It's a ludicrous thought. Not one stalker, but two. I can picture DS Church's eye roll already, and yet it makes sense, doesn't it?

I think back to the feeling in the car park at the trampoline party. I thought it was just my imagination, but it felt so real. And then there is DS Church's insistence that you were at work some of the times I was being followed. And just now, mugged in broad daylight on a quiet street. What are the chances it was random? But if someone is helping you, then who? And why?

I force myself to breathe, to calm down, to try to think.

I should report what happened to the police, but I'm sick of talking to them. It all feels so futile anyway. What can they do about it now? I still have my phone and my keys. It's only a bank card, a worn purse I've had for at least ten years, a bit of makeup, and some old receipts that are gone. I'll have to cancel my bank cards and get a new driving license, but there's nothing that can't be replaced.

But that's not all, I realize. My stomach knots. Hot tears burn at the edges of my eyes. My diary was in the bag. Every single thing you did, every torment, every sadistic gift you left for me to find, is written on those pages. I close my eyes, allowing the tears to fall. I know my diary isn't crucial to my case, I know the police have everything stored in evidence bags and logged in statements, but my diary could've been the difference between prison or not, and now it's gone.

It takes me ten minutes to calm down enough to call my bank to cancel my card and order a new one. Only then do I take a deep breath and look at Rachel's house—a detached Victorian house with a double driveway and big bay windows—and realize I've seen it before. There's a photo of this house on your phone. I remember seeing it at the hospital. You've been here.

I walk up the driveway, my mind still turning over what happened outside my house and the idea that you're not working alone. And for a second I can't remember what I want to ask Rachel. Still, I lift the brass door knocker and tap it three times. A moment later I hear movement from inside and a man throws open the door. He's big—the same height as Stuart but broader—a rugby player's physique. Handsome enough, but with a weak chin that makes his neck and face look like one.

"We have to think about the immediate impact. It's not all AI. EMS is crucial to stock pricing," he says, looking straight at me.

"I'm sorry?" I reply, glancing around. "Are you talking to me?"

He points to an earpiece sticking out of his ear. "Hang on one second, guys. I've got someone at the door."

He taps a button and sighs. "Yes?"

"Is Rachel here, please?"

"No, she's out at the moment. Probably collecting the kids." His eyes drop to my bloody knee and he raises an eyebrow but says nothing.

"Would you mind telling her that Jenna stopped by and ask her to please call me. It's important."

"Didn't you call the house the other day?"

"Yes."

"Then I'd take the hint." He taps his phone and starts talking again as he closes the front door.

Damn it! I climb back into my car. What next? My mobile buzzes from the seat beside me. The school's number flashes up.

"Hello?"

"Mrs. Lawson?"

"Yes," I reply, not bothering to correct my title.

"We . . . er . . . just wondered where you were."

My eyes shoot to the clock on the dashboard and I cringe when I see it's gone three. I'm late.

"Sorry. I've been trying to call. I . . . I just helped a man who collapsed on the pavement. I'm on my way now. I do apologize." The lie tumbles out and I feel bad for it, but it's the first thing that comes to mind.

"Oh my. How dreadful. Of course. We'll see you soon."

As I drive to the school, Beth and Archie consume my thoughts, pushing aside my questions for Rachel, my fear, and what happened outside my house.

CHAPTER 38

To: Jenna.Lawson@westburydistrict.org.uk
From: whereareyou@mailpalz.co.uk
Subject: Where are you?

I miss seeing you walk through the hospital. Always in such a rush, aren't you?

How are Beth and Archie by the way? Is Archie still wetting his pants at school like a little baby? Are they still running off to your childminder because they love her more than you?

* * *

To: Jenna.Lawson@westburydistrict.org.uk
From: YoudontloveBethandArchie@mailpalz.com
Subject: How does it feel?

NO ONE LOVES YOU, JENNA!!!!!!!!

You're a terrible mother. You can't see it yet, but you will very soon. When your children are gone and you'll have no one.

* * *

To: Jenna.Lawson@westburydistrict.org.uk
From: timeforfun@mailpalz.com
Subject: Did you think this was over?

It's only just begun. Tick tock, Jenna. Time is running out for you.

CHAPTER 39

Friday, June 21
JENNA

The storms started in the west of Britain last night. Flash floods and a barn in Wales hit by lightning. The news is showing rain falling in sheets, water pouring down roads, and fields that look like lakes. I wish it would hurry up and get to Westbury. I can't take much more of this heat.

The kids couldn't sleep last night. Too hot. They stayed up until ten, running through the house in their underwear, playing hide-and-seek and being the best of friends. It always amazes me how well Beth and Archie get on when the threat of bedtime is looming.

Stuart and I sat in the garden, him with a book and me with a glass of wine, the closeness we've shared these past months evaporating as fast as Archie's cup of spilled water on the paving stones. We didn't talk about DS Church or you. I didn't tell him about what happened outside the house or my theory about you. I wanted to, but something stopped me, like there was a barrier between us. When the e-mails arrived, one, two, three bullets aimed right at my heart, I broke the silence between us and handed Stuart my phone.

"I need to call DS Church," I said.

"Why bother? They can't do anything. He's getting desperate, that's all," Stuart replied with a shrug before handing the phone back to me. "Stop letting him get to you."

"He's threatening our kids, Stuart. He says something is going to happen. How can you be so relaxed about it?"

"I'm not relaxed, but I'm not rising to his bait. He's in hospital and will be for some time. Every time you're scared, you get distracted and the kids suffer and he wins."

"So you agree with him—I'm a terrible mother." The panic caused by your e-mails mutated into a dark rage and it was a fight to keep my voice low and even.

"No, that's not what I said. You're tired and upset and you're putting words in my mouth. But there's no way you would've forgotten the kids today if you hadn't been so distracted by this man. And he can't even get to you anymore. That's the crazy thing, Jenna. He's getting to you more now than he ever did before."

"I was only five minutes late."

"Beth said it was fifteen. And don't palm me off with some lie about helping someone, Jenna. I know you too well for that." Stuart closed his book and stood up. "I'm going to bed."

I gritted my teeth and stopped myself from screaming after him. What would I have said anyway? He was right. I did let you distract me and no one can make me feel worse about it than me. So I said nothing and let the kids stay up far too late, and now they're tired this morning, dragging themselves down the stairs and faffing over their breakfasts and I end up driving to school.

The bell is ringing as we reach the gates. I kiss them good-bye and they run off to their classes just as the parents start to move toward me in a slow stampede. I turn away and head for my car.

I wonder again about the e-mails and whether I should tell DS

Church. But I've been avoiding the detective, and if I send these e-mails to her then I won't be able to carry on dodging her calls.

I'm just starting the engine when I see Rachel jogging toward her Audi. She's wearing white shorts that show slender, tanned legs. Her hair is in a neat ponytail which swishes with every step.

Now is my chance to talk to her. She knows something, I'm sure of it.

Cars are pulling away from the side of the road, weaving between one another like the bumper cars, except everyone is trying not to hit one another. For a minute it seems like I can hear that familiar whine-like siren that signals their start at the funfair. Rachel joins the queue, heading in the direction of town and the hospital.

I put the car into gear and move away, and before I can think about it or stop myself, I follow her. We hit the morning traffic, and all around me the town is waking up. Shop workers are scurrying toward the high street in colorful branded T-shirts. Rachel swings her car into the cement shell of a multistory car park and I follow. Up and round. Up and round. I'm so close I can see her mouth moving. She's singing along to something and I flick through the radio stations until Abba's "Mamma Mia" sings out, matching the movement of her lips.

She parks one level from the top. I'm still on the level below and watch her climb out. I park where I am and sit for a minute whilst she grabs her bag and walks to the stairs. I wait, drumming my fingers on the wheel before deciding to follow on foot. I just want to talk to her, to make her see that you're going to get away with this unless we do something. And if she knows you, then she might know your friends. She might know who's helping you continue your torment.

I wait until the door to the stairwell and exit clangs before slipping out of my car. The air inside the car park is stifling, but for the first time today I feel alert, focused.

I listen to the tap of Rachel's feet on the cement stairs and try to walk in time to her skipping footfalls, but twice she stops and I'm caught out with a step that echoes through the stairwell.

The high street is quiet, the shops only just opening. A street sweeper motors by, sucking up cigarette butts and spitting out soapy water. I watch Rachel stride along, a shoulder bag slung over one shoulder. She looks like a woman on a mission.

I wonder how I can play this. After all my phone calls and turning up at her house, I doubt she'll believe me if I try to pretend it's a coincidence that I'm here.

I lose myself in my thoughts for a moment and when I focus again on following Rachel, she's gone. I keep moving, my gaze darting left and right. More people flock into the high street. I weave around a group of mums with strollers, and then suddenly she's right in front of me and I have to stop dead before I barge right into the back of her.

She whips around and when she sees me her face changes— her eyes widen, her mouth becomes a startled O. I recognize the look instantly; it's the same one on my face in one of the photos you've taken of me.

"Leave me alone. I don't want to talk to you," she half hisses, half shouts, running into the shopping center before I've so much as taken a breath, let alone had a chance to reply, to explain.

I start to follow, my cheeks flaming red, aware of the shoppers staring at me. I'm desperate to explain.

What was I thinking?

I wasn't; that much is clear. I wanted only to talk and she thinks I was following her, which is crazy, except of course it isn't.

From the corner of my eye, I catch a glimpse of Rachel standing outside one of the shops. She's talking to her husband and they both turn to look at me.

Hot tears teeter on the edges of my eyes as I dart back to my car. I can't believe what I've just done.

CHAPTER 40

SOPHIE, *age 15*

Sophie slams the front door and throws her school bag across the floor. She is quite sure today has been the worst day ever. Flick and Vicky have been absolute cows all week, whispering to each other about what they're going to wear to the nightclub on Thursday and bursting into ridiculous giggles every five minutes. Anytime Sophie asks, "What's so funny?" they shake their heads and say, "Nothing. Doesn't matter."

It does matter.

Sophie wonders if she can fake a sickness bug for the rest of the week. She doesn't want another day like today, and it's only going to get worse the closer they get to Thursday. And of course, the only thing worse than Flick and Vicky's excitement about going to the disco will be going to school on Friday and hearing all about the fun they had without Sophie.

Fat chance her mum will buy a fake illness though. For starters, her mum would have to actually notice Sophie exists, and that's never going to happen.

And it isn't just missing the night out now either. Sophie is missing out on the fun of getting ready. Flick and Vicky are meeting at Flick's house, and Flick has nicked some vodka from her mum and dad's booze cabinet so they can drink vodka and Coke before they go.

Plus Reece found out that Sophie isn't going anymore and has totally stopped checking her out at lunchtime. And now Vicky is all over Graham at lunch break so it's doubly certain that Flick will pull Reece on Thursday, and while they're all having the best time ever, Sophie will be stuck in Boresville looking after Matthew.

Sophie shuts herself in her room and turns on her music. She flops onto her bed and closes her eyes, trying to imagine what it would feel like to kiss Reece.

"Sophie," Matthew calls over the music before tapping on the door.

"Go away," she shouts, feeling instantly crappy about it. "What is it?"

"Can I come in?" he asks, opening the door a fraction.

"Fine."

Matthew opens the door and leans against her wall, his hands fiddling with the stupid camera Trevor gave him. Trevor gave Sophie the same one. It's digital with a screen at the back that shows the photo that's just been taken. Flick has still got the old kind with the film she has to take to Boots to be developed, and Sophie had planned to take her camera to the disco to show them how cool it is, not that she'd ever tell Trevor that.

"Are you going to say something?" Sophie asks Matthew.

Matthew smiles and then so does she. "You can go to that party."

"What party?"

"The one on Thursday. I heard you and Mum talking. I don't

need a babysitter." He holds the camera out and snaps a photo of Sophie on the bed.

"I hate it when you do that," she says, covering her face with her hands.

"Sorry."

Sophie moves her hands and watches Matthew for a moment. He's staring at the screen. Her mum's right. There is something about having the camera that seems to help Matthew.

"S'kay," she says. "What were you saying about the disco? I can't go. Mum said I have to stay with you."

"I'm old enough to look after myself."

He's not wrong. Matthew is almost thirteen.

"I won't tell her or anything," he adds.

"And you think she won't notice when she comes home from her dinner with Trevor and finds I'm out."

"I'll stay up and tell her you went to bed with a headache. You can make a lump under your duvet and I'll make sure she doesn't check. Then I'll sneak down and unlock the back door. She might hear if you come in the front, but I think the back door will be OK. She'll never know you went out."

Sophie thinks for a moment. Matthew has really thought about it. She's not sure she's ever heard him say so much in one go before. "Thanks," she says eventually. "That would be cool."

Matthew smiles and takes another photo of Sophie. She throws a pillow at him and he dives out of her room before it can hit him.

Maybe her life doesn't suck, after all. It'll be just like Matthew says. Her mum will never find out, and even if she does, the worst she'll do is ground Sophie forever and her life will be exactly the same as it is now. Wait until Flick and Vicky hear about this.

CHAPTER 41

To: Jenna.Lawson@westburydistrict.org.uk
From: areyouready@mailpalz.com
Subject: Not long now!

Tick tock, Jenna. It's almost time to finish this!

CHAPTER 42

JENNA

The front door bangs and I jump up from my stupor on the sofa, heart pounding in my ears, legs wobbling under me from the sudden shift in weight. Someone is in the house.

"Who's there?" I call out.

"It's me," Stuart replies, appearing in the doorway to the living room. "Don't shoot." He laughs before checking something on his phone.

The fear is gone, replaced with crushing panic. Have I fallen asleep and forgotten to collect the kids? I was sleeping, dreaming of you again and running. This time it was me who was chasing someone. You, I think. Or Rachel. Buses were flying past us and I almost had you. My hand was out and I could almost touch your shoulder.

I blink, the remnants of the dream disappear, and in its place comes the e-mail. *Tick tock, Jenna.*

I want to call DS Church and ask if she's been back to see you. Either you're sending these e-mails or you're asking someone else to do it for you. Whichever way I look at it, you must be in a fit state to be interviewed. But no matter how many times I pick up my phone to call her, I can't bring myself to do it. She's called me twice now, and both times I've not answered. I can't avoid her forever.

DS Church doesn't think you're my stalker, and while I know that you are, that there's evidence on your phone and in your house, I can't ignore the feeling I'm missing something.

"You're home early," I say to Stuart, checking the time. It's only two thirty. I rub a hand against my neck, stiff from my awkward sleeping position.

"It was too damn hot to work. I sent the boys to the pub and thought I'd walk with you to collect the kids."

"I wasn't going to forget to collect them." I mean it as a joke but my tone is snappish and it lands all wrong. "Sorry."

Stuart's phone buzzes and he frowns for a moment before tucking it back into his pocket. "Are you sure everything is OK? What have you been doing today?"

"Nothing much," I reply. I dip my head, hoping to hide the red glowing on my cheeks as I think about following Rachel. "Trying to sleep, mostly."

He smiles then, backing out of the room, away from the fight that's been building between us like the threatening storm. "I'm going to grab a shower and change, then we'll go. Or I can get them and you can stay here and rest if you like."

"No, it's OK. I want to come."

Stuart reaches for his phone again and heads upstairs.

THICK WHITE CLOUDS cover the sky above us as Stuart and I walk side by side, neither of us talking, but I'm glad he's with me after what happened yesterday. He hasn't noticed my grazed knee and I still haven't mentioned it.

Stuart hasn't said anything but I know he's worried about me. Does he think I can't be trusted to look after Beth and Archie? After what happened this morning, a part of me wonders if he is right to be worried. What was I thinking?

"Looks like the heat wave is almost over," he says, nodding at the sky.

"I hope so."

"Has Beth been OK with you this week?"

"Yes." My reply is quick, automatic. "Why?" What I mean is, why wouldn't she be OK? She's spent the week with me, but then I think of the insolence she shows at every little request I make, and I wonder if she's said something to Stuart.

"She's just seemed a bit grumpy lately, that's all. Do you think it's hormones?"

"Probably," I reply. Secretly I wonder if that's true or just an excuse we tell ourselves anytime the children act out. "You don't think this is her reaction to what's happened to me, do you?"

"What do you mean?"

"Archie has been an open book. The bad dreams he tells us about at breakfast and then not being able to go to the toilets by himself at school because he's scared a man is going to be waiting for him inside. Maybe Beth is having her own reaction. It's not been easy for them."

The gates of the school come into view as we round the corner. Stuart is just about to reply when I spot Rachel's husband climbing out of a car. My eyes look past him to Rachel, sitting in the passenger seat, staring ahead and pretending not to see us. My insides knot and I hurry Stuart along as though I can see the scene about to unfold.

"Can I have a word?" Rachel's husband says, striding toward

us and stopping only when he's close enough for me to see the blood vessels in his eyes.

A red heat prickles my skin. I know before he speaks that this is about earlier.

"Er . . ." Stuart glances at me and then to the car, toward Rachel. Even from here I can see her cheeks are as red as mine. "Maybe this isn't the best time." Typical Stuart, forever trying to placate and he doesn't even know why.

"I'm Bradley Finley, Rachel's husband. It's about your wife, mate."

"Excuse me?" Stuart frowns, turning to me for an answer I don't want to give.

I glance behind me. Most of the parents are walking through the gates for pickup, but there are still pockets of parents chatting by their cars and looking our way.

"Look." Bradley sighs, smoothing down the fabric of his shirt, which is straining so tight across his body that I can see snatches of his chest and gut through the gaps between the buttons. "I appreciate she's been through a lot," he says, looking at me and yet somehow talking about me like I'm not here. "But she needs to leave Rachel alone."

"I'm standing right here," I reply.

"What?" Stuart's mouth drops open. "Jenna, what's going on?"

"She's been harassing my wife, mate," Bradley replies, pointing a finger at me. "Phone calls day and night. Knocking at our door and now following her. It needs to stop or I'm going to the police. OK?" Bradley marches off toward the school without waiting for a reply.

When he's gone, Stuart turns to look at me, his face taut. "What the hell, Jenna?"

"It's nothing. A misunderstanding," I add even though it's not and I know it.

We walk into the school playground and choose a spot away from the groups of waiting parents.

"Have you been following Rachel?" he asks, looking at me as though I'm a plot twist he can't figure out in one of his sci-fi novels.

"I was trying to talk to her, that's all. It was important. I didn't mean to scare her."

"You of all people know what it feels like to be harassed." Stuart's voice is a whispered squeak. "What's gotten into you?"

"For Christ's sake, I wasn't harassing her. She got the wrong end of the stick, that's all. I'll explain it to her on Monday and apologize."

"I really think—"

"Let's talk about this later," I cut in, spotting Archie. He's on his tiptoes by the teacher, craning his neck to see us. When he catches sight of us he whoops and fist-pumps before racing flat out and leaping into Stuart's arms. "Daaaaddyyyyy," he cries like he hasn't seen Stuart for a month. I try not to let it bother me, but it does.

Beth appears a few minutes later, red-faced and teary eyed.

"Hey, what's wrong?" I ask.

"Nothing. Can we go?"

"In a sec. Tell me what's wrong first. Has something happened today? Shall I speak to Mrs. . . . er . . ." The name of Beth's teacher is a blank space in my head.

"Mrs. Claybourne." Beth sighs, eyes on my feet. "And no. Don't. I just want to go home."

"OK, let's go." I don't push it. I'm as keen to get out of here as she is. We start to move, Stuart first, then Beth, then Archie and me.

"Can you hold my water bottle, please?" Archie asks, pushing it into my hands. "We did art today. I want to show you a drawing I did of a stag beetle. It's really cool. I got two merits. Did you know stag beetles can grow up to twelve centimeters?"

I put my arm around him and hurry him on. "I'd love to see your drawing. Can it wait until we get home though?"

"OK," he says, still digging in his bag, feet moving slowly. We're at the gates in the mosh pit of other parents and children. There's a jam ahead—a boy has fallen off his scooter. I can hear him screaming in pain. I peer over to check if he needs any help, but it looks like grazed hands and humiliation more than hurt.

"This way," I say to Archie, tugging him around the fallen scooter.

I've lost Beth in the medley. I think she's up ahead with Stuart, but I look behind me just in case and catch a glare from Bradley. He's walking with a group of mums he seems to know. They're all staring at me like I'm some kind of monster.

As we leave the gates I catch sight of Beth and Stuart further up the road. Archie rushes after them and I follow close behind.

The moment we're through the front door Beth runs upstairs and shuts herself in her room. I don't stop her, but twenty minutes later I take her a snack and a glass of water.

"What's going on?" I ask, pushing her legs over and sitting on the bed beside her.

"Lacey says I can't go round to her house anymore." Beth's eyes brim with fresh tears. "We fell out at school."

"Oh."

"She said I can't come to her sleepover in the summer holidays and now I'm the only girl in the entire class who isn't going. So I said that she was stupid."

"Beth," I reprimand.

"I know it's not nice, I just said it because I was upset and because she said it first. I really really wanted to go to the sleepover. Can you speak to her mum and ask her to ask Lacey to let me come?"

"I . . . I'm not sure." Anger burns inside me. Has Rachel said something to Lacey about me? "It's probably just a misunderstanding. It'll blow over on its own. Besides, the summer holidays are still weeks away anyway."

Beth nods, causing two fat teardrops to roll down her face. I catch one with my finger before reaching out to hug her. She wraps her arms around me and I breathe her in. She smells of grass and sun cream and something Beth-like I can't describe that fills me with love.

"It's going to be all right." I try to believe my own words. "I promise," I whisper as the reality of what I've done sinks deeper inside me—a cement block plummeting into the ocean.

CHAPTER 43

Jenna

"What's wrong with Beth?" Stuart asks when I come back downstairs.

"Can we play a game, Mummy?"

"Sure," I reply to Archie. "She fell out with a friend," I tell Stuart in a low voice.

"Yesssss." Archie fist-pumps the air. "I'll be an astronaut and I've just crash-landed on a strange planet." Archie throws himself to the floor and skids across the kitchen tiles on his knees.

"How about snakes and ladders?" I plead, too tired for Archie's imaginary world today. "Unless you think I'll win?"

"OK, but I get to be the red counter." Archie jumps up and runs to the living room. "And it has to be best out of five."

Stuart says nothing and we spend another evening in a stony silence, broken only by the false jollities we put on for the kids.

Later, when I've checked Beth and Archie are asleep, their doors firmly shut, I tiptoe down to the kitchen, where Stuart is waiting for me. For once he's not shying away from the fight we've all but had scheduled since three p.m.

"What the hell were you thinking following Rachel?" he snaps as though we're still out on the grass verge and Bradley has just stormed off.

"I told you. It was a misunderstanding. I tried to talk to her the other day and she wouldn't listen to me. I was trying again and she got the wrong end of the stick."

"What did you want to talk to her about?"

I busy myself with pouring a glass of white wine from the fridge, using the time to get the words straight in my head. "It wasn't just photos of me I found on Matthew Dover's phone. There were photos of Rachel too. That's what I was trying to talk to her about. She's connected to him somehow. At first I thought he was stalking her too, but now I'm not sure what's going on. I think she might have been having an affair with him. I thought—"

"Oh, you thought," he cuts in, his voice rising. "Well, that's a relief. For a moment I was wondering if you'd lost the ability to think at all."

"Calm down, Stuart. You'll wake the kids."

"Me, calm down?" He rakes a hand through his hair. "I've found out my own wife is harassing someone and you want me to calm down."

"I'm not harassing anyone, and you're missing the point. He has photos of me and Rachel. There has to be a connection, a reason. And I'm going to find it."

Stuart swears under his breath. "This is a mum at the school, Jenna. Her children are really good friends with our children." He slides his glass onto the side with a loud sigh. "Jenna, I'm worried about you. You've become obsessed with this man."

Heat fills my body. The furious-rage kind of heat. It sweeps right over me, flushing my skin. "Don't be ridiculous. I was only trying to talk to Rachel. She's the one who's acting weirdly here. She's avoiding me, Stuart. Why would she do that if she didn't have something to hide?"

Stuart closes his eyes for a long moment and rubs a hand across his face. "You know what? You're right when you said it's affecting Beth. It's affecting all of us, and I don't mean the stalking, I mean you. You're not thinking straight. You've had a breakdown, Jenna. I don't know who you are anymore." His voice is so sodding calm, as though he's hammering home the point. I'm the irrational angry woman who is acting insane, he is the levelheaded man who is always right.

My fists clench together and hot tears form in my eyes. I brush them away before they can fall. "You've no idea what I've been through. You bury your head in the sand like you always do when you're faced with something that heaven forbid might pop the happy bubble you like to live in."

"That's not fair. I've been here for you through everything."

"Yes, you have, but the whole time you've been telling me to stop worrying, the police will get him, and even this week you've been trying to convince me it's all over and I should get back to normal. It's not over, Stuart. Nowhere near over. I wish you'd see that. You've seen the e-mails. He's never going to stop." My voice is no longer sharp but quivering. I grit my teeth and gain control of myself.

Neither of us speaks for a moment and all of a sudden the fight leaves me, the anger fizzling out like flat lemonade.

"Look at yourself, Jenna," Stuart says, moving toward me and pulling me into a hug I don't want. "You need help. You're not sleeping, are you? That's the problem here. You need to get some sleep. That's why you're not yourself."

I open my mouth to protest, but Stuart continues before I get the chance. "Please, Jenna, for us, please stop all this. You're living on coffee and adrenaline. Can't you see what this is doing to you and to all of us?"

"You make it sound like I've been deliberately staying awake all night."

"Take a sleeping tablet. Get a good night's sleep and in the morning you'll feel better. You have to trust the police to do their jobs and stop trying to help, because you're not, are you?"

I shake my head, freeing more tears from my eyes.

That night I dig out the sleeping tablets from the back of the bathroom drawer and take one.

"I love you," Stuart says as we climb into bed. "I'm doing everything I can to make this marriage work; are you?"

To which I say nothing, because I don't know what to say. Part of me wants to tell him I love him too, because I think he might be right. I wanted to prove you're a monster, I wanted to understand you, but everything I've done this week has made things worse.

But I say nothing because that's not all I feel. There's another part of me that is reeling backward, waving my hands in the air, shouting, *Wow wow wow, how did I find myself married to a man who doesn't understand me?*

CHAPTER 44

SOPHIE

The grass on the lawn is lush green and soft under my trainers. The garden is in full bloom, with a riot of color and richness. It looks particularly beautiful in this early-evening light. Nothing is drooping or dead, nothing is yellowed from the sun, and I feel a pang right in the middle of my gut for how far away I am from ever having a garden this nice. The house that goes with it is equally exquisite. Giant furniture in giant rooms with carpet that feels bouncy under my feet.

Being in this garden has made me realize how much I'm going to miss my lovely new apartment. It has been a tiny glimpse into a future that isn't mine anymore.

"Bradley spends hours out here with a hose," Rachel huffs from beside me, nodding toward the stretch of garden I'm admiring before dropping into another push-up. "That's why it looks like this."

"It's gorgeous." I turn toward Rachel and give her an encouraging smile. "You're doing great. You're over halfway."

"Thanks so much for fitting me in at short notice," Rachel says. "I hope I didn't ruin any Friday-night plans with Nick."

"Not at all." I swallow hard, pushing back the fear that rears up when I think of Nick and what I'm planning to do. I know he suspects something. I've had to keep up a steady stream of chat just to stop him asking me what I'm thinking every time I fall silent. It's exhausting. He always seems to be right by my side, breathing down my neck.

I caught him going through my drawers last night when he thought I was cooking a stir-fry in the kitchen. I wanted to scream at him to stop, to get out, but I couldn't. I was too scared of what he'd do, so I backed away and shouted that dinner was ready before he could look under the bed and find the bag I've started to pack.

Am I really doing this?

Tears fill my vision and I blink them away, focusing on the timer on my phone. "Ten more seconds, Rachel. Really push the ground away as you come up each time."

The timer beeps and Rachel flops to the floor with a groan. "God, I hate push-ups."

"You've got sixty seconds' rest and then we're moving on."

Rachel turns onto her side and reaches for her water bottle. "Hey, my friend is looking for a personal trainer. I've given her your number. I hope that's OK."

I pull a face and Rachel's perfectly arched eyebrows shoot up. "Have I done the wrong thing?" she asks. "I didn't think you'd mind."

"It's not that. Of course I don't mind. It's just . . . I'm planning to leave Westbury."

"What? Oh, don't say that. Who will yell at me to get fitter? How long are you going for?"

Forever is what I want to tell Rachel, but I shrug instead. "I'm not sure yet."

"Is everything OK?"

"Not really." I drop to the floor beside Rachel. "Please don't say anything to anyone, but things with Nick aren't great. He . . . he's not the man I thought he was. I'm going to get a fresh start." My voice quivers. It's the first time I've said the words out loud. It's also the first time I've confided in anyone about anything for longer than I can remember, and I feel exposed and stupid. I shouldn't have said anything. *Good one, Soph!*

Rachel reaches over and pats my arm. "I'm sorry."

I smile, leaping to my feet. "Thanks. Now come on. You've got sixty seconds of burpees. Go."

I push Rachel hard for another thirty minutes. There's something in the set of her face that tells me she needs it.

"How's everything with you?" I ask when she's lying on the lawn, her face crimson and gleaming with sweat. She looks like she's trying to make snow angels in the grass. "Is everything all right with Bradley?"

"Yeah, fine. There's just stuff going on at the school. One of the mums is acting weird. It's rattled me, if I'm honest. Bradley has taken the kids to the cinema tonight so I can have a break, which is a treat. But sometimes I wish he'd suggest getting a babysitter and taking me out, you know? He couldn't keep his hands off me when we first met." A wistful smile pulls at her lips.

"When he sees you in a bikini on holiday next month, I bet his jaw is going to drop to the ground."

"This session really helped. I'm going to be aching tomorrow."

"That's what you pay me for." I pass Rachel a fresh bottle of water and watch her carefully. There's a tension in her body. Something is bothering her, and before I can stop myself I ask about the affair. "So, no more fun with the other guy then?"

"God, I wish." Rachel shakes her head. "No, I don't wish that. It was so wrong. A blip. I was just lonely after the move and he was just so available." Rachel's smile widens. "There was something intense about it. About him actually, like when he looked at me, I was the only thing in the world that existed. There was once when he turned up at my door. No phone call or warning. Bradley had just left, so I guess he must've been watching the house. We had sex right there in the entrance hall. Like I said, intense.

"But I'm trying to pretend it never happened, which isn't easy right now. Whatever problems Bradley and I have, I don't want to throw our marriage away."

"Well, once Bradley sees you in a string bikini, you'll be like newlyweds again."

"If he looks up from his phone for long enough to notice." Rachel sighs. "But, God, I hope so. I've booked the children into an activity club at the hotel so we can spend some time together. Actually, I'd better grab a shower, they'll be back from the cinema soon."

"Do a few stretches first, OK?" I say, gathering up my bag.

"Hey, I've had a thought. Are you busy tomorrow night? I'm going out with a few of the mums. It was supposed to be a PTA thing, but now one of them is bringing her sister and a few have dropped out so it's more of a general night out. I can't promise it won't descend into drunken ramblings about our kids"—Rachel laughs—"but it will be fun and you look like you need a bit of that."

I smile at her final comment, and even though I know Nick will hate it, I find myself nodding. "Thanks. Where shall I meet you?"

"At the top of the high street outside the cinema at seven. I don't know the bars in Westbury yet, but someone will know a good one."

"See you then," I say with a wave good-bye.

I drive slowly back toward the apartment and imagine Nick watching me on his Find My app. The thought makes my skin crawl, a thousand ants under my skin. I'm desperate to turn my phone off, park the car, and go for a run, but it will only make Nick more suspicious, and I don't want that. I have a plan forming in my mind, and if it all goes well then I'll be long gone before he even notices.

Just a few more days to get things straight.

An image of Matthew pops into my head and the old guilt rises up inside me. I didn't go to visit him today. I know he'll have waited for me, ready with more questions. But that's the thing, the guilt is old. Matthew is all grown up now and so am I. I can't keep feeling responsible for him, no matter how many times I promised Mum.

My heart aches at the thought of leaving Mum. She doesn't care about me. She doesn't want to see me and won't even know I've left, but it still hurts.

A single tear traces its way down the side of my face. I really wish I could undo everything that happened that night.

CHAPTER 45

Saturday, June 22
Jenna

The sleeping tablet pulls me into a deep black hole of nothing. I don't dream, I don't think about you, but when I wake six hours later, in the early hours of the morning, I don't feel refreshed either. My head is groggy and my mouth is as dry as the earth in the garden.

I fumble my way downstairs with a drunken room-spinning feeling. I desperately want to close my eyes, but that makes it worse, like I'm on the teacups at the fairground and Beth and Archie won't stop turning that damn wheel in the middle.

Water helps. I guzzle it back until I can hear it sloshing in my stomach. Outside the sky is dark but I can just make out the first rays of dawn in the distance.

I press my hands to my face. My skin is hot, feverish, and I drag myself to the doors, twist the lock, and open them a fraction. The air is cool and I lean against the doorframe and feel my eyelids close.

I'm not sure how long I stay there for—a minute, an hour—but something jolts me.

My eyes shoot open. The garden is dark gray, more shadows than anything. What made me open my eyes? A noise? I think it was a noise. Yes, definitely a noise. A rustling and a thud, or was it more human than that? Did I hear a muffled sneeze? The truth feels just out of reach, hiding behind the fog of the sleeping tablet.

I hold my breath and listen to the silence. I hear nothing, and yet there's something out there. I can feel a presence.

I step back and take a breath—a quick in and out. My hand reaches for the handle to shut the door and just as I'm yanking it closed something moves. A shadow that leaps out from behind one of the rosebushes. I yelp, turning the lock as the thing jumps over the back fence and disappears.

I stand frozen, unable to move, my eyes fixed on the back fence.

A minute passes before I realize I'm holding my breath and my lungs are on fire. I breathe out and try to pull in a deep breath, but nothing happens. It's like I'm still not breathing. I try again, in and out, waiting for the relief of oxygen moving into my body, but it doesn't come.

I can't breathe.

I spin around and stumble to the breakfast bar.

My legs give way and I cling to the counter. Black spots fill my vision and I know it's only a matter of seconds before I collapse to the floor.

In the back of my mind I know this is a panic attack. I'm a doctor and I know I'm going to be OK. I fight to bring the knowledge forward, to slow my breathing.

Then a sob catches in my throat and I breathe again before covering my mouth with my hands. Shoulders heaving up and down, tears welling in my eyes and falling down my cheeks.

I force myself to look at the glass doors again and the still of the garden beyond. A part of me wants to snatch up the phone and call the police, but I'm not sure what I saw. My thoughts are jumbled and dreamlike.

I catch sight of my reflection in the glass and don't recognize the broken face of the woman staring back at me. My cheeks are red, but the skin beneath my eyes is dark gray, like smudged eyeliner. I look like I haven't slept for a week.

What was out there? A fox? A person?

My hands are shaking so hard I can barely grip the door handle, but I do and despite the fear rampaging through my body, I unlock the door and step outside.

The air is cooler than it has been for weeks and is heavy with the smell of the salty estuary.

"Who's there?" I call out into the silent night, swinging the flashlight from my phone toward the fences and searching for any movement.

I inch further into the garden, away from the safety of the kitchen, but there's nothing out here.

I'm turning around, back to the house, when my flashlight catches on something on the ground near the fence. I step closer. It's a pile of sticks. They're leaning against one another like a miniature bonfire, and that's what it is, I realize. A small fire ready to be lit.

Last time you came into my garden, you burned the grass with weed killer. This time you were going to set a bonfire. Except it can't be you. You might be sending e-mails, but there's no way you're capable of running across my lawn and jumping over the fence with a broken leg.

The thought rears up so fast this time it's like a punch to my gut. I've been thinking it for days. Ever since I smacked down on the pavement outside and my bag was taken, but thinking something and knowing something are two very different things. Here is the proof staring me in the face—someone is helping you.

CHAPTER 46

Sophie, *age 15*

What do you mean?" Sophie asks, the smile fading from her face. The bounce she felt on the way to school that morning drops and becomes a dead weight, rooting her to the spot. "I'm saying I can come tonight."

Flick opens her locker before glancing at Vicky, the pair sharing one of their stupid looks.

"It's just . . ." Flick shrugs, pulling out a book from her locker and closing it again. "My mum said I can only have one person over to get ready with me. We're not saying you can't go to the club or anything, are we, Vicky?

"No, course not. It'll be great if you can come," Vicky chips in, making it sound anything but.

"But last week you said I could come to yours first," Sophie says, hating how whiny she sounds.

"Sorry. My mum's changed her mind."

"Oh." Sophie bites her lip, fighting the tears building behind her eyes. "Never mind. I guess I'll see you guys there then."

"How will you get home?" Vicky asks.

"What do you mean? I thought your dad was collecting us."

"Yeah, but you said you weren't coming so I've offered Reece and Graham a lift home. My dad can only fit four of us in his car."

Sophie smiles like it doesn't even matter. "I'll figure something out."

The bell for registration clangs above their heads. "See you later, yeah?" Flick says, hooking arms with Vicky and heading for their classroom.

"Sure." Sophie scoops up her bag and walks away.

But Sophie doesn't see them later. Not properly anyway. Flick and Vicky don't turn up to their usual spot by the trees at break, or lunch. They don't even wait for her before lining up for food like they normally do. Sophie sees them eating chips and gravy in the canteen and messing around with Reece and Graham.

That's why they don't want Sophie to go tonight—she'll spoil their foursome. Maybe she should go anyway. Get a bus to the club and walk home if she has to. She could wear something really amazing and look ten times better than Flick and then Reece would fancy her again.

Except Sophie can't do that. She doesn't have anything amazing to wear. She doesn't even have any makeup because her mum says she's too young. She was planning to borrow Flick's, but now she can't.

Sophie leaves school the moment the bell rings and cries as she walks home.

Matthew is sitting on the doorstep waiting for her, taking photos of the sky.

"Don't you have a key?" she snaps.

"I lost it."

"Mum's going to kill you."

"No she won't."

He's right too. Her mum never tells Matthew off. *It's not fair,* Sophie thinks. Nothing is fair.

"You still going tonight?" he whispers even though their mum won't be home until really late.

"No," she snaps. "And it's all your fault. There's no way I can leave you, is there? Mum never tells you off, but she's always laying into me and she'll kill me if I go out tonight. So thanks for that."

Sophie waits for a reply she knows won't come.

"I wish . . ." she says, feeling the hurt from Flick and Vicky's betrayal tear through her chest. "I wish you'd never come to live here. I wish it was just me and Mum and Dad, like it used to be. They'd still be together if it wasn't for you."

Sophie stomps up the stairs, already feeling crappy, but too angry to turn around and apologize.

At the top of the stairs she glances down to the front door, where Matthew is still standing. His eyes are screwed shut tight and his hands are two tight fists by his sides. She hasn't seen him do that for years.

Sophie almost says something then, almost backs down, but then she thinks of Vicky and Flick and the night out she's missing, she thinks of Matthew's smug *"No she won't"* comment and storms into her room, slamming the door behind her. She's sick of everyone tiptoeing around him. She sick of her mum treating them both like babies.

Sophie yanks the wardrobe and pulls out her favorite black denim skirt that her mum lets her wear only if she puts leggings on underneath because it's so short. She throws it on the bed and pulls out a green halterneck which makes her boobs look great. Flick and Vicky can't stop Sophie from going out, and it's not as if Matthew isn't old enough to look after himself.

CHAPTER 47

To: Jenna.Lawson@westburydistrict.org.uk
From: Timeisrunningout@mailpalz.com
Subject: Are you ready?

Neither of us can escape what's coming. ARE YOU READY?

CHAPTER 48

Jenna

My eyes shoot open and I sit up, staring frantically around the bedroom. How did I get here?

The sun is streaming in through the gaps in the curtains and the air is humid and smells of sleep. Images of the bonfire in the garden zigzag through my thoughts. I saw someone in the garden, I saw the sticks, but now I'm in bed and I don't remember how I got here.

Was it all a dream?

I leap out of bed and run down the stairs. The house is still. Empty. I glance at the kitchen clock and see it's already gone ten. Stuart must've taken the kids to their swimming lessons and decided not to wake me.

I throw open the doors in the kitchen and step out into a wall of heat that causes a queasiness to tumble in my stomach. I reach the fence where I saw the sticks at dawn and a gasp escapes my mouth.

They're gone.

I stumble back inside and turn on the coffee machine just as Diya calls.

"Hey," I say. "I'm sorry. I was meant to call you, wasn't I?"

"Yep. You cow," she says, and I hear the grin in her voice. "I thought I'd done something to upset you."

I draw in a long breath before I answer. "Don't be daft. You could never upset me. It's just been a tough week."

"A&E isn't the same without you. Are you missing us yet?"

The question throws me. A part of me craves being in the thick of an emergency, to be wholly and completely immersed in my job, but I have loved spending more time with Beth and Archie, and it's a relief to not feel torn in two by the guilt of trying to work and take care of the kids.

Then I remember the look of pity on Nancy's face when she spoke to me. *Are you aware that your colleagues are concerned about you?* I feel angry every time I think about it.

"Jenna?" Diya prompts.

"Sorry. I miss it a bit, I guess," I say in the end. "I miss you more."

"Ah, well, it's funny you should say that because I'm phoning to remind you that it's my birthday night out tonight. Not that I think for one second that you've forgotten."

"Of course not," I lie, scrunching my eyes shut. "And happy birthday."

"Thanks. So you'll come?"

It's the surprise in her voice, the unexpected hope, that makes me say yes.

"Great. We're meeting at the Kings Arms at seven thirty," she says.

"I'll see you there."

We hang up and I collapse against the counter, wondering how I'll make it out tonight.

By the time Stuart and the kids traipse through the door after lunch I'm on coffee number three and a headache is hammering in my temples.

"Hey, there you are," I say, scooping Archie into my arms. "Have a good time?"

"Yeah. Dad took us for fish and chips after swimming and a seagull stole some of Beth's battered sausage."

"Oh no." I look to Beth.

"I didn't want it anyway." She shrugs.

"How was swimming?" I ask her.

"Fine. Can I watch something?"

"Sure." I nod. "Just for an hour, OK? Then we'll do something together."

Beth rolls her eyes but says nothing as she drops a damp swim bag on the floor and throws herself onto the sofa.

Archie wriggles out of my arms and races up to his bedroom. The door closes and I hear the thud of him jumping across the floor, fighting aliens on his planet Bong, no doubt.

"Feeling better?" Stuart eyes me with concern.

"Much better," I lie, wishing it was true. I'm quite sure I look my absolute worst right now, and the polar opposite to Stuart, who is wearing a dark red T-shirt that hangs perfectly on his athletic frame.

The words, the truth about what I saw in the garden, swirl in my head and form in my throat. I wait for them to spill out, blood from a wound, but they don't. I'm not even sure what I saw anymore.

"It's Diya's birthday drinks tonight," I say as Stuart pours himself a glass of water.

"Are you going?" he asks without turning around.

"Is that a problem?"

"No, of course not. I just thought you wouldn't be up for it."

"I'm not really, but she's my best friend."

He nods before collecting his book from the counter and stepping into the garden. I watch him leave and feel yesterday's argument lingering between us like a bad taste in my mouth.

I spend the afternoon locked in a three-hour battle of Monopoly with Beth and Archie, pretending the sleeping tablet helped, pretending not to be scared by this morning, pretending everything is fine again. It's good to see them both laugh, especially Beth, when I landed on her Mayfair hotel.

By the time I leave the house Stuart is humming again and kisses me good-bye. "You look gorgeous," he says with an admiring glance to my black maxi dress. "Have a good time."

I walk fast, glancing behind me every few steps and wishing I'd got a taxi. By the time I arrive in the high street I'm red-faced and clammy all over.

The shops are closed, shutters down and dark. Only the yellow arches of McDonald's glow bright. But the place is still buzzing with people. Teenagers huddle in groups around benches, smoking and taking selfies. I cut down a side road where three men with bare chests stagger in the direction of the seafront. It's like a Spanish holiday resort except for the ugly gray buildings and the scratchy fumes from the passing buses.

My pulse quickens as the men weave into my path. I look behind me. The street is deserted. My muscles tighten, my hands balling into fists. I try to step out of their way but they separate, staggering across the pavement. One drops off the curb and they laugh like a pack of cartoon hyenas.

Only after they pass by do I breathe again.

The King's Arms is on a corner plot, one road back from the main high street. Bus stops line one side of the road beside delivery bays for the shops. The pavement is covered with bird crap. Stale scents hang in the air. Stale food, stale bodies, stale everything.

The pub is busy. The noise and the people have spilled out onto the pavement. The beat of unrecognizable dance music fills my ears as I fight my way through the door.

Every table is filled with people shouting at one another to be heard. Others linger in the middle of the floor, drinks in hand, one eye on the door to check out the newcomers and one eye on the tables, waiting to pounce should one become free.

I'm smacked with nostalgia the moment I push through the crowds. I met Stuart in this bar, on a night just like this one, and we danced and talked for hours. I thought it was just for fun. Someone like Stuart—the rugged builder, up for a laugh, always smiling—and me, fiercely driven and serious. But after that night Stuart asked me for dinner and I said yes. Stuart has never understood my drive, my desire to save people, but it never used to feel like it mattered.

"Jenna," a voice shouts, interrupting my thoughts. Diya's slender arm shoots in the air from one of the booths by the windows.

Diya leaps up and wraps her arms around me, holding me tight for a second. "I'm so glad you came," she shouts in my ear.

"Me too," I lie.

"You look gorgeous."

I pull a face. "You're the one who looks gorgeous." And she does. Diya is wearing her favorite red polka-dot dress and is radiating energy. "Happy birthday," I say, handing her a neatly wrapped box.

She opens the box and squeals at the simple gold chain with a lightning bolt charm at the end. "I love it," she says, just like I knew she would. "Thank you."

Diya pulls me to the table and I smile at the people sitting around it. Eight altogether. A mix of doctors and Diya's friends

I've met before. Thomas Carrick is wedged right in the corner, looking out of place among the others. His face lights up when he sees me and he waves.

Diya follows my gaze to Thomas and laughs. "I invited him along to break him in a bit. He's so nervous all the time," she says in my ear, "and besides, he's rather cute too."

"My round then," I call out, pasting a smile on my face.

There's a ripple of approval and I take requests. A bottle of white wine, two pints of lager, three gin and tonics. Diya offers to come with me but I shoo her away. "It's your birthday," I shout.

I repeat the drinks order in my head as I push through the crowd and join the throng waiting to get their drinks. The hairs on the back of my neck tickle and I glance around me suddenly, searching for the eyes on me.

No one is looking my way.

I need to relax. That's why I've come out tonight, isn't it? To relax? Or have I just come to prove to Stuart that I'm fine? I wish the music wasn't so loud. The beat of it is pulsing through me, rattling my bones.

I reach the edge of the bar and squeeze myself in between a hen party wearing pink fluffy tiaras and dresses made out of toilet roll, and three girls in tube tops and miniskirts who are too young to be here and hiding their age behind fake eyelashes and heavy makeup. I stare for a second too long at one of the girls, my insides knotting as I think of Beth. The girl catches my eye and looks at me with a resting bitch face before turning to her friends and laughing.

It takes an age to get served. Younger, prettier people with wide smiles and flirty eyes catch the bar staff's attention long before I'm able to. In the end it's Thomas Carrick who comes to the rescue. Pushing up beside me and shouting a loud "Oi" at one of the men behind the bar.

"Thanks," I say after our order is taken.

"Purely selfish reasons. I wanted my pint," he says, making me laugh. "It's really good to see you, Jenna. The hospital is boring without you."

Thomas takes the two pints and I take the wine and gin and tonics on a tray. I'm almost at the table when I spot Christie just ahead of me. I shout a "Hello, fancy seeing you here." She turns, her expression sheepish.

Then my gaze drifts and I spot Rachel, watching me with narrowed eyes, and a few other mums from the school I sort of recognize.

"Oh, hi," I call with as much cheer as I can muster. "Of all the pubs, eh? I'm just out for birthday drinks with a friend." I lift the tray as if backing up my story with evidence. *I'm not following you*, I want to shout at Rachel.

For a split second I wonder if I should try to talk to her now, but I squash the thought back down. It's too loud in here, and by the look on her face, she's more likely to tip her drink over my head than listen to anything I have to say.

"Are you having a good night?" Christie asks, fidgeting a little as though she's not sure where to stand.

"Yes, thanks. I'd better get these over to my friends. Have a good night." My eyes pull back to Rachel and we stare at each other for a long moment before Christie steps aside and I move through them.

"What took you so long?" Diya asks.

"I hung around hoping for a better offer, but it looks like I'm stuck with you lot tonight," I reply, handing her the wine bottle. The group laugh and I'm grateful they do. I can still feel the mums watching me. There are dozens of bars in Westbury. This isn't even the nicest one or trendiest, and yet here they are.

I perch on the edge of the booth and pretend I'm listening to Diya and Thomas talk about work. I've been away from the hospital for less than a week, but already I feel out of touch.

My gaze is desperate to move back to Rachel and the group. I'm on my second gin and tonic when I can't bear it anymore and look for her. For a moment I think they've gone. The bar is quieter now as the drinkers move on to the seafront clubs. But then I spot them at a table in the far corner. Rachel has her back to me and I try not to stare at the strands of sleek blond hair that fall over her shoulders.

It takes me a moment to realize that the woman I recognize sitting beside Rachel isn't one of the school mums, but Sophie. Your sister, Sophie.

Her gray-blond hair looks silver in the light of the bar and is tied up in a high ponytail. She's deep in conversation with Rachel and it's obvious they know each other. But how? Rachel said she'd never heard of you, and yet she clearly knows Sophie.

"What do you say, Jenna?" Thomas's voice breaks into my thoughts.

"Huh? Sorry, I was miles away."

"We were just arguing over which is worse to have land on your shoes—vomit or shit? In fact, don't answer that. How the hell did we get to talking about this?" He looks at Diya, who falls into drunken giggles.

"Are you OK about taking the time off?" Thomas asks me then, his expression serious.

"I guess so. The hardest part is knowing someone I work with went behind my back and complained about me to Nancy. I just don't get it. What was I doing? And why wouldn't they speak to me first about it? This is my career. My whole life. We've all worked so hard to get to where we are, and to put my job at risk . . ." My voice trails off. I'm looking at Diya as I'm speaking and the sudden panic widening her eyes makes something click in my head.

"It was you?" I say, taking a sharp breath in.

"We've all been worried about you, Jenna," Thomas says.

My fingers curl into two fists and I say nothing as I wait Diya out. She didn't, I tell myself. She's my best friend. She wouldn't do this, and yet the guilt on her face says it all.

"You haven't been yourself," Diya says in voice so low it's hard to hear.

"So you thought you'd tell our boss and have me put on leave?" I snap, anger buzzing inside my head.

"It wasn't like that. Nancy asked me outright how I thought you were coping at work and I had to give her an honest answer."

I stand up suddenly and catch Rachel and the other mums staring at me, but right now I don't care. "And was that based on your professional opinion or on the things I told you because I thought we were friends?"

I push my way outside, past the huddle of smokers and into the muggy night. My pulse is racing. I can't believe this. Diya's betrayal stings worse than I could ever have imagined. I trusted her, and now she's turned around and used it all against me.

"Jenna, wait!"

I spin around to find Thomas jogging toward me. "Diya wanted to come out but I told her I would talk to you. Let me walk you home."

"No need. I'm a big girl." I stride ahead, alcohol building a confidence I know could shatter any second.

"Please. I want to. I think you're . . ." His Yorkshire accent sounds suddenly thicker as his sentence trails off. He looks at me with a sheepish expression that makes me want to groan inside. "I think you're amazing. After everything that's happened to you, you're still the best doctor I know. You know, if you ever want to grab a drink sometime, just us, we could . . ."

I cringe and do nothing to hide it from my face. Is Thomas really trying to ask me out? Here, now, when I'm clearly pissed off, not to mention married with kids. "Go back inside, Thomas," I snap, adding a force to my voice that he can't ignore before dashing across the road to the taxi rank and diving into the first car I see.

But as the taxi pulls away, it's not Diya I find myself stewing over, it's Rachel and Sophie and the fact that they know each other. What does it mean? How are they connected to what you've been doing to me?

CHAPTER 49

Monday, June 24
SOPHIE

Nick takes forever to leave for work, which is weird for him, but typical that it should happen on the one day I need him to get out. The seed of a plan that planted in my head just days ago has grown—a forest in my thoughts that I can't see past. I can't wait anymore. I have to escape right now.

The hospital called me yesterday. I didn't answer, but later, while Nick was doing some weight training in the living room, I slipped into the bathroom, locked the door, and listened to my voice mail. My skin grew hot and I stared at my wide-eyed reflection in the mirror as Matthew spoke, low and urgent in my ear. *"There's something we need to talk about,"* he said, reminding me of that day we met near Rachel's house. *"I'm getting more mobile. I can walk on crutches now, and I've remembered a lot of stuff, Sophie. If you don't come visit tomorrow then I'm busting out of here and coming to you."*

I knew in that one moment that if I didn't leave the very second Nick was out of the way then I'd be stuck with him and with Matthew, the pair of them fighting over me like a play toy.

I check the time again. It's 6:31 a.m. Only a minute has passed since I last looked at the bedside clock. I can't lie here much longer. Nick is normally up and out the door by six, but I can hear him in the kitchen, opening and shutting drawers.

"Sophie, you'd better get up," he yells. "You're seeing Greg at seven."

No, I'm not. I canceled last night, feigning food poisoning. There's no way I can work today. I'm too jittery, and the voice in my head telling me to get my fresh start is so loud, I can't think of anything else.

"Greg just texted to say he's running twenty minutes late," I shout back. "I've got a bit of time."

"Well, I'm off," he calls, and I hold my breath while I wait to hear the sound of the door bang shut.

The moment it does I leap up and head straight for the shower. Then I pull on an old pair of jeans and a T-shirt I've not worn for ages. Both feel strange against my body after months of wearing mostly activewear. As I stare at my lean frame, my extensions, the silver of my hair in the mirror, I realize just how much of myself I've changed to be Nick's girlfriend. I've always changed things about myself, but this is the first time I've done it for someone else.

I don't know who I am anymore. But maybe that's a good thing. I'm leaving the old me behind. I'm really leaving Westbury. Finally.

The next hour is spent rushing through the rooms, frantically packing. Only when I'm done do I reach under the bed and pull out my old school backpack. I don't know why I've kept it all these years. The pink fabric is faded and yellowed, and when I lift it to my face I can still smell the smoke. It was one of the only things that survived the fire.

I fill it with the essentials and hurry to the kitchen to make myself some breakfast. I'm not hungry, but I know I should eat while I have the chance.

It's just as I'm slipping on my trainers, a slice of half-eaten toast in my hands, ready to leave, that I hear the front door open. I stand frozen in the kitchen, my eyes scanning the living room. My backpack is on the sofa but the rest of my things are still in the bedroom. Nick's probably forgotten his gym bag. If I'm careful, I might be able to get him out of here without him learning the truth.

"Sophie?" he yells as his feet pound down the hall.

"Yeah." I try to sound relaxed while inside I'm a wreck of nerves and desperation. *Just let me go, Nick*, I want to beg.

"I was just in the gym and who do you think I bumped into? Greg," he says before I can answer. "Imagine how surprised I was to see him there and imagine how stupid I sounded when I reminded him of his PT session, only to be told that you canceled him last night."

"I . . . I'm not well," I say, clutching at my stomach and hoping he'll get the hint and not ask any questions. "I didn't want to disappoint you. I'm sorry."

He eyes me up and down from the doorway, taking in my different outfit. "You look fine to me."

"It's Matthew," I blurt out, another lie. "The hospital needs me to be with him this morning while they run some tests. I knew you'd be mad so I didn't tell you."

I feel my eyes drag to my backpack. Panic shoots through my body and I move a fraction, trying to get to my bag before Nick sees it.

"That's total bullshit," Nick growls, stepping closer so that his body now blocks my way. "What's really going on?"

I lean back against the counter, my hands behind me on the drawer where we keep the knives. I picture the stainless steel points and wonder how far I'll go to get free.

"Sophie," Nick barks.

"I'm leaving you." The words fall from my lips and I can't believe how amazing the truth feels. My head spins with it and I bite my lip to stop the smile spreading across my face. "I'm leaving Westbury."

"What? When?"

"Right now." My eyes move again to my bag and this time Nick's gaze follows.

Before I can stop him, Nick is across the room and plucking my bag from the sofa.

"Leave it alone," I shout, leaping toward him.

"What is this stuff?" he asks, holding the bag away from me. The frown on his face deepens. My heart leaps into my throat as I picture my precious things. The photo of Mum, an old schoolbook, a shell from the beach. Things that are meaningless to everyone but me.

"It's personal. Please give it back."

He looks at the bag again and then to me. "So you were going to leave without saying good-bye? Why would you do that to me?" Hurt crosses Nick's face and for a horrible second I feel myself waver.

I clench my fingers into two fists and force myself to keep going. I'm not going to give in this time. "Because you're a bully," I tell him.

"No I'm not," Nick says. He frowns again and shakes his head.

"Really? You call me constantly, you always want to know exactly where I am, and now you've put a tracker on my phone. That's not normal behavior. You know that, right?"

Nick drops my bag to the floor by his feet and sinks onto the sofa. "Of course I do. But you've left me no choice, Sophie. It's not me who's been acting strange around here. It's you. You never tell me where you're going or when you'll be home. You work for me, remember? If I'm going to book you in to meet a client then I need to know you're going to turn up."

"It's called trust, Nick. How many other employers do you know who make the people that work for them have a tracker?"

"Yes, trust. That's exactly my point. You have to trust me. You go running at night. You go to visit that weirdo brother of yours alone, and to top it all off, you totally shut down when I ask things. You never talk to me, Sophie."

"I talk to you all the time."

"About nonsense crap. Don't you think it's strange that I've no idea what happened between you and your mum? I've lost track of how many times I've tried to get you to open up to me. What did you do that was so terrible that she won't talk to you anymore?"

"I don't want to talk about that."

"That's OK. Can we take a moment? I'm sorry." He holds out a hand for me to take. "You're right. I've been acting crazy. Everything that's happened with your brother has brought a lot of stuff back for me. I've never told you this, but I got in trouble when I was a kid for shoplifting. After that it was like I was labeled. This one local copper started hounding me all the time about burglaries and other stuff he thought I'd done. So when the detective started asking questions, it spooked me. I didn't push your brother in front of the bus, but I was in town and I knew they'd think I did it."

Nick sighs, his eyes pleading with me to stay. "We can work this out. I'm not going to let you run away from me like this. I love you."

I feel my resolve shrink, my courage with it. He's right. He's never going to let me go and neither is Matthew. Maybe it would be easier if I just accept my fate now.

"Sophie, come sit with me." Nick's hand is still in the air, waiting for me to take it, and I know that if I let him get hold of me then I'll never be free.

I nod and step closer, pulse racing like a jackhammer. At the last second, I snatch my bag from the floor and hold it to my body. Anger flashes across Nick's face and in that moment I realize that all I need for my fresh start is right here. What the hell was I planning to do with all my stuff anyway?

"Sophie," Nick warns. "Come and sit down now."

I spin around and sprint down the hall. Nick's footsteps are right behind me but I keep going.

"Where do you think you're going?" His voice is close.

I fly into the door and yank it open just as his hand reaches it. But he's too slow, I'm too desperate, and I squeeze through the gap and shove the door back into him. I hear the smack of wood and Nick's cry of surprise but I don't stop to see the damage I've done.

I run down the corridor and straight into a waiting lift. As the doors pull slowly closed, I wait for Nick's hand to appear between them, and only when they close with a gentle thud do I breathe out.

I'm free.

I hug my bag to my pounding chest and gulp in heaving breaths of relief and freedom.

Just one more place to go and then I'm gone forever and there's nothing Nick, Matthew, or anyone else can do to stop me.

CHAPTER 50

JENNA

Stuart wakes me up with a light shake. "Time to get up, sleepy-head. The kids are up and I've got a breakfast meeting at the council. I've got to dash."

I mumble a good-bye and check my phone. It's gone seven. I've slept for over eight hours for the second night in a row.

There are no e-mails waiting for me this morning. No sick promise that something is going to happen. The more sleep I get, the more certain I am that Stuart is right. These e-mails are the desperate empty threats of someone who can't get to me anymore.

Has your phone run out of battery? Is that why you've stopped?

I don't care anymore. Do you hear that? I don't care about the e-mails. I don't care about you. I want my life back. I'm going to talk to DS Church today and tell her I was in the high street on that Thursday you were pushed into the road. I'll tell her about the mugging too and my theory that someone has been helping you. I can't keep hiding from her calls anymore. If she's discovered that I looked through your phone and went to your house, then I'll have to face the consequences. Then I'm going to book an appointment with the occupational health team like I was supposed to days ago, and speak to Nancy about when I can return to work.

Diya called me yesterday with a tearful apology. "I'm so sorry, Jenna," she said the moment I answered. "You were right. I shouldn't have gone behind your back, but I was just so worried about you. I knew you'd never forgive yourself if you made a mistake."

Without the gin and tonics and the anger, I could see Diya's actions were those of a friend. She was trying to protect me from making a mistake that really would end my career, and if I'm honest with myself, I know there were times when I was so strung out, so scared, that I shouldn't have been working. I still wished she'd told me afterward, or gone about it a different way, but I can't deny that time off from the hospital has given me more time to think, and finally I'm sleeping better.

I said sorry too and we both ended the call laughing about her attempts to teach Thomas the Macarena.

Thomas is another person I'll need to apologize to. I woke on Sunday morning red-faced at my behavior toward him. Did I really think Thomas had a crush on me? He was just trying to be my friend.

I'm starting to wonder if everything I've done over the last week really has been the result of some kind of breakdown, as Stuart suggested. A combination of the months of terror you subjected me to, exhaustion, and no longer having my job to focus on. The thought turns over in my mind as I tidy up the breakfast dishes.

We leave for school early and walk under a heavy gray sky. After endless weeks of sunshine, the world looks dull this morning. The sea in the distance is no longer glistening but dark, almost black with flashes of white foam and turbulent waves.

It's still hot though. The fabric of my summer dress sticks to my skin and I'm glad for the French braid keeping my hair away from my face and neck.

In the playground, Archie and Beth drop their bags at the start of their class lines and stand by the gate, waiting for their friends. The playground fills up with the usual drop-off chaos and the cacophony of four hundred schoolchildren, but something feels different. Like I'm the last one dancing in a game of musical statues, wiggling about, arms in the air with no idea that the music has stopped and everyone else is staring.

I say good-bye to Beth first. I'm relieved to see she's hand in hand with Lacey and they are giggling together. My eyes scan the playground, searching for Rachel, but I can't see her anywhere. I don't even know what I would say to her now.

"Bye, Mum," Beth says without looking up. "Don't forget it's the dentist today."

"What?"

"The dentist."

"That's not today, sweetheart."

"It says it's today on the calendar," Beth replies.

"Oh, I thought . . ." My voice trails off. I meant to change it. The day you walked into my house pretending to be a buyer and snooped around. I was going to change the appointment, but I forgot. I don't suppose it matters now.

Beth looks at Lacey and they both giggle. "It's at two thirty p.m. so I get to miss boring assembly."

"Right, I'll pick you up later then."

I move over to Archie and kiss him good-bye. He rubs his palm across his cheek where my lips touched his skin, but he's smiling at me as he does it.

"You've got the dentist today," I tell him. "So I'll pick you up after lunch break."

Archie frowns, sticking out his bottom lip. "I thought you'd forgotten."

"So you knew and weren't going to tell me?" I tickle him under his arm and he wriggles away with a happy yelp. "You can thank your sister for reminding me."

"I don't want to miss assembly."

"How about we get some fresh donuts on the seafront afterward, assuming you get a thumbs-up from the dentist, that is."

"Promise?"

"I promise."

I watch them walk into school and feel my body unwind a little, like it always does. You can't get to them now. And if you are working with someone, then I feel happier knowing the children are safe in school behind locked gates and rigorous safeguarding protocols.

I'm just walking out of the gates when someone taps my shoulder and I jump, jerking my body away as my hands fly up, and only then do I see it's Christie.

"Sorry," Christie says. "I didn't mean to scare you."

"It's my fault, I was miles away. How are you?" I ask, taking in Christie's pale face and hollow eyes.

"Er . . . actually have you got time for a quick cuppa?"

It's on the tip of my tongue to say no but there's an urgency sparking in Christie's gaze that makes me agree.

"Did you have a nice time the other night?" she asks as we walk the short distance to her house.

"I think so. I feel a bit old for that place now. What about you?"

"Yeah, it was nice to get out."

We make small talk about the kids and the looming six weeks of summer holidays as we walk to Christie's house.

The moment the front door is closed behind us, the atmosphere changes and Christie crumbles before my eyes. Fat teardrops roll down her cheeks and drop onto the doormat.

"Hey, what's happened?" I guide her to the sofa, expecting her to tell me about a health scare she's having that she wants my advice on. I'm gearing myself up to reassure her about a smear test with abnormal results or a lump on her breast. "You can tell me," I add, taking her hand.

Christie sniffs, pulling herself together. "It's about the other night. The mums I was with, I like them, but . . . Rachel, she . . . the thing is I don't think they realized that I'm friends with you and when they started talking, well, I couldn't just walk away." Her voice cracks and her shoulders start to shake. "I'm sorry." She sniffs. "I'm not sure whether to tell you this."

"Christie, it's OK, just tell me."

She nods. "Rachel . . . Lacey's mum, do you know her?"

"Not really." Despite everything that I've done this week, I realize it's true. I don't know anything about Rachel or you.

"She . . . she only moved to Westbury a year ago, and by the sounds of it her marriage is in a bit of trouble." Christie pauses then, watching my reaction like she's told me some big secret. "Rachel got really drunk. We all did. Except, you know what I'm like. By ten p.m. I'm ready for a cup of tea and my pj's." She gives me a weak smile. "So I moved on to lemonade and the others kept drinking. Then this guy starts trying to chat Rachel up and we all had a laugh about it, but then she starts crying and telling us that she had an affair."

"I know," I reply, thinking of the photos on Matthew's phone,

the sense that Rachel was lying to me. It's just as I suspected—
they were sleeping together.

"You do?" She sits back and gawks at me. "And you're OK
about it?"

I shrug. "I only found out recently. I don't know all the details.
Did she tell you how they met or how long it went on for?"

"Er . . . I think they met in the school playground," Christie
offers, her eyes still staring at me with disbelief.

"What? What was Matthew doing in the school playground?"

"Who's Matthew?" Christie asks.

"Matthew Dover. My stalker. The man Rachel had an affair
with. I've been trying to speak to her, but she won't talk to me."

I wait for Christie to say something but she doesn't for a long
time. Fresh tears well in her eyes.

"What is it?" I ask.

"Rachel didn't say at first who it was with, but then one of the
mums kept asking if it was someone we knew, and then another
mum joked about how they wouldn't kick Stuart out of bed in a
hurry, and Rachel's face, well, it was obvious. We all knew by
then so she admitted it."

A sour taste fills my mouth. "I don't understand what you're
telling me. One of the mums fancies Stuart? What's this got to do
with Rachel and my stalker?"

She shakes her head. "I'm sorry, Jenna. I don't know anything
about your stalker. It was Stuart that Rachel admitted she had
an affair with. She swears it's over. She said she asked you to join
the PTA as a way to talk to you. She was curious about what kind
of person you were, but wishes she hadn't now because she thinks
you've guessed about the affair and you're following her places,

trying to scare her. She's terrified you're going to tell her husband."

The world stops for a moment. A piercing noise whines in my ears. Stuart and Rachel had an affair. My husband, the father of my children, was sleeping with someone else right under my nose, at a time when I was trying to deal with the worst experiences of my life. At a time when I thought we were closer than we've ever been. It doesn't make sense.

A year or two ago, maybe I'd have believed it, but not recently. We've been so close. This last week hasn't been our best but . . . my thoughts trail off as the reality of Christie's words sinks in.

Stuart's voice echoes in my thoughts. *I'm doing everything I can to make this marriage work.*

Hurt spreads through my chest and my thoughts darken like the clouds outside.

"I'm so sorry," Christie says. "Did I do the right thing telling you? Jason told me I shouldn't interfere, but I couldn't bear it. It'll be all round the school now and I wanted you to hear it from a friend."

"Thank you," I manage to say through the rock cutting into my throat. "I mean it, Christie. Thanks."

"Do you think . . . Will you tell Rachel's husband?" Her voice is so soft, almost a whisper, but she's staring at my face with such wide, watery eyes that it makes me wonder if Rachel put her up to this.

An image of Stuart and Rachel kissing punches through my thoughts. *He wouldn't do that to me*, a voice whispers. I shut it down, picturing instead the way Bradley jabbed his finger at me last week when he accused me of harassing Rachel. But it's not his ugly scowl I'm thinking of, it's the look of horror on Stuart's face when Bradley approached us and his desperation not to make a scene. At the time I put it down to Stuart being Stuart, dodging confrontation, but now I think about his reaction, and Rachel's pale face from the car, refusing to look our way. I wonder if they were both in panic mode. Stuart because he thought Rachel had told her husband about them, and Rachel because she thought I knew and was going to tell Bradley.

Christie says something but I'm not listening.

"Sorry?" I say.

"I said if you need me to have Beth and Archie at any point, you know I will, don't you? I love them like my own. And Niamh thinks of them like a brother and sister. Honestly, I'll take them anytime, day or night. Do you want me to collect them for you after school? In case it's too hard to face people in the playground?"

The thought hadn't even crossed my mind. My cheeks burn thinking of the looks from this morning. Now I know why.

"I'll be fine," I say, standing up. "They've got a dentist appointment this afternoon. I'll be collecting them early."

For a moment my knees feel as though they might buckle, the weight of the truth too much to bear. Christie must see it as she reaches out and hugs me.

The tears fall. Great heaving sobs of them down my face and soaking into the shoulder of Christie's T-shirt.

"There, there, let it all out," she says, patting my back, and I feel the warmth of her care, the same she's given to Beth and Archie for so many years now, and I reach out and hug her back.

"I'm sorry for being such a mess." I sniff, pulling away.

"You don't have anything to be sorry for. I'm here for you, OK? Whatever you or Beth and Archie need."

"Thank you. I don't know what I'd do without you."

A smile lights Christie's face and she kisses my cheek before I open the front door and walk into the oppressive heat.

A part of me wishes she hadn't told me, and another part of me doesn't want to believe it, but I know she's telling the truth and now I have to deal with it.

CHAPTER 51

Jenna

I walk home from Christie's house lost in thoughts of Stuart and Rachel and how blind I've been. As I near the house, something pink catches in the corner of my vision.

My head turns and I see the flower—a single pink carnation tucked under the windscreen wiper of my car, its baby pink petals squished between the wiper and the glass.

My skin tickles in the warm wind now whipping through the trees and I shudder, my eyes roaming every space between the cars, looking for the eyes that I'm sure are watching me.

Two more steps and I see more pink petals scattering the pavement too.

Stuart's car is parked outside the house and I wonder why he's home. Then I reach the doorstep and stop dead. Shredded pink carnations fill my doorstep like confetti. There must be a hundred flowers here. And lying beside them is Archie's dark green book bag he lost all those weeks ago.

The book bag is open. There are no books inside anymore, but sticking out of it are three plastic dolls.

The first one is like all the other red-haired dolls you've left me. The face of this one has been melted into a gloop. But it's the other two dolls that I can't tear my eyes away from. One has long orange hair and the other is a boy doll with brown hair. They're both wearing tiny green school uniforms.

Beth and Archie.

There's something else too, nestled to one side, half-buried in flowers. It's only when I step closer that I recognize my diary. What's left of it anyway. The pages have been completely destroyed, burned to nothing but a charred mess.

A feverish panic presses at me from every direction. My head whips around, back to the street. "Who's doing this to me?" I scream out as my eyes dart one way then the other. I see no one.

I've been stupid. I've known for days that someone was helping you, but I did nothing, I told no one. And now this has happened.

My hands are shaking as I unlock the front door. I look up to the CCTV camera but it's gone.

"Stuart?" I shout out.

"Yeah," his voice travels from the kitchen.

"Where's the CCTV camera?"

"Huh?" he asks, appearing in the hall still wearing his suit from his breakfast meeting. The anger of the affair rears up so suddenly it brings a wave of nausea with it, but I can't think about it right now.

The front door is wide open and bits of flowers are blowing across the wood floors.

"The CCTV camera is gone. Someone's taken it."

"I took it down last weekend." He frowns, his eyes widening as he draws nearer and takes in the mess.

"What? Why?"

"I had to unscrew it from the wall in order to get all of the sticker off and I haven't got round to putting it back yet. I didn't think it mattered anymore. What the hell is all this stuff?" he asks, peering through the door.

I swear under my breath. "Another gift." I grind my teeth together. The fear I felt outside is morphing into a slow rage.

"But—"

I hold up my hand and he stops talking. "What are you doing here?" I stare at Stuart and for the first time I see the nerves twitching on his face.

"I told you, I had a meeting. I thought I'd pop back and get changed out of my suit before going to the site. It's like a dust pit at the moment. Is everything OK?"

The question feels loaded. The truth dawns on me slowly, a wave of knowing washing over my thoughts. His question isn't about you, or this mess on our doorstep, it's about Rachel. She must have told Stuart about her drunken slip and he's come back to see if I've heard. For a crazy moment I wonder if Christie, Rachel, and Stuart are in on it together, but I squash it down. I'm being paranoid.

"Did you do this?" I throw a hand at the petals on the floor.

"What? Of course I didn't. Jenna, I—"

"You had an affair with Rachel." It's not a question, but still I search his face for an answer. The color drains from his face, his shoulders slump, and just like that I have my answer.

CHAPTER 52

Jenna

Anger—pure, undiluted rage—is bubbling inside me. I step into the living room and pace across the room.

"All that stuff you said at the weekend about how you're doing all you can to make our marriage work, making me feel like I'm crazy. And all this time you've been shagging someone else."

"I'm sorry," Stuart says, following me into the living room and collapsing onto one of the sofas. "I was trying to protect you. It's over now and I didn't want you to get hurt. I meant what I said. I am doing everything I can to make us work."

"You didn't want me to find out, you mean. How much did you tell her?" I ask.

"About what?"

"About what was happening to me?"

Stuart is silent for a beat and then he shrugs. "I don't know. A bit, I guess. It was hard to stand by and watch everything that was happening to you. I had to talk to someone."

I think back to Rachel standing outside the gym that time and how nervous she seemed. Was it all about her affair with Stuart?

No. There is something more, a missing puzzle piece. Rachel is friends with your sister and there are photos of her glued to your bedroom wall. Bernie said you were seeing someone for a while. An older blond woman. What's to say she wasn't sleeping with you as well as Stuart?

"Did you tell her about the burned grass in the garden?"

"I don't know. Maybe." Stuart buries his head in his hands and I stop pacing and drop onto the sofa opposite him. "Why?"

I ignore his question as wave after wave of understanding, humiliation, and horror crashes against me. "When did it start?"

His words are muffled but still hit me hard. "After Christmas."

"So just after Matthew Dover had thrown that doll at me and we'd gone to the police? At a time when I was at my most vulnerable, when I thought we were giving our marriage a second chance, that's when you decided to start sleeping with someone else?"

"I didn't plan for it to happen."

"How could you do that to our family? How could you pretend that our marriage was strong and we were fine when it was a lie?"

"It wasn't like that."

"Then what was it like?"

Stuart lifts his head from his hands but doesn't reply.

"I mean it, tell me," I say. "How do you go from chatting to someone for two minutes in the school playground to shagging?"

"I don't know how it happened. I honestly don't. Beth and Lacey begged me and Rachel for a playdate and so Rachel came over to the house after school with the kids and we got talking."

"Tell me you didn't have sex in our bed?" I spit out the words and wonder what difference the answer actually makes to the depth of Stuart's betrayal.

"Of course not."

"And I'm just supposed to believe you, am I? After all the lies you told me?"

"For Christ's sake, Jenna." Stuart's voice is loud and makes me jump. "Do you have any idea how lonely it is being your husband?"

"Right, this is my fault. Great cliché, Stuart."

"I'm not making excuses for what I did, but you want me to explain, so at least give me the chance to speak."

I wave my hands in the air. "Go for it."

"You . . . make me feel like hired help. You're always reminding me how much smarter you are than me and how you save lives every day. You work long hours because you love it and because you have to. And you come home and expect everything to be done. The washing, the dinners. Most weeks I feel like a single parent. I didn't use to mind. I know your job is more important than mine and it's more important than remembering our wedding anniversary and more important than being home more than two evenings a week to kiss the children good-night."

Guilt digs hard in my stomach. Two evenings a week? I know my shifts run over sometimes, but I'm home more than that, aren't I?

"So what changed?" I ask.

"Nothing. Nothing ever changed with you, and I got sick of it. This can't possibly be news to you. We almost separated before Christmas, but then things with that guy . . . Well, you needed me and I couldn't leave you. Then Rachel was there and . . . we were both lonely, I guess, and looked for comfort in the wrong place."

"Everything I've been going through." I shake my head, a lump forming in my throat. "And you've been sleeping with someone else. I can't believe this. So the only reason you didn't leave after Christmas was out of pity?"

"No. I stayed because I love you. And having the affair with Rachel made us both realize how much we have to lose. It made me realize how much I do still love you."

"How long did it go on for?"

"A few months."

"How many?"

"It's over between us and it has been for ages," Stuart says. "We both ended it because we didn't want to destroy our families. This last week, we've both been in hell worrying about—"

"You've been talking to her?" I shake my head, picturing all the times Stuart's been on his phone. It didn't even cross my mind that he was being unfaithful. Not for a single second.

"A couple of times. She thought you knew about us. Look, I'm sorry, Jenna. I'm really really sorry. If you'll give me another chance, I'll spend my whole life proving to you how much you mean to me."

His words sound corny and I let them hang in the silence as I stand up and walk out of the room.

"What are you going to do?" Stuart calls after me. "About us?"

"I don't know." It's the truth. "Can you call DS Church and tell her about this mess on the porch? Someone is helping him." I grab my bag and leave without waiting for an answer.

My mind is churning over everything I know and everything I don't. I can't think about Stuart anymore. The flowers and the dolls, it's a message. I don't know what it means, but I have to find out before anything can happen to Beth and Archie. And if Rachel won't talk to me then maybe you will.

CHAPTER 53

JENNA

Traffic is heavy and it takes me nearly an hour to crawl across town. By the time I reach the hospital the sky above me is no longer gray but inky blue, and a distant rumble of thunder growls from somewhere far away. I park and check my phone.

There's a missed call from DS Church. She's left a voice mail asking me to call her. "We've had a development."

I swallow hard. At last. My hands shake as I return her call, but instead of ringing, it disconnects. USER BUSY, my display tells me. I'll have to try again later.

I walk quickly to the brain injury unit on the ground floor and press the intercom as thoughts of seeing you again consume every inch of my mind.

A long thirty seconds later a voice squawks from the microphone. "Can I help you?"

I stutter for a moment and the words come out in a jumble of who I am and who I want to see. It occurs to me as the door unlocks that they might not let me see you, but I have to try.

"Good morning," a nurse greets me from behind a desk. "It's

room four," he tells me. "Mr. Dover is happy to see you, but we are limiting visits to ten minutes."

I swallow hard and force my feet to move.

The door to room four is open. It's a simply furnished room with a hospital bed and two armchairs facing each other. Your neighbor, Bernie, is sitting in one chair and you are in the other.

Bernie stands when he sees me, his face lighting into a smile. He's wearing a hospital dressing gown and looks a lot better than the last time I saw him.

"Here she is. My hero. Didn't even know I was having a heart attack until this lady showed up. Thank you very much." He takes my hand in his and shakes it gently and I wonder if he notices the tremor.

"My pleasure." I smile, despite the tightness in my chest. The desire to run returns. That fight-or-flight burst of adrenaline. Except now I'm choosing fight. I have to for Beth and Archie. The dolls from this morning flash in my thoughts.

"Well, I need to get back to the ward," Bernie says. "I promised I wouldn't go far. Got my angio-whatnot tomorrow."

Bernie squeezes my hand and says another thank-you before walking slowly away.

A silence falls. All the questions I want to ask you bubble up inside me, but now that I'm standing before you, I don't know if I can ask them.

"Do you want to sit down?" you ask, waving your cast arm at the chair.

I inch into the room, fighting the images of your hand grabbing out at me. You look different from the last time I saw you. You've shaved and your hair is pushed away from your forehead.

"The nurse told me that you're the doctor who saved my life. Thank you. But I've forgotten what name they gave me?"

"I'm Jenna Lawson. And I'm not just the doctor who saved your life, am I?"

You frown, titling your head to the side. "What do you mean?"

"You've spent the last eleven months stalking me." There. I lay it out, exposing the truth like ripping off one of Archie's Band-Aids, quick and steady, revealing the wound underneath.

You close your eyes in a childlike expression, as though you can block out my voice, but you can't and I carry on.

I'm aware of the heavy sound of my breathing and the tears dripping down my face. "You stand behind trees or in shop door-ways, or outside my house, my home. You send me e-mails. You say horrible things about my children. You leave sick things on my doorstep. You take photos of me on your phone."

There's more I want to say. The words are not enough to con-vey the destruction you've caused—a wrecking ball to my life—but your eyes open again and you stare at me with an intensity that steals my voice.

"I don't think so." You shake your head. "No, definitely not. I would remember if I did things like that. I'm not like that."

"Take a look at your phone if you don't believe me."

"I don't have my phone. It got lost when I was hit by the bus."

"You're lying. I saw it before."

"I'm not. I haven't seen it since I woke up." Your cheeks flush and you fidget in your chair and push a finger in between the cast and the skin on your arm.

"This itches like hell," you say as though the last few minutes haven't happened.

A part of me wants to jump up then and search your things, but what is the point? I'm not here to prove what you've done. I know that already.

"When you were hit by the bus, it stopped for a while. And now it's started again. Who is doing this for you? Is it Rachel?"

"Who?"

Frustration throngs through my body and I sigh.

"Rachel Finley."

"Do I know her?" you ask. Your lips twitch at the edges just a little, but I see it. You're fighting a smile. You're enjoying this.

"Yes."

"My memory is still a bit sketchy, especially the new stuff. Did you know someone pushed me into the road? The police came to talk to me."

I pull out the crumpled photo from my bag and throw it over to you. "I took this from your bedroom wall. It's Rachel."

"You've been in my house?" Your face changes, the mask slipping just long enough for me to see a darkness, like a storm cloud blocking the sun. Your eyes narrow and your jaw tightens.

The moment passes and you find your mask, your lost Boy Scout look.

"You've been in mine," I shoot back, sounding stronger than I feel inside.

Your eyes stare at the photo of Rachel and then back to me. "I like to take photos."

"Who is helping you? Who left the dolls on my doorstep this morning?"

"I'm getting tired now."

The nurse from the front desk appears as though you've said the magic words. "That's your ten minutes, I'm afraid. We do like to be strict here as rest is so critical to brain injury recovery, but we do encourage you to come back."

He holds the door open for me and I've no choice but to leave.

"Jenna," you call as I reach the doorway.

I turn around and you push yourself off the chair and stand. "I remember watching you."

A chill travels down my spine and my mouth drops open but no words come out.

"It's not what you think," you say, reaching for a pair of crutches.

"What is it then?"

"I don't know. I can't remember."

The nurse touches my arm, shooing me from the room, but I glance back a final time and see your eyes scrunched up tight and your free hand clenched into a fist.

I came here for answers, to find out who is helping you, but all I have are more questions.

CHAPTER 54

Sophie

I stare up at the house for a long time, trying to imagine what it would've been like to live here like Mum had planned before the fire. It's a semidetached at the end of a quiet cul-de-sac, and way nicer than my dad's shitty little flat that me and Matthew ended up in.

The front garden is so Trevor. Perfectly cut borders and symmetrical flower beds that make me want to stomp all over them for no reason whatsoever other than that they belong to the man who turned my own mum against me.

Hurt pours out from every cell in my body. I'm being unfair, but I can't help it. It's been a long time since I was at this house. Trevor's hissing remark from the last time I was here still stings. *"She doesn't want to see you or your brother, Sophie. Surely you can see that with your own eyes. It's too painful for her and I don't want you causing any more problems for your mum. Haven't you done enough damage?"*

Paving stones cut across the grass and lead to the front door. They're set too widely for my stride and I end up leaping from one to the other and pressing the doorbell before I lose my nerve. I've faced up to Nick already today. I'm not going to back down now.

A shadow moves behind the door and I watch Trevor press his face to the glass. A moment later the lock clicks open and he appears in the doorway.

Trevor looks older than I remember. His hair is completely white and the skin beneath his eyes is puffy and sags to the top of his cheekbones. He's clean-shaven and wearing a neatly ironed shirt tucked into a pair of dark blue jeans.

"Hi," I say, feeling fifteen again under his glare.

"Oh, Sophie, you shouldn't be here." I thought he'd be angry to see me, but all he seems is apprehensive, a little scared maybe.

"I know, but I'm leaving today and I won't be coming back. I just wanted to say good-bye to my mum."

Trevor continues to look at me and I see the weary distrust in his eyes.

"Please," I beg. "Just two minutes, I promise."

He gives a small nod of his head and opens the door. "But I'm not leaving you alone and if I think for a second that you're upsetting her, you have to leave."

"OK. Thank you."

Where Trevor has aged since I last saw him, his house has remained a time capsule. It's the same pale green carpet on the floors from the first time I came to see Mum here—not a piece of fluff to be seen—the same busy floral wallpaper and the landscape watercolor paintings in gold frames on the wall.

"You've got a visitor, love," Trevor says in a loud voice as he leads me into the living room.

He steps to one side and I see her. A weight lands on my chest. My throat aches and I know I'm going to cry.

"Hi, Mum." The words are a croak as I shuffle closer.

She's sitting on a cream leather sofa that is almost swallowing her up. Her auburn hair is cut short around her face and streaked with gray. She is so small, so frail, but she's still my mum.

Her eyes are distant, her gaze focused on a point on the wall near the TV. I desperately want her to turn her face and look at me and I feel suddenly winded, unable to breathe. There is so much I miss, but mostly it's what we could've had that really gets to me. Twelve years of love and support that she's not given me.

"Mum, it's me, Sophie." I perch beside her on the sofa, ignoring Trevor's disapproval wafting at me from where he's hovering in the corner. He never understood why I've stuck by Matthew all this time. In his eyes we're both to blame.

"Please, Mum. Please say something."

"Sophie." Trevor's one word is filled with worry.

A tear rolls down my cheek. I bite back a sob. "I'm leaving, Mum. I'm going to make everything right, I promise. I won't . . . I won't be back, unless"—I bite the edge of a nail and taste blood in my mouth—"unless you ask me to stay, Mum. Please ask me to stay."

I put my hands over hers. Her skin is warm but slack and nothing like the hand that used to hold mine.

Trevor steps forward and I know my time is up, but I can't pull myself away. "Mum, say something, please? Haven't you shut me out for long enough?"

My mum's hand trembles beneath mine. I lean close to her ear. "I know you can hear me and I'm begging you to forgive me."

The tremor spreads to her arm and up her body. Her head begins to shake and I pull back just as Trevor leaps toward the sofa.

"Good-bye, Mum," I say.

"You need to leave," Trevor says, his voice a desperate whisper. "Oh, love, it's OK. Take deep breaths for me."

I scurry to the doorway and watch as Trevor wraps his arm around Mum's shoulders, whispering soothing words in her ear. Her gaze is still fixed on the point on the wall above the TV and I wish she would look at me just once.

More memories surface. The aftermath of the fire. Mum's coma. The days of sitting by her bed, begging her to wake up. Then she did and I thought everything was going to be OK, but it wasn't. She never came back.

The doctor called it a catatonic state. I can still remember his words. *"While she looks awake, she's in a state of stupor and is unresponsive to external stimuli. We don't know if it's permanent or if it's something she may wake from one day. Your mum suffered cerebral hypoxia, which means her brain was starved of oxygen during the fire. This is the likely cause of her catatonic state and her seizures. However, it is also possible that her condition is the result of PTSD following the fire and she may get better in time. I'm afraid it will be a case of wait-and-see."*

I always thought she'd come back one day. I told myself this was her way of punishing us. I used to believe that if I just held her hand enough, if I could just keep talking to her, that she'd forgive us and wake up.

Trevor stands up and guides me toward the front door. "I'm sorry, Sophie. I know this must be hard for you, but you have to leave. You and Matthew trigger something in your mum's head, causing these seizures whenever you're here. It could kill her one day. Please go now." His eyes are moist, and for the first time I take in the gray pallor to his skin.

"Thank you for taking care of her," I say, forcing out the words.

There is more I want to say, more I should say to him, but I can't. I may have only just realized how hard the last twelve years have been for Trevor, but they've still been harder for me.

I run from the house and into the road. A cool wind has started to blow through the trees. The sky is dark and threatening, like the memories I can no longer keep locked away. At the end of the road I pull my backpack to my chest and slow to a walk. Mum didn't forgive me, but at least I said good-bye. There's nothing else for me here. I have to leave before Matthew can stop me.

As I make my way back toward town my phone rings from inside my backpack. I pull it out, expecting it to be Nick or the hospital. I've already disabled the Find My app, but I wouldn't put it past either Nick or Matthew to find me anyway.

Instead, Rachel's name fills my screen and I answer, telling myself there's time for one more good-bye.

CHAPTER 55

SOPHIE, *age 15*

There's smoke everywhere. A thick gray wall of the stuff she can't see through. Where is it coming from?

Sophie's eyes sting and she closes them for a moment, feeling her way along the wall. "Matthew?" she croaks, her voice lost in a fit of coughing. She crouches lower to the floor as the insides of her lungs burn.

Something sharp bites her knee. She reaches to touch it and feels a sliver of glass poking out. She pulls it free and tries to keep going.

For a moment Sophie is lost. Is she upstairs or down? Which room is she in? Panic sweeps through her, freezing her muscles. She reaches out, hands banging the wall and the floor for anything familiar. Her fingers knock against a doorknob. It's small and round—the cupboard under the stairs where her mum keeps the cleaning stuff and the board games. She's downstairs.

"Matthew?"

She can't see the fire but can feel the fierce heat of it pouring out from somewhere. Her skin tingles and she can smell it burning, like it's meat on a barbecue.

"Matthew?"

She crawls on all fours, away from the source of the heat, trying to navigate her way through the house she's lived in all her life. It feels like she's trapped in a maze.

"Help," she screams, spinning around. Which way? Everywhere feels so hot.

A huge bang sounds from behind her. She turns toward the noise just as a fireball of orange leaps out at her. Sophie screams, pushing herself against the wall.

Her lungs burn. There's no air left. Just fire and smoke and heat.

A strong hand grabs at her wrist and yanks her forward. She tries to stand and run herself but she's moving too fast and her feet can't find the floor.

Suddenly there's a whoosh of air and Sophie can sense the open front door is just ahead of them. The fire is nipping at her bare feet and there's a moment she thinks it's too late. The fire is so big, bigger than anything she's ever seen and the heat is unimaginable. She can't breathe. There's no way she'll make it out. But the hand on her wrist is gripping her tight and pulling so hard it feels like her arm is going to be ripped right off.

A second later and she's outside. Sophie's skin is burning and she doubles over coughing, but even so she can feel the cold dampness of the grass on her feet and the air soothing her lungs.

There's someone beside her coughing just like she is. Sophie opens her eyes. The night air stings but she forces herself to look. "Matthew?" she says, her voice a hoarse croak.

Lights flash. More people arrive. Neighbors in dressing gowns and slippers. Someone puts their arm around her, guiding her onto the street. Matthew still has hold of her wrist and she doesn't want him to let go. A blanket is put around the both of them, and all they can do is watch the smoke pour out of their home.

"Is there anyone still in the house?" a voice yells at them.

Sophie turns to the voice and the firefighter looming over them in a black coat and a yellow helmet. He yells the question again and Sophie wants to cover her ears.

"No," Sophie croaks. "Our mum's out with her boyfriend."

"Are you sure?"

Matthew says something, but the world is spinning and Sophie can't make sense of it.

A paramedic ushers them to the back of an ambulance and hands them an oxygen mask each.

Time passes, although how much, Sophie isn't sure.

Then a firefighter appears in the doorway of the house. He's carrying something on his back and as he reaches the front garden he drops it to the ground. Two more paramedics rush toward the lump. They think it's a body, Sophie realizes. She wants to shout at them, tell them they've made a mistake. It can't be. Her mum's out. But her throat is so sore from the smoke. Tears are streaming down her face.

"She's still alive," someone shouts.

A stretcher appears and they're gone so fast Sophie is still trying to process what's happening.

"I . . . what?"

"Mum," Matthew whispers.

"No. She's out with Trevor."

He shakes his head and tears spill from his eyes. "She came home early because she had a headache."

The world turns suddenly dark. Sophie can't breathe again,

like in the house with the smoke everywhere, except there's no smoke now.

She pulls her arm away from Matthew. His body is rigid beside her, his face dark and angry.

"What have you done?" She lets go of the blanket and stumbles away from him.

Time passes. People come and go from their homes, handing out water and cups of tea. More questions come, this time from a police officer with an open notebook. Sophie thinks she gives her dad's address, but can't be sure. She wants her mum.

CHAPTER 56

JENNA

I leave the hospital and drive to the seafront. There're still a few hours before I need to collect Beth and Archie, and I can't go home and face Stuart yet.

I should cancel the dentist. I'm in no fit state to deal with Archie's fear of the dentist's chair, but I promised donuts on the seafront afterward and something about Stuart's affair makes me want to keep this one promise more than ever.

The waves smack and pound the shore like pummeling fists. The air is still unbearably muggy but another rumble of thunder churns in the dark sky. It isn't raining, but it's in the air.

Snatches of my conversation with you flit through my thoughts. You said you don't know who I am, you said you're not my stalker, but you remember watching me. I know it was you tormenting me, but it's not that simple anymore. Someone left those dolls and flowers on my doorstep this morning, and if it wasn't you, then who?

I stare at the sea for a long time, trying to make sense of it all. Everything I thought I knew about you, about my job, about

Stuart and our life together, is sand slipping through my fingers. The only certainties are my children and how much I love them.

My phone vibrates in my bag and I dig it out. Eighteen missed calls from Stuart, five from DS Church, but it's the text message on my screen that I'm staring at. It's from Thomas.

An alert has gone around the hospital to watch out for patient who's left the BIU. Think it could be your stalker. Watch out! x

A chill spreads over my body and my eyes dart instinctively around. What the hell are you up to? I start the car and drive as fast as I dare. When I reach the school car park I call DS Church again and this time I reach her voice mail. I hang up without leaving a message.

At reception, I press the bell and wait for the receptionist to unlock the door. Her head bobs up by the window for a second and then disappears before I hear the click of the lock and pull at the handle.

The waiting area is small. A green sofa takes up most of the space. There are self-portraits painted by the year threes on the walls and a glass-partitioned hatch into the school office.

The receptionist leans forward in her chair and slides open the window. She's in her fifties with black hair and glasses on a string that swing out when she moves.

"Can I help you?" she asks.

"Yes, please. I'm here to collect Beth and Archie Lawson for a dentist appointment. Archie is in class 2b and Beth is in 4c."

The receptionist—Vanessa, according to her name tag—looks at me as though I'm off my rocker and laughs nervously.

I offer a polite smile and try not to show the desperation I feel squeezing me too tight. "I'm running a bit late," I add, hoping she'll get the hint and dash off to get them.

Vanessa looks behind her as though my children might be lurking in the back of her office and gives another nervous laugh. "I'm sorry, Mrs. Lawson, you're too late. Beth and Archie have already been collected for their dentist appointment."

"What do you mean? I'm here to collect them now."

"I'm sorry, but somebody already collected them. It says so right here in the signing-out book." She twists the A4 notebook around on the desk and pushes it toward me.

I stoop down and read the scrawl.

Name:	Time in:	Time out:	Reason:	Signature:
Beth Lawson		14:02	Dentist	
Archie Lawson		14:02	Dentist	

"No one has signed it," I say.

Vanessa twists the notebook back toward her and pops her glasses on her nose before peering once more at the words. "Yes, but their names are here and Mrs. Patel told me they left."

"Would I be here right now if I'd already collected them? More to the point, who did sign them out?" The first fluttering of panic dances in my stomach. Where are my children? I think of you no longer at the hospital. How far could you get? What are you capable of?

"I don't know. I was helping Mrs. Lark with a toilet accident. Sharon—I mean Mrs. Patel—must have overseen the sign-out."

"Where is she?"

"She just left."

Vanessa sits back as though the matter could possibly be closed, as though I'll shrug my shoulders and walk away and not care where my children are or why someone other than me collected them. I have a sudden desire to reach my hands through the window and shake her until she sees that these are my children she's talking about, who are supposed to be in school, they're supposed to be safe, and they're not.

"I'm not sure what to do," she says, her voice quivering.

I swallow the feeling down like a bitter pill. "OK. I'm going to call their dad and our childminder. Please call Mrs. Patel and find out who collected my children."

Stuart is the last person I want to talk to right now but he is still Beth and Archie's dad.

"Stuart," I say the moment he answers.

"Oh, Jenna. Where have you been? I've been waiting for you to come home. We need to talk. There is so much I need to say. I've been writing it down. Can you come home?" he asks.

"Have you collected the children?"

"No. I've been at home all day. What's going on?"

"I'm at the school," I tell him, the fever of panic creeping into my voice. "But the kids aren't here. Someone else has already collected them for their dentist appointment."

"Have you called Christie?"

"I'm calling her next. But I can't see why she'd have taken them."

"Maybe you arranged it with her ages ago and forgot."

There's a pounding in my ears, a "how dare he say that to me?" thought. "No, Stuart. I didn't forget. I spoke to Christie this morning when she told me about your affair and I told her I was collecting them today."

"All right. I'm sorry. Let me know, OK?"

"Sure," I reply, already hanging up.

I find Christie's number and my fingers fumble with the touch screen so it takes twice as long as it should. It rings and rings but Christie doesn't answer. I hang up, aware of Vanessa placing the office phone back into its receiver.

"What did she say?" I ask.

"It's all sorted. Panic over," she says with a clap of her hands and an "I told you so" look on her face. "Rachel Finley collected them. She said you'd been held up at work again and she'd offered to take them to the dentist for you."

"I didn't."

"She said you did."

"And I'm standing here telling you that I didn't." My voice is growing louder by the second. "Why didn't Mrs. Patel call me to check?"

"There was a lot going on. One of the year six kids was having a nosebleed and Mrs. Patel was trying to deal with that and when Mrs. Finley came in, well, I mean, it's not like we don't know her, is it? She's here all the time, what with the PTA and helping on the school trips."

I stare at Vanessa, unable to comprehend what she's telling me. I'm now facing the absolute worst nightmare of any parent and I can't process it. My children are gone. Rachel has taken Beth and Archie, and while a huge part of me still wants to believe that this is a silly misunderstanding, I know it isn't. Someone has been helping you. Someone was in my garden the other night. Someone put those dolls on my doorstep this morning. It has to be Rachel. Whatever happened with Stuart doesn't change the fact that she's connected to you, and now you're out of hospital.

The second passes, the world pulls back into focus. "Call the police," I shriek at her so loudly that Mr. Bell, the head teacher, appears from his office.

"What's going on?" he asks.

"Rachel Finley has taken my children out of school without my permission."

"I'm sure there's a logical explanation," Mr. Bell says in a calm voice that does nothing to quell my panic.

"Rachel Finley is working with my stalker. You need to call the police."

I call Stuart and rattle off the same information again. I wait for him to insist I'm wrong, but he doesn't. "I'm on my way," he says.

I hang up and stare at Vanessa's teary eyes. Mr. Bell has the phone pressed to his ear and is speaking to the police operator.

The trajectory of the next critical hours plays out in my head. I see the police arriving at the school, Stuart not far behind them. Cups of strong tea being pressed into our hands as the police reassure us that they're doing everything they can to find our children. Another image elbows into my thoughts. Stuart and I being driven back to the house, someone making us more unwanted drinks. Sitting in our living room and waiting for news as the darkness creeps into the night.

I can't let it happen. I won't be the victim anymore.

I turn to the door and leave without a word. Mr. Bell calls after me to come back, but I'm already running to my car. A drop of rain hits the top of my head as I move. Then another. It's tentative. One droplet, then a pause, then another. As if the sky has forgotten how to rain.

The downpour starts a second later, like a burst pipe, and by the time I reach the car I'm soaked.

Two police cars pull into the car park. I know I should stay and talk to them, but I can't.

I grab my phone and find the number for the estate agents. A woman answers and I ask for Wayne. She puts me on hold and I listen to a nonsense tune while my heart continues to pound in my chest.

The dentist appointment on the calendar. I should've changed it, but then you were brought into hospital. It didn't seem important, but now I think of the unidentified fingerprints and DS Church's insistence that they're not yours.

The music stops and then I hear Wayne's gruff, "Hello?"

"Wayne, it's Jenna Lawson. Can you describe the buyers who came to the house the other week?" The words spill out so fast I'm not sure I'm making any sense.

"Er . . . sure," he says after a pause. "I told the police everything at the time. The bloke was in his thirties, I think. Shortish blond hair. Normal-looking."

"And the other ones? The couple."

"It wasn't a couple, it was a woman."

"But you told Stuart it was a couple."

"I said a couple were booked in to see it, and then he asked about the second viewing and I forgot to tell him it was just a woman. Her husband couldn't make it."

"What did she look like?"

He lets out a puff of air as though I've asked him the square root of seventy-four. "She had blond hair, I guess. Pretty."

It's Rachel. It all keeps coming back to Rachel.

"She—" Wayne continues just as my phone buzzes with a text message and I hang up and stare at my screen in horror. Blood rushes to my head. The world around me disappears. All I see are the words on the screen.

Rachel: I have Beth and Archie. If you want them to live, come to Matthew's house. ALONE! If I see any police, they're dead!!

CHAPTER 57

Jenna

I throw my phone onto the passenger seat and drive away. The wipers are useless. I can barely see through the rain falling in sheets on the windscreen.

The traffic is slow and I sound my horn, screaming for people to get out of my way. I have to find my children. They are all that matter to me. I thought being a doctor was who I am, but I was wrong. Horribly, horribly wrong.

The drive to your house takes twenty minutes. Twenty precious minutes in which I don't know where my children are and I don't know if I'm doing the right thing anymore. Maybe I should have waited for the police. My phone is buzzing nonstop. I ignore it and carry on.

Every few minutes lightning streaks across the sky in brilliant white flashes. The thunder is a growling dog, a constant noise with no break in between, and all I can think about is how scared Archie must be right now, Beth too.

I tear down your road, bumping my car onto the curb outside

your house and jolt to a stop. The sky is as dark as night and there are no lights on inside.

My hands shake and all I want to do is race into your house and hug my children, but I call DS Church first. I leave a voice mail, my words streaming out a hundred miles an hour, but I hope she'll understand. Rachel has threatened to kill Beth and Archie if she sees the police, but I have to believe that by the time the police arrive I'll be with them, I'll protect them.

I pull out your keys from the glove compartment and grip them in my hand. I don't know what awaits me inside. The truth, for one thing, but all I want right now is Beth and Archie and I'll do anything to keep them safe.

The salty wind rushes over me as I step out of the car. The heat has finally been driven away by the storm and the air is now cool.

Your door key is gripped in my hand and I run through the rain. I don't knock, I don't even wait, I just jam the key into the lock, open the door, and rush into the living room in a fury of panic and desperation. My arms are up, fists clenched. I'm panting and ready to fight.

I see Beth and Archie first, crammed together on one side of the sofa, their legs wrapped around each other. My children. My beautiful children.

"Mummy," Beth cries out from the sofa.

Archie lifts his face from where he's hiding it by her side and bursts into tears. "Mummy."

The love wells up, pure and raw, and I rush forward and drop to my knees before wrapping my arms around them both.

"I thought you wouldn't come," Beth sobs.

"There is nothing in the world that could stop me getting to you," I whisper. My eyes roam the floor and the photographs covering every inch of the carpet.

It's only when I pull myself away and stand that I notice Rachel cowering in the armchair by the window.

"What the hell do you think you're doing?" I shout at her.

"I . . . I'm sorry," she stammers. "Help me. My ankle. I fell on it and think it's broken." Her voice is weak. Tears and snot are streaming down her face. A beat passes between us. Something isn't making sense, but I don't care. For all I know you are on your way here right now.

"Come on, kids, we're leaving." I gather Archie into my arms, resting him on my hip, and wrap my other arm around Beth.

"I was forced to do it," Rachel snivels. "Please help me. I'm sorry. I'm so sorry."

There's movement behind me. A figure appears in the doorway. Rachel yelps and the children push their bodies closer to me, their arms gripping me tight as though at any moment they think they'll be ripped out of my arms.

I turn and stare at eyes filled with hate and malice, and a chill spreads over my body as though I've been submerged in ice. "Sophie?"

"Hello, Jenna. Nice of you to join us at last."

CHAPTER 58

Sᴏᴘʜɪᴇ

A force pushes through my body and I laugh. It's not funny. I'm being deadly serious, but after all this time I can't believe I'm finally here with Jenna, Beth, and Archie.

"I don't know what you're doing here, but I'm taking my children out of this house right now," Jenna says. Her face is fierce—a mama bear protecting her cubs. At last, she's doing something right. Shame it's too late.

"You can drop the act now," I say. I step into the room and close the door behind me, careful to keep myself within swinging distance of the doorway. I don't want this to be over too soon.

Jenna's eyes fall to the baseball bat in my hand and she takes a step back, putting Archie on the floor and pushing the kids behind her. Archie whimpers like a scared kitten. The noise annoys me. He's such a baby, just like how Matthew used to be.

"What act?" she asks like she doesn't know.

"The good-mother routine."

"I don't know what you're talking about."

"Of course you don't. That's my point. You know, I really liked you at first. You were so kind to me the first time we met. And you looked so much like my mum that I felt this crazy connection to you. Then you told me all about Beth and Archie and I couldn't believe it. Two children, a girl and then a boy, eight and five they were then, the same age as me and Matthew when he first came to live with us."

"I never told you any of that." Jenna shakes her head, frowning like she does when she doesn't like something. It's normally Stuart who makes her look like that, or the kids when they're giving her lip, but today I guess it's me.

"You really don't remember treating Nick in A&E last year, do you? I came in with him when he had his appendicitis. You were so nice to me, and you really do look just like my mum. I left you a thank-you card, and then it was like I couldn't stay away. I kept going back to the hospital, hoping to see you. And one day there you were on your way home and I had to follow you. I had to see where you lived and what your family were like.

"I wanted to know everything about you, but then the more I saw, the more obvious it became—you don't just look like my mum, you act like her too. Always so busy, aren't you? You work all the time and barely see your own kids. And I knew, I just knew, it was history repeating itself. The more I watched you the angrier I felt."

I kick at the piles of photographs from Matthew's bedroom that are now covering the carpet and find the one I'm looking for. I reach down to pluck it from the pile, staring at the fear on Jenna's face. "See here?" I say, holding the photo up and showing it to Jenna. "Matthew is such a freak with his photos, isn't he?" I say. "He takes photos of everything." I wave the bat over the piles. "And I mean everything. Just look at this one of you, here. Can you see me in the background in the cap and gym kit?" I toss the photo to Jenna but she doesn't try to grab it.

"You never saw me, did you? I was a lot better at blending in than Matthew was, obviously. He did me a favor, really. You've been so busy looking for him that it made it a lot easier for me to watch you. That's what I mean. You're just so focused on yourself. No one else matters, do they? Certainly not Beth and Archie."

"Sophie, please. I love my children. Whatever this is, let them go," Jenna begs. Her voice is trembling and I feel her hurt. Am I really going through with this? I've wanted this fresh start for so long, but now that I'm here it doesn't feel like I thought it would.

"I just want to do it right this time. A different ending," I say.

I grip the bat tighter in my hand and screw up my courage. I will not be a coward anymore. I will not let people push me around anymore. I'm here now. It's time to rewrite the past. Any minute now and she'll see what I've done.

"This is insane. You have to let us go," Rachel sobs.

Jenna moves then. A step to the right. I eye her carefully and see the thought running through her head, and the emotions playing on her face—hope then disappointment. She's wondering if she can get past me to the door. She can't.

"You know what, Jenna? For a doctor, you really are quite dense. I really thought you'd recognize me when I came to see Matthew in the hospital and you were there. I was properly freaking out.

"Have you worked it out yet? Matthew wasn't even following you. You see that now, right? He figured out what I was doing and started checking up on me, taking his stupid photos. Back in May, wasn't it? I'll admit it shook me up seeing him and knowing he knew what I was doing. I tried to stop, to go back to a time before you. I even managed it for a week, but in the end I had to see you again." The moment the words are out, I realize how much I'm going to miss watching Jenna.

I suddenly remember Matthew's phone in my pocket and pull it out. Jenna's mouth drops open.

"Sorry, have you been looking for this?" A thrill—a buzz of nervous energy—shoots through me and I smile. It really shouldn't matter now, but it feels good to get one up on Jenna and the police. "I had to take it. Matthew recorded our chat, you see."

There's no reason to listen to it, except to kill time, and that's all I've got left. I open up the recording and a second later the noise of traffic crackles in the microphone.

"Sophie." Matthew's voice echoes out so clear that for a moment it feels like he's in the room. "We need to talk."

"I can't right now. I'm right in the middle of something."

"Following that doctor, you mean?"

There's a silence. In the background the sound of a bus rushes by. "Whatever."

"I know she looks like Mum, but she isn't."

"I know that." My reply is sharp and I feel the same anger now as I did then. Matthew was standing in my way, stopping me from getting to Jenna.

"What are you planning to do?"

"Nothing. I just like watching her, that's all."

"You're lying. I know you too well."

"So what if I am? What are you going to do about it?" I remember the way my heart pounded through my whole head and how trapped I felt with Matthew standing over me, but his voice as it carries into the room is strong.

"What I should've done twelve years ago. Tell the truth." The noise of the road grows louder and I picture him holding up his phone to me. "I've recorded everything. I'm going to the police right now before someone gets hurt."

"It's too late for that."

Air rushes in the microphone. I picture Matthew's free hand swiping the air, trying to grab me to steady himself. Me leaping away, but not before he grabbed my umbrella right out of my hands.

A horn beeps, brakes screech, then nothing. No deafening thud of Matthew's body as the bus smashed into it, no sound of my panicked cries as I ran away.

I drop Matthew's phone to the floor and grip the bat in both hands, slamming the top of it down until the phone is a mess of broken glass and wires. I wish my own memories could be erased just as easily.

"Mummy, I'm scared," Archie whines, burying his head in Jenna's dress.

I look from the floor to Archie. "I didn't mean to hurt Matthew." The words are a whisper. I don't know who I'm talking to now. I couldn't have him spoil this for me. Tears burn in the corners of my eyes. The familiar guilt rushes through my body.

"It's your job to protect him, Sophie."

No, Mum. It was your job to protect us.

"Please," Jenna begs. "Let us go now."

I shake my head, ignoring the worry worming through my insides. Can they smell it yet? I can. But then I can always smell the smoke. Memories elbow their way unwanted into my thoughts.

"There was a fire in this house once," I tell Jenna. "You wouldn't know it now, would you? I couldn't believe it when Matthew said he was going to rent this place—our old family home. Matthew says it helps him feel close to Mum, but this place gives me the creeps. I think he lives here as some kind of weird way of punishing himself for what happened. He blames himself, obviously. I blame him too as it goes."

My eyes are itching. It's starting.

Archie coughs. Then Beth.

I watch Jenna's eyes look from her children to the door where a thin layer of gray smoke is seeping in from underneath.

"Oh my God," Rachel screams. "She's going to burn us all alive."

"Shut up," I hiss, wishing Rachel weren't here. I only posted the personal-training flyer through her door as a reason to get close to her house. I wanted to see where the woman who was shagging Jenna's husband lived. I never expected her to phone me. Still, she was useful in the end.

Rachel stands up, hobbling beside Jenna. Fear slithers snake-like up my body. I'm outnumbered. I raise the bat just as Rachel tries to leap forward and grab it. For all her fitness, she is too slow and I raise the bat out of her reach before bringing it down on her shoulder with a thwack that makes her scream in pain.

"Get back." I kick her where the bat hit and Rachel screeches again, staggering out of my reach and back to where Jenna is standing.

"I tried to warn you," I say, turning back to Jenna. "I left so many warnings, I even pushed you over last week—"

"That was you?" Jenna cries out.

"Don't you get it?" I say. I'm shouting but my voice is muffled by the throbbing of my heartbeat in my ears. "It was all me, but you didn't listen. I tried to make you see how dangerous it is to ignore your family. You don't pay attention to what your husband is doing or how your kids are feeling. I knew it the moment I read all those little notes in Archie's school diary." I reach into my backpack and pull out Archie's book. The shell drops out with it. A beautiful pearly white shell I took from the bowl in Jenna's living room when the idiot estate agent showed me round.

"He's just like Matthew. It won't be long before he starts acting out. Both of them will when they realize you don't love them. The same thing will happen to them as it did to me. I'm just speeding up the process.

"It really would've been better if we'd have all died that night. That's what I realized when I met you, Jenna. Then my mum wouldn't be trapped in her own head, hating us, and I wouldn't have to live every day—"

"I love my children," Jenna says, her voice angry now. "They're not like you and Matthew. I'm not like your mum."

"Yes they are." I move to the door and press my weight against it. Smoke is clawing at the back of my throat and my eyes are watering but I won't stop now. This is my fresh start, my chance to end what I started twelve years ago.

CHAPTER 59

SOPHIE, *age 15*

Sophie opens her eyes slowly. They're sore from crying and for a second it feels like they won't open. The CD has stopped playing and the house is silent. She looks at her clock, expecting it to be late, but it isn't. It's only nine thirty. She must have cried herself to sleep.

Vicky and Flick will be dancing now. Sophie imagines Flick's arms snaking around Reece's neck and stealing Sophie's first kiss. The clothes she was going to wear are screwed up on the floor. She tried them on earlier and stared at herself in the mirror before changing again and crawling into her bed to sulk. She wished she'd had the confidence to go out alone, to walk straight up to Reece and pull him onto the dance floor. It was a stupid plan. Stupid. Stupid. Stupid.

Sophie sighs, her thoughts turning to Matthew. She waits for the regret to hit. She'd been cruel, but he deserved it. She's starting to see his behavior for what it is—an act. All of his silences and strops, the way he listens and watches but doesn't speak—it's all fake, a way to wrap her mum around his little finger and dodge the telling-off that Sophie seems to walk right into.

Matthew deserves everything he gets from now on and there's no way she's going to cover for him anymore. Her mum needs to see what he's really like. All those little bowls of paper Matthew is always burning in his bedroom. One day it's going to land him in a world of trouble and there's no way Sophie is going to protect him any longer.

An idea drifts through her thoughts. What if Sophie leaves a bowl of burned paper in the kitchen where her mum will see it? Her mum would have to react then, she'd have to do something. It's not even like Sophie will be setting him up, not really. She's just showing her mum what Matthew has been up to.

Sophie sits up, wide awake now. Her mum said Trevor had ordered a taxi for ten p.m. She'll be home in forty-five minutes. Plenty of time to set things in motion. Sophie digs in her bedside drawer for the matches she took from Matthew ages ago.

Without making a sound, Sophie opens her bedroom door and listens to the noises of the house. The hot water tank is clicking and she can hear the soft murmur of music playing in Matthew's room.

Sophie slips downstairs to the kitchen and spots the vase of pink carnations sitting on the table. Her mum's favorite. A gift from Trevor, no doubt. Sophie grabs Matthew's school bag from the floor and pulls out a few loose sheets of paper.

She tears the paper into long strips and piles them in a china bowl just like Matthew does.

She drags the match across the box and touches the flame to the paper, watching it come alive, folding in on itself and turning brown, then black. Other pieces of paper catch the flame. Smoke starts to waft upward, taking tiny pieces of paper with it.

Sophie grabs a chair and drags it across the floor until it's beneath the smoke alarm. She leaps up and pulls out the battery before it can beep and tell Matthew her plan. At the last moment, she swipes the photo of them from the fridge—the one Matthew refused to smile for—and puts it in the bowl. Her mum will hate that. Then she hurries to the living room to turn on the TV.

"Matthew was in the kitchen doing his homework the last time I saw him," she says, practicing what she'll say to her mum when she gets back.

There's an old *Friends* episode on the TV and Sophie curls up on the sofa to watch it, her ears primed for the sound of her mum's key in the lock.

It's ten minutes before Sophie notices the smoke. She blinks and rubs her itchy eyes. Where is it all coming from?

She stands too fast, knocking a glass from the table where it smashes on the floor. The smoke is everywhere. She swallows and tastes it in her mouth.

Sophie bites her lips, knowing she's going to cry. This is bad. This is very bad. She didn't mean for this to happen. It was only a small bowl of paper. She didn't mean . . . Sophie coughs, doubling over and dropping onto all fours.

This is Matthew's fault. He drove her to it. She only wanted to show her mum what he's really like.

CHAPTER 60

JENNA

There's a fire. Sophie has set a fire. My heart is beating so fast
and I know I have to get Beth and Archie out of this house.

"Sophie, please. My children are innocent. Let them go, I beg
you. I'm the one you want."

Sophie tips her head back and laughs again. It's a horrible
sound. More like a scream. Her eyes flick wildly around the room
and she's spinning the bat in her hands.

I risk a quick glance to Rachel. Tears have streaked two black
lines down her face and she's cowering on the floor just behind me.
I was wrong about her on so many levels, but there's a rage still burning inside me. She took my children. She put them in this position.

"This is obviously about them, Jenna," Sophie says. "You must
see that. It's always been about them. It's history repeating itself,"
she says again, rubbing one of her eyes.

Archie coughs from behind me and whimpers. The sound cuts
deep into my heart. I turn and look at them. Their arms are wrapped
tightly around each other, and seeing their beautiful faces cements
something inside of me. I will get them out of this.

"It's OK, kids. Get down on the floor as low as you can," I tell them. "Cover your mouth and nose with your clothes.

They move quickly to the carpet, and Rachel pushes herself closer to them, her face screwed up in pain as she reaches a protective arm around my children and whispers to them to cover their mouths. When I turn back to Sophie, the room is hazy with smoke.

I remember Sophie now. That first time we met. Her hair had been bleached blond and cut short, and she'd seemed so nice, so sweet. I'd enjoyed our chat.

"Are you a mum?" she asked me.

"Yes. I have two children. Beth is eight and Archie is five."

"My mum won't talk to me anymore. We've not spoken for twelve years."

"Oh, that's a shame." I didn't ask why. It was none of my business, but I remember the hand I put on her arm and the smile I gave her. *"If you love your mum, don't give up on her. There's nothing that can't be fixed, including your boyfriend's appendicitis."*

"Promise?"

I laughed because she reminded me so much of Beth in that moment. *"Promise."*

Beth coughs and gags. The noise forces me to move. I take a step forward. Then another.

Sophie lunges at me, swinging the bat and missing me by an inch. "Don't you dare try it," she shouts.

"What about Nick?" I plead. "What would he say about this?"

"Nick." Sophie growls the name. "He was always checking up on me. He hated it when I left the flat at night when I wanted to come sit in your garden just to be close to you. I should never have agreed to live with him. He was getting so suspicious. I couldn't bear it anymore." Sophie reaches into her pocket and pulls out a lighter. Her eyes never leave mine as she crouches down and holds it to the corner of a photograph lying on the floor.

The flame leaps up before almost disappearing. The edges turn black and slowly the photograph is swallowed up until it's all black. The photo beside it catches even slower, and then the one beside that.

"Your mum wouldn't want you to do this, Sophie," I say, desperate now to talk some sense into her. "No matter what has happened in the past."

"Don't talk about my mum." Sophie's eyes cloud with tears. Her shoulders slump.

In the sky above us thunder roars, and when the noise dies away I think I hear the distant wail of a siren. Too distant, I think. There isn't any time.

"You don't have to do it. The police are on their way. Don't get in more trouble than you're already in. I . . ."

"I, I, I, me, me, me. That's all you think about, isn't it? What about what your kids want? What I want?" A sob catches in her throat. "I just want my mum to love me again."

"Sophie—"

"I thought this would be a fresh start for all of us. I'm sorry. I'm really sorry." As Sophie speaks, her gaze roams the room, her thoughts now elsewhere and I inch slowly, very slowly closer.

Two more steps.

One more step.

"Get back," she screams suddenly, swinging the bat toward me. I jump away, but not fast enough. The tip of the bat smacks into my side. The blow knocks me off-balance, pain shooting out, and I fall to the floor in a fit of coughing. A sharp pain hits my thigh and I realize I've fallen on the burning photos. The smoke is everywhere now.

"Just let me think for a minute. I don't . . . I'm not sure what I'm doing." Sophie's face starts to crumble. Tears streak down her face and she's shaking all over. Her eyes dart between the door and us. "Maybe we can talk some more. I thought I wanted this."

Is she changing her mind? Is she going to let us go? I'm rooted to the spot, waiting. Every second feels like a minute. Beth and Archie's coughs fill my ears. We're out of time. The fire is growing. We'll die if we stay here much longer. Resolve hardens inside me. I jump up and throw myself at Sophie. There's a split second where Sophie is staring at me and I'm flying through the air and all I see is pain and regret in her eyes.

She crumbles from the force of my body and we both fall back, landing in a heap by the bookcase.

"Beth, Archie, get out. Rachel, get them out."

The bat drops out of Sophie's hands and she comes at me with her fists as her body writhes underneath me.

"Stop, Sophie," I shout.

"No." She lashes out, punch after punch landing all over my body. My face, my stomach, my chest. I feel the air rush out of me and the pain everywhere. Sophie is strong, but I will take it if it means my children are safe. I hear Rachel reach the door. Beth and Archie are with her. I'll take all the punches Sophie can throw at me if they'll just make it to safety.

"I'm not leaving without my mum." Beth's voice cuts straight to my heart.

"I'm right behind you, Beth," I shout to her.

More smoke fills the room from the open door. Sophie's fists drop and suddenly she bucks, tipping my weight, and I fall to the floor. Sophie scrambles up and leaps across the room and a scream pierces the air.

Beth.

I squint through the haze and see my daughter lying on the floor. Rachel has her hand and is trying to pull her out, but Sophie's grip on Beth's ankle is holding fast.

I snatch up the bat and rush at Sophie, swinging it hard and fast at Sophie's arm. The crack of bone echoes through the room, followed a split second later by Sophie's screams.

I reach for Beth and help her up and together we rush out of the front door.

The sound of sirens echoes down the street. So many sirens and louder now too. A police car turns into the road, followed by the red bulk of a fire engine.

I gasp for air and feel Archie and Beth press their shaking bodies up against me. "It's OK," I tell them. "You're OK. You're going to be OK. I love you," I tell them, over and over.

CHAPTER 61

One month later
JENNA

Bernie's living room looks the same as the last time I was here. I take a seat on the sofa and stare at the photos of soldiers posing by trucks, and a schoolboy growing older in each shot. I peer closer, searching for more, like I always do now. The photos on your wall are never far from my thoughts. If only I'd looked closer, searched every photo more carefully, then maybe I'd have seen Sophie in the background on some of them, and Beth and Archie would've been spared the trauma she put them through. But I didn't. I saw what I wanted to see. I saw myself and nothing else.

Memories of that day rise up, smacking into me like an unexpected wave over the seawall. I feel the shaky relief of holding Beth and Archie in my arms, all of us sobbing. My eyes didn't leave that front door though, not for a second, watching for Sophie to emerge from the fire. But she never did. DS Church told me later that she barricaded herself in the living room, pushing the furniture against the door before starting another fire. The fire crew couldn't get to her in time.

Then the bustle and noise of the hospital, sounding so alien when it was me who was the patient. I was discharged quickly, but they kept Beth and Archie overnight to monitor them for any smoke damage to their lungs. Stuart and I slept on foldout beds beside them. I lay awake all night, staring at the polystyrene ceiling tiles as my heart raced and silent tears rolled down my face, thinking of my children and how close I came to losing them.

Only when dawn was breaking and the nurses began moving between the beds, doing the early rounds, did I think of Sophie and the look on her face as I threw myself at her. If I'd waited just one more minute would she have let us go? Would she still be alive too?

Nick found me in the canteen later that morning, as if I'd summoned him with my questions. He looked broken. His muscular frame somehow shrunken by grief and shock. His eyes were red and wet, and when he begged me to tell him what happened, I took my coffee and steered him to a quiet corner table. I told him everything.

I thought he'd break down, cry, sob, crumble beside me. Instead he stood and leaned over me. "You're lying," he hissed.

"Nick, I realize you're grieving, but I'm not—"

"I spoke to Rachel," he said with a sudden flash of triumph on his face. "She told me Sophie was changing her mind. She was going to let you go, but you attacked her. Why couldn't you have waited?"

"I . . . I didn't know for sure she was going to let us go. She might've been trying to buy more time. There was smoke everywhere. My children were struggling to breathe and I had to get them out. There wasn't any time to wait."

"You're the reason she's dead." He jabbed a finger at me, poking it hard into my collarbone. His touch was an electric shock of fear that zipped through my body. "She was mine. She was everything to me."

"Don't touch me." The words flew out of me, a low growl. The coffee cup was in my hand and I tightened my grip, ready to throw it at him.

His eyes drew to the cup and he stepped back, his face contorted with pain and anger. Diya appeared then, a plate of breakfast in her hands. "Everything all right?" she asked me, glaring at Nick. "Do I need to call security?"

I shook my head as Nick took another step away and Diya slid into the seat beside me, her arm wrapping protectively around my shoulders. Nick turned to leave, but not before glaring at me a final time. His eyes ablaze with a fiery hate.

From Bernie's kitchen, the kettle finishes boiling. I pull in a deep breath, gripping my hands to stop them shaking, and focus on why I'm here. I listen to the clink of a spoon and the fridge opening, then closing. My heart jitters when you walk into the room wearing a black T-shirt and black jeans, just like you always wore when I saw you watching. Your casts are off and your hands are full with two mugs and liquid spills from the top.

"I never leave enough space for milk," you mutter.

"It's fine." I take the mug, careful that my fingers don't touch yours. I know you're not who I thought you were, but I'm still a mess seeing you. Coffee runs down the china, dripping brown blotches on the bright yellow of my top.

A silence settles over us. I don't know how to start.

"How are you?" I ask.

"Getting there. Bernie has been great letting me stay here. He should be back from the shops any minute. He'll be glad to see you."

I nod, but I hope I won't be here long enough to see Bernie.

"I'm looking for somewhere else to live. I can't be in that house now." His expression hardens. "I'm going back to work next week. Just part-time. I still get so tired."

"Head injuries are a long road to recovery."

"Are you still working at the hospital?" he asks.

"No. I'm locuming as a GP now, filling in at local practices where I'm needed. It's better hours for the kids."

I did try to go back to work, I tried slipping back into my old life, but like a pair of outgrown shoes, I couldn't make it fit. Suddenly the shifts were too long, the days too stressful, and I worried about Beth and Archie constantly. I thought it would be hard to leave emergency medicine after all the years I put into it, but actually it was easy in the end.

We fall silent. Mr. Barnaby strolls into the room. He brushes his soft fur against my leg before jumping onto your lap and purring.

"You had something you wanted to ask me," you say.

"Yes." I take a breath. "I've been thinking a lot about what happened." Tormenting myself with all the things I did wrong, the clues I missed. "And I have to know why you did what you did. You must have known I saw you taking photos of me. You knew what Sophie was doing and you did nothing about it."

"I was trying to protect her. She spent her whole life looking out for me. When I saw it was going too far I tried to get her to stop."

"Not hard enough. My children could've died—" My voice becomes a squeak and I swallow hard. Now is not the time for emotion.

"I almost died trying to stop her, Dr. Lawson."

"Why did you let her do it, and why did you follow her so much? I thought it was you. I thought you were stalking me. All those photos you took and put on your wall."

You close your eyes. "I like taking photos. It doesn't mean anything. It's just the way I make sense of the world. I know I'm not normal. I see the way people look at me, but I can't change who I am."

Neither of us speaks for a moment.

"Do you know Rachel Finley?" I ask then. The answer doesn't matter but it's been bugging me.

"No," you say, looking at me again. "The first time I heard the name was when you asked about her in the hospital and then when the police came to tell me what happened. Rachel was with you in the house, wasn't she?"

"She was one of Sophie's clients. Her kids go to the same school as mine and Sophie used her to get my children from school."

You nod and I realize you know all this already.

"You took a lot of photos of Rachel, and Bernie said he saw an older blonde coming to the house sometimes. Was it her?"

You pull a face and give a light snort. "Good old Bernie. Nothing gets by him. I think he must have seen my boss from the restaurant. She came to the house a few times to taste some new dishes I'd worked on. We didn't do it at the restaurant because she didn't want to upset her head chef. We had a bit of a thing, but it didn't last long. She's going through a divorce and it got too complicated. As for the photos of Rachel, I was keeping a close eye on everyone Sophie saw in the end and that's why I have photos of Rachel."

I want to push the point. A close eye? Is that what you call following your sister wherever she goes and taking hundreds of photos of her and everyone she sees?

"I'm sorry for what happened to your children," you say then.

"And I'm sorry about Sophie." The reply is automatic. It's the kind of throwaway comment that is easy to say when someone is gone, but deep down, in a place I don't like to go, I'm glad she's dead. I know now that Sophie was very ill. I think in her head she saw me and the children as though we were living her life over again and thought she could change history and stop her guilt. I'm sorry for the pain her death has caused Matthew and Nick, but whether she was ill or not, I can't forgive her.

I wait for Matthew's next question. Why didn't I wait? Why didn't I do more to save Sophie? I wait for Matthew's anger to rise up, his recrimination just like Nick's, but it doesn't come.

"Poor Sophie," he says in the end. "I feel so guilty about what happened. I wish I could change things."

"Don't you blame her for what she did to you? She pushed you in front of a bus."

"She panicked, that's all. I was threatening to go to the police and she was scared. Sophie had it tough growing up too. Mum put all her energy into me and I know Sophie was left out a lot, and then she had to look after me after school when our nan couldn't do it anymore. My childhood improved astronomically when I was adopted by the Dovers, but Sophie's didn't.

"After years and years of it, she blamed me and wanted to get me into trouble by burning some paper to show our mum how I used to set fire to things. It went horribly wrong and the kitchen curtains caught fire, and she never forgave herself. I've always felt responsible for what happened as well. If the Dovers hadn't adopted me then Sophie would still have her mum. Sophie wasn't perfect, but she was my sister and I will always love her. I know she didn't want to be saved but I want to keep her memory alive and remember the good in her."

A silence settles over us. I try to process everything you've told me about your childhood and Sophie. Maybe one day I'll feel some sympathy for you and Sophie, but I don't have it in me right now. It's still too raw.

I stare at you and the dark eyes I still see in my nightmares. You might not have been my stalker, but when I think of the hundreds of photos on your bedroom wall, I can't see you as innocent either.

"I'm sorry," DS Church had said to me the last time we spoke about Matthew. "The Crown Prosecution Service think it's too difficult to prosecute Mr. Dover for harassment. All the evidence we have points to Sophie, and the photos you've mentioned burned in the fire. I'm afraid there isn't enough evidence."

DS Church filled in the gaps from that day. "After Stuart phoned me to report the dolls and the flowers on your doorstep, I had a colleague phone all the florists. I was sure an order for that many pink carnations would be remembered, and it was. A florist on Long Mead Road remembered the purchase. A cash buyer, but they had Sophie on CCTV coming in to collect them."

"And Matthew?" I asked. "Where did he go?"

"He never made it further than the car park. He told the hospital staff he was worried about his sister."

"What will you do now?" Matthew asks, pulling my thoughts back to the room.

"I'll carry on."

I thought coming here would give me closure, but all it's done is rip open the wound again. I stand to leave, my coffee untouched. "Good-bye, Matthew."

"Good-bye, Dr. Lawson. Thank you for saving my life."

I walk out of Bernie's front door and to the car where Stuart is waiting. The day is blue skies and sunny, but there's a slight nip to the air. A typical summer's day by the sea now that the heat wave is over.

At the last moment I turn back to the house and see you, a shadow behind the net curtains.

"OK?" Stuart asks, leaning in to kiss my cheek.

"Yes."

"I've got the Canadian work visa applications through. We can fill them in tonight if we want to."

"That's great." I smile. It is great. It's another step closer to moving, to a new way of life, if I want a new life. I know Stuart wants to stay, and so do Beth and Archie. I'm not sure why I'm trying to drag them halfway around the world when there is nothing to run from anymore.

Sometimes I wonder about leaving Stuart and making a clean break, just the three of us—me, Beth, and Archie. The children and I have grown so close these past few weeks. Beth and Archie have both taken to sleeping in bed with me since the fire, leaving Stuart to stay in Archie's bed.

I lie awake and watch my babies sleeping for hours, heart beating too fast, barely able to breathe, thinking of that day, thinking how close I came to losing them. When I do sleep, I dream of Matthew and Rachel, Sophie and Nick, and I wake up drenched in sweat and gasping for breath.

"Are you sure about us?" Stuart asks, throwing me a worried look as he starts the car.

"I'm sure," I lie. "Come on, we need to get some food for dinner before the school pickup."

"We should see if we can get some Canadian maple syrup. Archie will love it."

"That's true."

We drive in silence, lost in our own thoughts. Stuart is trying hard to earn my forgiveness. Sometimes I think his affair is nothing, not after everything else we've been through. Other times, I want to scream at him to leave. I can't forgive him yet, but I'll find a way to live with it until I do. Beth and Archie have been through enough and need us both right now.

An hour later we park on the road by the school and Stuart cuts the engine. It's the last day of term. The last time I'll ever come to this school if I decide to leave.

As we walk toward the gates, I spot Rachel. She's wearing a pair of jeans and a loose T-shirt and she's limping slightly from the damage to her ankle.

"I'm sorry. I'm so sorry," she had cried to me over and over. "Sophie said . . . she said she was trying to help you. She called me on Monday morning and left this panicky message, begging me to call her. So I did. She said she knew your stalker was out of hospital and was going to get Beth and Archie if we didn't get them first. I thought I was helping. I went along with it at first but then just before I went into the school I tried to suggest we go to the police. She went ballistic. She said if I didn't help her, then my kids would be next and he'd kill them and the police wouldn't be able to stop him. I didn't want to do it, but I was scared, and then she said if I didn't help her, she'd tell my husband about me . . . me and Stuart. I didn't know she was going to hurt them. I really didn't. You have to believe me."

A familiar anger burns inside. I can forgive her for sleeping with Stuart and I can forgive her for lying to me, and avoiding me, for making me think I was crazy, but I can't forgive her for walking into the school and collecting Beth and Archie. It's her fault they were in that house, her fault they wake up crying for me in the night.

I draw in a breath and let it out slowly, trying to focus on the Rachel who pulled Beth out of the house when she didn't want to go.

Rachel and her family are moving back to London over the summer. Beth is devastated to be losing her best friend, but I know she'll get over it.

The bell signaling the end of school is ringing as we step into the playground. The classes start to flock out, a sea of green. Beth and Archie race toward me. I open my arms to them and they jump into me and we hold one another tight. The love pours through me, dousing my anger toward Rachel, Matthew, the memories.

"Mummy, Mummy." Archie jumps by my side. "We did art today and I got a merit for my picture." He holds up a piece of paper and I crouch down for him to show me properly. "I did all of us playing at lunch break. See—there's the older boys playing football, and there's Beth with a skipping rope."

"It's very good, Archie. I like how you've drawn the trees. What's this?" I ask, pointing to a black shadow next to where Archie has drawn the dark green railings that border the playing field.

"That's the man, Mummy."

"What man?" I ask, my mouth suddenly dry.

"The one who's been watching me."

"Oh, Archie," I say, pulling him into my arms. "There's no bad man anymore. It's all over, I promise." I swallow back the emotions threatening to burst out of me and pull myself up.

"I saw him today, Mummy. And at the weekend," Archie says in his singsong matter-of-fact voice. "He called my name and waved to me," Archie says before skipping ahead to catch up with

Stuart and Beth. I follow close behind, my eyes on the drawing and the smudged shadow of a figure standing on the outside of the railings, watching the children.

A shiver races down my body and I hurry to reach my family.

It's the trauma of everything that's happened to him, to us, I tell myself. While Beth has been an emotional roller coaster—angry, lashing out, sobbing, and begging me not to leave her side—Archie has seemed fine. No bad dreams. No accidents at school. And yet the coloring in my hands, the shadow, it's not OK. I'll talk to him later and explain again that he's safe now.

On the road, the groups of parents and children disperse and we walk side by side toward the car, my hand slipping into Archie's, keeping him close.

"Who wants an ice cream when we get home?" Stuart asks.

"Meeeeee," Beth and Archie shout together.

They clamber into the backseat and I'm opening the passenger door when something changes in me. For a moment I can't place the feeling crawling over my body, and then I gasp and spin around, my eyes darting across the road. Did something just move by that tree? A shadow?

ACKNOWLEDGMENTS

My first thank-you is to my readers. Thank you so much for reading *One Step Behind*. I write stories because I love it—I always have—but it's in your minds that the words come to life, and that feels a lot like magic to me. If you've enjoyed Jenna and Sophie's story, then do let me know, either on social media or by leaving a review. It really does make an author's day! And to the book bloggers who go the extra mile to help authors—thank you. You are awesome!

They say the second book is the hardest. They are right. There were times when I thought this book would be impossible to start, let alone finish. The fact that it is here now is due to the perseverance, support, insight, and encouragement from my two fantastic editors: Natasha Barsby and Danielle Perez. Thank you both!

To my agent, Tanera—you've been by my side for every step of this book. Thank you. Knowing you're in my corner makes every day that much easier. Thank you for always supporting me and challenging me to be the best writer I can be.

Publishing a book is a team effort. So thanks must also go to the marketing and publicity teams and everyone else at Berkley, Transworld, and Darley Anderson Literary Agency. A special mention should also go to Faceout Studio for my stunning cover.

I have so much respect for the emergency services and the jobs they do, and I've been lucky enough to receive some great input from those who know far more about police matters than I do. Thank you to Matt Carney (and Laura Carney) and Julie Fountain for answering my messages and always being happy to chat at the school pickup. At least, I hope you've been happy to chat, and I've not been badgering you too much.

I hope you'll forgive me for taking a few liberties with Jenna's career path. She and Diya should have continued to move to different hospitals during their specialist training years, but I kept them together at the same hospital to make things easy for Jenna's family and the story. I'm indebted to Hannah Litchfield for sharing her knowledge of A&E with me, and reading umpteen versions of chapter 5. Thanks also to Beckie Edwards and Jim Fisher for their knowledge on paramedics.

Westbury District Hospital is a fictional hospital, but I hope I've reflected the intensity of A&E shifts and just how hard our amazing doctors and nurses work. I will be eternally grateful to every single nurse, doctor, porter, and administrator who keeps the hospitals running day and night, and provides us with fantastic health care and kindness when we need it. "Thank you" are not big enough words.

When this book was just a whisper of an idea, I was fortunate enough to receive some great plot advice from Neil D'Arcy Jones. Thank you for taking the time to listen and for your insights.

To the Savvy Writers' Snug and the Psychological Suspense Authors' Association, thank you for making me feel part of an amazing community and for all the virtual cheers and hugs.

In July 2019 I met three fantastic authors, and for the first time in my life I felt as though I'd found my tribe. Nikki Smith, Laura Pearson, Zoe Lea—I've dedicated this book to you, because you've kept me going through every chapter and every new draft. You're the first people I want to share my good news with, along with my writing woes, and I'll forever be grateful that we met. Our chats always brighten my day.

As always, a huge thank-you to Kathryn Jones for her proof-reading skills and friendship, and for making me laugh so much. And to Carol, Sarah, and Catherine, for always listening to me ramble on about writing. I'm lucky to have friends like you.

I owe a special thank-you to Lottie and Lola for lending me (and Archie) their magical world of planet Bong.

Thank you to my Facebook friends, who answer my random research questions, tell me the name of the thing I can't remember, or chip in with jokes when I need them (Sarah Bennett—thank you for Jenna's joke in the bar). Helen Edwards, you always give great answers! Lynsey Dunsby—as promised, your name made it into the book.

Thanks to my dad, Steve Tomlin, for planting the seed of Jenna in my mind. To Maggie Ewings (aka my mum) and Mel Ewings—thank you for your support, and for always opening your doors to a writer and her dog in need of a place to write. Tony Ellingham—thank you for your endless encouragement, for all you do for us, and of course for all the Twix bars.

The final mention is for my family—Andy, Tommy, and Lottie. I love you so much. Thank you for understanding the roller coaster world of a writer's life, for distracting me with shopping trips and board games, and for making me laugh every day.

ONE STEP BEHIND

LAUREN NORTH

DISCUSSION QUESTIONS

1. What were your first impressions of Jenna and Sophie? Did these change over the course of the novel?

2. Early in the story, Jenna is faced with an ethical dilemma when she meets her stalker for the first time. Did you sympathize with her point of view? What decision would you make in that situation?

3. What kind of mother is Jenna? Do you think this changed as the story progressed? Are mothers judged differently or more harshly than fathers?

4. In Jenna's chapters, she talks to her stalker as though telling the story to him. Why do you think the author chose to write the novel in this way? Did you like it?

5. Which character did you relate to the most, and why? Did this change at any point in the novel?

6. The story is set during a heat wave. How big a part do you think this played in the novel? Would the novel have felt the same if it hadn't been as hot?

7. How does Lauren North create a sense of tension and unease in *One Step Behind*?

8. What did you think of Matthew as a young boy? Did your opinion of his character change as the novel progressed?

9. What do you think the future holds for Jenna and Stuart?

Photo by Laurie Ellingham Author Photos

Lauren North studied psychology before moving to London, where she lived and worked for many years. She now lives with her family in the Suffolk countryside. *The Perfect Son* was her first novel.

CONNECT ONLINE

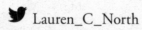 Lauren_C_North

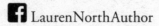 LaurenNorthAuthor